WATCHERS OF THE BELOVEDS

Book Two: Legends Returning

by

Stori Fallon

Dedicated to 2025
the year that asked for everything
and left nothing unchanged

where pain became passage,
healing shaped the memories,
and transformation was unavoidable.

Where Joy became no longer a choice, but a decision.

And to my Aurora Borealis
my northern lights,
who never stopped shining, even when my skies were dark.

One .

Two..

Three...I love you the most.

I thank God for you and his unfailing love and mercy.......

Jessahme and Mom, thanks for being my cheerleaders.

And For those who remember who they were

before the world told them who to be.

The Epistle of Jude (KJV)

Jude

1:6

And the angels which kept not their first estate, but left their own habitation, he hath reserved in everlasting chains under darkness unto the judgment of the great day.

1:11

Woe unto them! for they have gone in the way of Cain, and ran greedily after the error of Balaam for reward, and perished in the gainsaying of Core.

1:14

And Enoch also, the seventh from Adam, prophesied of these, saying, Behold, the Lord cometh with ten thousands of his saints,

1:21

Keep yourselves in the love of God, looking for the mercy of our Lord Jesus Christ unto eternal life.

1:22

And of some have compassion, making a difference:

1:23

And others save with fear, pulling them out of the fire; hating even the garment spotted by the flesh.

1:25

To the only wise God our Saviour, be glory and majesty, dominion and power, both now and ever. Amen.

There was a woman who asked for power to be young and loved.
The darkness gave her promise, but not the price.
She was meant to take, yet she would refuse.
And when the final child was placed before her,
she would close the gate and let herself be hunted instead.

There was a warrior forged into a weapon before he knew his own name.
His hands were trained for destruction, his loyalty purchased with blood.
He never sought forgiveness from the One he wounded most.
Until at last he knelt, and the ground received his confession.
The sword he laid aside did not break—it was left behind.

Among the guardians was one who fell not through rebellion,
but through grief.
Their power forgotten, their seat abandoned,
They walked the world believing she was lost.
Yet guardianship waits for the child of promise,
and when they rise, the sky will wear her colors.

There was a child born of darkness, who loved too deeply to obey.
When he glimpsed the end, he tried to bend time to his will.
Time resisted them. Not all deaths are undone,
not all love is permitted to save.
This child lives to remember,
and to watch what is lost unfold.

When the gate refuses, and the sword kneels,
and the forgotten rises,
the legends have returned.

LEGENDS RETURNING

Chapter One

Eva

I stood there watching as Remiel hefted his duffel bag into the back of the truck. The soft creak of the tailgate and the echo of gravel beneath his boots felt deafening in the quiet of the morning. I kept my arms wrapped around myself, not for warmth, but for the illusion of composure. I didn't want to fall apart. I didn't want to beg. But I was close. Close to suffocating, unable to breathe thinking about his departure. About the emptiness without his presence.

Michael had come to him in the hospital. *Michael.* The archangel, appearing with a direct command that Remiel hadn't been able to ignore. It had been the kind of calling he used to receive from the heavens. There was a time when Remiel had walked with light in his veins. He had been a Watcher once…but that part of him was gone now, not stripped away in disgrace, but laid down willingly. God, in an act of mercy, had granted him descent. A rare gift, to become mortal. To know love, to know choice, to walk among those he once guarded.

And now he was being called to war again, not in celestial armor, but in worn boots and a mortal body. A mercenary in this earthly world, fighting battles that were gray and that blurred the lines between good and evil. Still a protector. Still fighting for something bigger than himself. But now every breath, with every step, with every wound…. it all would carry the weakness of humanly flesh. It would also carry him away from me.

Sometimes the reality of my life, of who we were and how we came to be was so surreal that it threatened my peace. I couldn't speak of it. Not to friends, not to family, not to anyone. Remiel had once told me that some truths aren't meant to be shared. They're meant to be carried in silence, close to the heart, even if it meant breaking it.

Remiel walked back toward me, worry in his eyes. I stood on the porch, leaning against one of the wooden posts because my legs felt too hollow to hold me. He climbed halfway up the steps, paused, and looked at me like he was memorizing my face… every line, every shadow. Then, without a word, he placed his hands on my hips and pulled me down one step so we were level, chest to chest.

The way he held me…..as if it would be the last time. I wrapped my arms around his neck, and he pressed his face into my shirt, breathing me in. The heat of his breath soaked through the fabric, branding me with the memory of his closeness. He moaned softly, the sound was pulled from someplace deep, one part ache, one part surrender. His arms encircled me so tightly that I felt my ribs would crush beneath it. We didn't speak for the longest moment. Finally I laid my head against his, lips brushing his hair. "Remiel…" I whispered, but it sounded like a silent scream. He didn't move. Didn't respond. He just held me tighter, his silence held all the things he didn't know how to say … or didn't dare to.

We had only been married for three months. Three months full of moments of uncertainty. And now he was leaving again, called to some faraway conflict, some shadowed place where mortals like him were needed. He was going as a man…a mortal. And I was the woman left waiting, wondering how to breathe in the spaces he'd leave behind. Waiting for the day he might return. Praying that he would return.

As if reading my doubts and fears, his voice wrapped around me, pulling me from the edge of the nightmare I had been silently falling into. "Eva, I will come back to you. I promise." The sound of his voice was low and hoarse. The desperation, love, longing, and a fear neither one of wouldn't…didn't dare name. His arms tightened around me once more, like he could hold me in place and time, and maybe he could. I buried my face in his shoulder, then pressed a kiss against his beating heart, trying to pour everything I couldn't say into that one touch. I didn't care that the grip of his arms made it hard to breathe. I didn't want air if it didn't have him in it.

His hands shook slightly as he pulled back, just enough to look at me. His gaze searched mine, hungry for something. Was he needing reassurance, courage, maybe even forgiveness for leaving again? And I could only give him what I had which was whispered words, touches, and the raw ache of our love. "I'll be here, Remiel," I whispered, even though the words nearly choked me. This wasn't just a goodbye……

I wanted to tell him. About the life growing inside me. About what Michael had said. But Michael's words still rang loud in my ears, *not yet, not now*. The understanding of what Michael had commanded, made it so difficult. Knowing that I was letting Remiel leave without telling him. Remiel stepped back only enough to cradle my face in his hands, the tips of his fingers feathering across my cheekbone. Light but electric. I closed my eyes for just a second before opening them to look deep into his storm clouds.

"Penny for your thoughts?" he asked, his smile soft and coaxing.

I shook my head, a gentle smile tugging at the corner of my lips. "No," I teased, "but for a kiss, I might tell you."

His laughter rumbled through his chest like distant thunder. A sound that I loved. He instantly picked me up, my legs instinctively wrapping around his waist.

"Remiel!" I gasped, half laughing, but he was kissing me and I didn't want him to stop. He kissed me with the kind emotion that made the world of worries disappear. Every fear, every question, every painful what-if melted beneath the weight of his lips. As if reading my doubts and fears, his groan broke through the uncertainty.

He carried me out to the swing on the back porch, it creaked slightly when the breeze moved through it. This was our favorite spot and it held so many memories. He sat with me curled in his lap, and for one moment, the world felt still. It was just us. I leaned into him, head tucked beneath his chin.

He rested his cheek on my hair, rocking us slowly, back and forth, back and forth. No words. Just the rhythm of the swing and the steady beat of his heart beneath my hand.

He started humming, something old, maybe a hymn, maybe something from before his descent. I didn't know the melody, but it lulled around me like a lullaby. The scent of him filled my senses. I tried to remember the scent as I tried to etch every part of this moment into my memory.

"I don't want to leave you," he said eventually, his voice barely above a breath.

"I know," I whispered. I wanted to tell him everything. I wanted to scream that he couldn't go. But I didn't. I couldn't. My silence was the price of his return. I laid my head against his chest and he wrapped his arms tighter around me. I yawned despite myself, the swing lulling me, his warmth pulling me under.

"Go to sleep," he murmured, brushing his lips against my curls. "I'll be here when you wake up."

And I believed him……….

When I awoke, a blanket was on top of me, but his warmth was gone. I was no longer outside but in our bed. I sat up in alarm, heart pounding. "Remiel?" I called, practically stumbling from the bed. "Remiel?"

Panic clawed at me, had he gone without saying goodbye? I stumbled blindly down the dimly lit hallway, but then I saw him. Sitting at the kitchen bar holding a cup of coffee like he'd never leave. Relief rushed through me in a wave so strong it almost buckled my knees. He turned on the stool, then seeing my worried expression, he opened his arms.

I didn't hesitate. I went to him. "I thought you left," I said against his shoulder. "I panicked. I…"

He held me tighter. "I'd never leave without telling you."

I pulled back, studying his face. Those storm-gray eyes, the lines of weariness and tenderness. He was once an angel, yes, but in a way he was now my angel on earth. The one that had led me to salvation and a closer walk to God. Teaching me how to forgive and love myself. Running my fingers through his hair, I watched as he grabbed my hands and then he pressed his lips against the back of my hands.

"It's time," he said, soft and low. "I have to go, Eva."

Tears stung, but I nodded. I'd known this moment would come. We had pushed it off as long as we could. His hands found my waist. "You're holding something back."

I hesitated, I couldn't look at him. "I just… don't want to lose you." But that wasn't the truth. Not all of it….. If Remiel knew, he wouldn't leave. And if he didn't leave, he wouldn't return. That was the cruel balance of it all. The *ifs.*

I walked him to the door, each step a countdown I didn't want to finish. He turned, pulling me into one last embrace. His kiss this time was different. Less fire, more ache. Like a hidden goodbye... His hands curved around me, one at the small of my back, one in my hair and I clung to his shirt like I could keep him from vanishing.

"Just come back to me," I whispered.

He gave me a sad, crooked smile. "Eva, we found each other in the realms. That doesn't end there." He kissed my forehead, and I closed my eyes….when I opened them, he was already walking away. I stayed there, arms empty. And then I placed a hand over my stomach, over the life growing quietly inside me. No matter the distance, we were still connected. Always.

I watched him drive away until slowly, I walked back inside. I closed the door and leaned against it, struggling to control my ragged breaths. I took a deep breath, willing myself to stay strong. I had survived worse, after all my life had been a relentless road of trouble until Remiel arrived…but even then the road after had not been exactly smooth sailing.

Closing my eyes, I took one deep breath. ***You can do this Eva, you have been through worse.*** I knew I couldn't stay here all day wallowing in despair. I needed to get out of the house. A visit to Mariana and the baby would help. I shook off the thoughts of how to tell Remiel about the baby when he returned, and walked down the hallway. I would take a quick trip to town, get some things, go see Mariana and then swing by the stable to check on Nevada.

When I arrived at Mariana's house, the warmth inside hit me immediately—a small sanctuary from my life's chaos. Little Carlos was perched on the rug, giggling at the way a toy rattled in his tiny hands. He was growing so fast. Already, his dark hair, golden-brown eyes, and bronze skin bore a striking resemblance to his father. He squealed when I crawled close and began playing peek-a-boo, his laughter filling the room like sunlight.

Eventually, he crawled onto my lap, his tiny hands exploring my curls. I winced and laughed as he tugged at them, delighting in the way they bounced back.

"What's on your mind, Eva?" Mariana asked, her voice soft yet insistent. She settled cross-legged in front of me, gently lifting Carlos into her lap to keep him from yanking at my hair. "You're here, but you're not here. I know Remiel left today, but this… this is something deeper."

I slowly sat up, dragging my hands down my face in a tired, defeated way. "I didn't tell him something that was very important…now I wonder if it was a mistake?"
She shuffled little Carlos around to keep him from grabbing and

pulling her hair. "It can't be that bad, I mean, it's Remiel, you two live for each other, literally."

I offered a faint chuckle, but it sounded so hollow and fake. "It's serious. I didn't tell him he's going to be a father."

Mariana stopped playing with little Carlos and looked at me, her face was suddenly somber and serious. Mariana's fingers brushed Carlos' hair absently, but her eyes never left mine. "Eva, I am happy for you but as your best friend, you should have told him."

Her voice held a slight tremble of sadness, and I knew she was thinking of Carlos and how he died.

"I know, Mariana, but if I had told him, he never would have left." I said, putting a hand over my eyes, hoping to hide the tears that wanted to burst forth.

"So, Eva, so what if he had stayed? You work and he works, I know Lisa pays him well, Her stable is completely filled, and she has never had so many people coming to take riding lessons."

I wanted to tell her the truth but I could not. How could she possibly understand? It was not about money. It was about souls.

Three months later

"You lied to me." Remiel's voice was low but full of raw emotions that shattered the angry silence of the room.

"Why would you lie to me?" His eyes darkened, filled with pain and accusation. He clenched jaws in anger and I understood. I could not be angry with him. I had no words of defense.

I reached out instinctively, placing a hand on his arm, but he jerked away as if my touch burned him. "Remiel, please, you have to listen. It's not what you think. I couldn't tell you. I—"

He cut me off, his voice sharp as he pointed a finger at me. "You let me leave knowing the truth. You stood there and let me go." The betrayal in his tone was like an emotional blow, each word a dagger to my heart.

"I never thought that you would keep something like this from me, Eva." His words were like ice, slicing through the air between us.

"I have to leave, this is too much. I have to breathe somewhere away from you." His words hurt me and his expression was a mask of agony as he turned and walked too calmly out the front door. I expected that he would slam the door but no, he didn't even do that. I heard the start of the truck's engine and the crunch of gravel as he drove away.

I sank onto a kitchen stool, my legs suddenly weak. I could not hold it back any longer. The emotions cascaded inward and my sobs came out as shuddering gasps, each breath a painful reminder of my guilt. It was true. I had lied by omission. When Remiel returned, he had learned the truth from Matthew, not from me.

I wondered if Matthew had purposely orchestrated this rift between us. I could not understand why he would want to do that? Or perhaps it was just an innocent mistake. I wasn't sure. I couldn't think straight. My emotions were everywhere. They were confusing me and Remiel's hurt was punishing me.

My cellphone started ringing and I instantly knew it was Matthew. I looked at the number and hit the decline button, I didn't want to talk to him right now. I walked to the hallway and picked up my purse and keys. I needed to get out of the house away from the mess I had made.

I was sure I knew where Remiel had gone, but I wasn't going. I drove aimlessly for a while, my mind a whirl of despair and regret. Then I decided to go to Mariana's. But as I turned into her driveway, my heart sank when I saw Matthew's truck parked in front of her brick house. I should have known that he would be there.

Panic surged through me. I immediately put the car in reverse, but as I was halfway out, I saw Matthew emerging from the house, his gaze locking onto me. Of course he sensed I was there, I continued to back out but parked on the side, I couldn't just be rude and leave but I had to make up something.

I rolled my window down as he approached the car. "Eva, are you going to come in? Is everything ok? I tried calling you earlier."

His voice sounded concerned, but I couldn't offer an explanation without pointing fingers at him.

"I was bringing something for the baby," I lied, my voice catching. "But I forgot it at home. I need to go back and get it."

He frowned, worry etched on his face. "Eva, are you sure you are ok?"

I tightened my grip on the steering wheel, avoiding his gaze. "Matthew, I… I need to go." I saw his expression change to one of confusion and hurt as I began to roll up the window and shifted the car into drive.

"Eva, wait…I am sorry. About telling Remiel. I didn't know." He had put his hand on the window.

"Eva, I hope I haven't caused any confusion." His tone was genuine but at this moment, I didn't care for genuine or sincere.

I silently shook my head as I put the car in drive. Out of the corner of my eye, I saw him back up. I drove around for what seemed like hours but I knew it was only thirty or forty minutes. I finally returned to the house and Remiel's truck was there. I turned the car off and sat there looking at the cottage. Would he still be angry with me? Would he talk to me or ignore me? I felt like my stomach was in knots that continued to tighten and twist.

I stepped inside, my breaths shallow and uneven. He was sitting on the couch, his head buried in his hands. The moment the door clicked shut, he lifted his head, his eyes meeting mine. The silence between us was a suffocating blanket. I was unsure if he was going to come to me or if we would remain distant, our relationship hanging by a thread.

He stood up, his movements stiff with unresolved anger. We exchanged a long, painful look before he turned and walked down the hallway. I remained frozen, my heart aching with the knowledge that my silence had deepened the rift between us.

Remiel

I had been home for only a few hours, and already it felt like my world was unraveling. I had stopped by a flower shop on my way back, hoping to surprise Eva with a gift. She didn't know I was back, and I wanted to make the homecoming special. With a bouquet of sunflowers in hand, I headed towards the bookstore, my mind drifting to thoughts of seeing her again.

Suddenly, Matthew appeared with that wide, enthusiastic grin of his. He clasped my hand firmly, his joy very evident. "Congratulations, Remiel! I know you and Eva are over the moon. Mariana's planning a big celebration for you both and the baby announcement."

Confusion washed over me as I looked at him. My gaze dropped to his hand that he was still shaking mine and then back to his face. His smile faltered as he noticed my reaction, his demeanor suddenly changing from excited to worried in a heartbeat as he realized his mistake.

"Remiel, have you spoken with Eva? Have you seen her yet?" Matthew's tone went from congratulations to serious in about 5 seconds.

"No, I have not. But thank you for the news of our upcoming joy. Now if you will excuse me, I need to speak with my wife." I shoved the bouquet of flowers into his chest as I turned on my heels walking away.

Rapidly, I mentally pieced together the fragments of the puzzle, Eva was pregnant. I had been gone a little over three months, which meant she must have known before I left or discovered it shortly after. The realization that she hadn't mentioned it when I called, gnawed at me, till there was an ache in my chest. Why would she keep that from me? What was she hiding?

Somehow, my truck seemed to drive itself back to the cottage. My thoughts were consumed by Eva, the world outside became a blur. I sat in the truck for a few moments, gripping the wheel tightly as a fierce tide of betrayal and hurt surged within me. I wasn't just angry; I felt deeply wounded, as if a part of me had been taken without my consent.

She had kept this from me. Everybody knew but me. The feeling that she had known kept eating at me. The more that I thought about the day I left, everything made sense. For a few weeks, Eva had not eaten well. She played it off as the spring flu but on the day I was to leave, I felt like there was something she wanted to tell me but wouldn't.

I entered the house quietly, expecting to see her in the kitchen, but instead Eva was curled up on the edge of the couch, her head resting on her hand. She had been reading, but the book had slipped out of her hands and onto the floor. I approached her with a tenderness that contrasted sharply with the storm inside me. She looked so serene, she was wearing one of my gray cotton t-shirts and a pair of her leggings. Her curls, now longer and fuller, spilled over her shoulders and down her back.

I gently picked up the book and set it aside, my heart began racing as I noticed her slightly rounded belly beneath her shirt. I eased down beside her, careful not to wake her. My hand reached out almost of its own accord, resting on her stomach. The evidence was undeniable….she was carrying our child.

The realization sent a wave of awe through me, mingled with pain. I traced the small curve of her belly with my hands, the realization of our future sinking in. The thought of our child, the product of our love, filled me with both joy and anguish.

Eva stirred, her eyes fluttering open. The moment she saw me, a look of shock and panic crossed her face. Her hand instinctively moved to her stomach where it met mine, her gaze darting from our joined hands to my face. "Remiel, I can explain," she stammered, her voice trembling slightly with uncertainty of how to explain.

I pulled my hand away, the motion feeling like a blade cutting through the fragile thread between us. "You don't have to explain. Matthew already has." The bitterness in my voice was sharp.

She opened her mouth, searching for words, and I could see the hesitation—the delicate line between fear and guilt—but I pressed on, my voice rising, trembling with both anger and vulnerability. " I knew that

Matthew once loved you. I knew at the mountain. But I never thought you returned his affection. I never wanted to believe that. But is that what has happened?

Her eyes widened, shock colliding with hurt, and I saw the flicker of guilt there. "Remiel—no, what are you even saying?"

"Tell me the truth! You love him more than me, don't you? Is that why he was the first to know? Are you having regrets being married to… a descended angel? Or have you been pretending all this time, for my sake?" My insecurities all came pouring out.

Her eyes widened, shock colliding with hurt, and I saw the flicker of guilt there. "Remiel—"

"Don't! Don't speak!" I cut her off, the ache in my chest twisting into raw, human frustration. "I've returned, Eva. I came back. Everything I am, everything I've fought for, everything I've left behind. I came back for you. And you… you've been looking at him, thinking of him, sharing parts of your life that I should have been part of. And I—" My words faltered, the divine part of me warring with the human, claws of insecurity scratching at my soul. "I can't… I can't just stand here and act like that doesn't matter!"

She softened, her lips trembling, her gaze dropping as if she still carried the weight of all her shame—the past with Dagon, the taint of being a Beloved who had known a fallen angel. I could feel it, the pain and the fear in her eyes, but it only stoked the fire of my own insecurities. A descended angel, and yet I felt… unworthy. Incomplete. The shadow of my otherness reminding me …

"Answer me!" I demanded, my voice low and dangerous, but quivering with the vulnerability I refused to show. "Do you love him?"

Tears welled in her eyes, and I saw the faint quiver of her lips as she shook her head, voice trembling. "No, Remiel… it's not like that. You know it's not like that. After everything that has happened to us, how could you even think that, let alone say it?"

My chest heaved, the tension of anger, jealousy, and longing constricting me, yet beneath it, I felt the fragile hope that perhaps, despite everything, we could bridge this chasm. But the fear—the fear that my descent made me less…less worthy to be with her. Because I was not a Beloved by birth. I was a descended angel and clawed at me relentlessly.

She shook her head, voice trembling, "No, Remiel… it's not like that. He is our friend. You know that. He helped us and—"

"And he's Nephilim, Eva," I said, quieter now, trying to calm the storm inside…but more afraid than angry. "Do you even understand what that could mean? What his connections with other Nephilim–could mean?"

Her face went pale. Because now she understood what I was asking. "Matthew isn't like that. He would not turn on us, Remiel. He is not part of the darkness that we fight–that you fight." Her voice was soft but still uncertain.

I stared at her, heart hammering, the bitterness still clinging to my words. I walked out, seeking refuge at the stables. I could still hear Eva's pleas for me to listen, but my anger clouded my judgment. I needed distance, time to cool off before I said something more that I would regret.

Learning to control these mortal emotions was not the easiest thing. At the camp it was easier, we were all soldiers there with one purpose. There was no time to think about love or romance. It was strictly battle and survival. Now being back here, emotions were pouring in like a flood. I was angry because I had been denied the news of my child, I had been denied the celebration of knowing.

I stepped into the barn, and the familiar smell of hay and leather was a small comfort. Nevada lifted her head, nickered softly, and I ran a hand along her neck, letting the steady warmth anchor me. And then—before I could process it—Lisa was there. There in my space, there in my face.

"Remiel!" she exclaimed, almost throwing herself at me in her enthusiasm. She wrapped her arms around my neck in a tight hug, pressing close enough that her breasts were pressed against my chest in a way that was not accidental—or maybe just unthinking. "I can't believe you're back! You don't know how long we've been waiting!"

I froze for just a moment, caught between surprise and the flood of mortal sensation I was still adjusting to. Her embrace lingered a second too long, her body brushing subtly against mine as she laughed, the sound warm and bright. She pressed her lips to my cheek and I stiffened, gently easing her back just enough to create space.

Lisa's hands dropped to her sides, but the excitement in her eyes didn't waver. "I'm sorry," she said, still smiling.

"I didn't mean to smother you—I'm just... so glad you're here. Honestly, the whole team will be so glad that you're back." Lisa continued to run her hand up and down my arm, a gesture that was making me very uncomfortable. This was something she had never done before.

I nodded, keeping my voice calm. "It's good to be back," I said carefully, forcing myself to focus. Nevada's steady breathing under my hand helped, but a part of me remained alert, aware of the pull of her energy, the too-close warmth of her hug.

Lisa finally stepped back a pace, brushing imaginary dust from her sleeve, still smiling like she could light the whole barn on fire. Her riding shirt was unbuttoned just a little too far and her pants were extremely tighter than what she usually wore. "Well, I'll let you get settled. But I am just so glad to see you. Let me know when you have time and we will start going over the new project horses."

I exhaled slowly, "Thank you, Lisa." I could feel trouble brewing with her already. Something told me a lot had changed at her stables in the time that I had been gone. I wondered if Elliot, her last boyfriend was still around or had she gotten rid of him?

She lingered a heartbeat longer, too happy to let it end neatly, and I reminded myself why I needed to stay focused. The work, Eva, the life waiting for me outside this barn—it all demanded my attention. Nothing else mattered, not her friendliness, not her excitement, not the natural surge of longing that came with human contact. Yet even in her excitement and my denial, I felt the *pull of mortal emotions*, the tiny friction that reminded me how fragile control could be.

Eventually, I found myself back at the cottage, sitting on the couch, my head in my hands. When Eva came in, I rose to approach her, but when she remained silent, I turned and headed towards the back porch, needing to escape. Just as I reached the door, her voice stopped me. "Remiel, please. Please just talk to me."

I hesitated, my hand on the doorknob. Memories of the past flooded my mind. I had left her so many times before, and she had always been there waiting for me. Shaking my head, I turned around. As I walked toward her, the emotions on her face were overwhelming. Yet the one thing that stood out was her love. It radiated from her and I could still feel it even underneath her pain.

I opened my arms, and she came to me immediately, burying her face against my chest. I inhaled the familiar scent of her, lavender and a mixture of warmth and tenderness. I wrapped my arms around her, my heart literally aching with the need to comfort and be comforted. Her body trembled slightly, her emotions barely contained. I felt her take a deep breath and then exhale slowly.

Gently, I took her by the shoulders and pulled her a little away from me, needing to see her face clearly. "Why, Eva? Why didn't you tell me? Did you know?"

She would not look at me, so I pulled back and placed my hand gently under her chin, lifting it, till those sunflower eyes were gazing into mine. Her eyes were pools of unshed tears as she searched for the right words. The vulnerability in her gaze mirrored the pain I felt. The space between us seemed to shrink, but the gulf of misunderstanding remained.

"Michael told me…" Eva's voice trembled as she took a shuddering breath, her eyes glistening. "Right after I found out, he came to me. He told me that I couldn't tell you, because if I did, you wouldn't go and then… then…" Her words faltered, the weight of her unspoken fears hanging heavily between us.

"Then what, Eva? What else did he tell you?" My voice came out harsher than I intended, laced with frustration and desperation.

She moved away from me, as she pulled out of my embrace, tears began to spill, breaking my heart. Her arms crossed protectively over her chest, which only emphasized the gentle curve of her belly even more.

"He told me that if you stayed and didn't go as you had promised, as you had vowed...that you would become like the Fallen…" She wiped angrily at her tears. "Why? Why did you keep that from me? I never wanted you to become mortal if that meant you would become a Fallen."

"He had no right to tell you." I stepped toward her, wanting to close the distance. My heart began to race rapidly and uncontrollably.

"He had every right to tell me," she shot back, her voice quivering with emotion. "He was trying to protect you… protect us." She crossed her arms once more as if trying to shield her heart from the truth.

I closed the distance in two strides, my hands framing her face, my thumb brushing away the tears. "Do you have any idea what it did to me?" I murmured.

"Coming back and realizing the one thing that should have been shared between us… was kept from me?" Her breath shuddered as my forehead rested against hers.

"I felt shut out," I confessed softly. "Like you didn't trust me with your fear… or your hope."

"I was terrified," she whispered. "Of losing you."

The confession shattered what little restraint I had left. I pulled her back into me, harder this time, my mouth brushing her temple, her cheek, my breath warm against her skin. She gasped softly, fingers curling into my arms, her body fitting against mine like it always had—like it always would.

And I knew that she was right, Michael, my once celestial brother, had always tried to protect me. I sighed, running my hand through her hair. "Eva, please, I don't want to argue."

My gaze lingering on her, filled with both longing and remorse. She looked so beautiful, so intensely alluring, even now. The sight of her, so close yet so distant, drove me wild with a need that had been unfulfilled for far too long. I pressed a slow, lingering kiss to her forehead instead of her lips, because this wasn't just about desire. This was about *relief.* About having her here, safe, after everything.

She didn't pull away, but she didn't lean in either. Her body was tense, like she wasn't sure she could trust this moment yet. I didn't blame her…I kissed her, wishing I could kiss away all of the harsh words and pain that I had caused.

Then I let my lips trail to hers, it was slow. Deliberate. A kiss meant to ask, not take. My lips brushed hers once, barely there, before pressing again—deeper this time, fuller, as if I were pouring every unsaid apology and every sleepless night into that single connection.

She inhaled sharply, and her body softened against me, the tension melting like she had finally allowed herself to feel what she'd been holding back. Her hands slid into my shirt, gripping the fabric as though she needed proof that I was real, that I wasn't leaving again.

The kiss deepened, not frantic, not rushed—just aching. A meeting of longing and restraint, of desire tempered by love. I tasted salt from her tears, felt her breath tremble against my mouth, and I held her closer, one hand firm at her back, the other cradling her face like something precious. When we finally parted, our foreheads rested together, breaths mingling, hearts racing in uneven rhythm.

The evening breeze drifted around us, soft and warm, carrying the scent of honeysuckles and the faint hum of crickets singing in the grass. After our conversation in the hallway, we had stepped outside, hoping to leave the arguments and doubt behind, to reclaim a fragment of calm.

We walked slowly, side by side, letting the fading sky guide us rather than our words. The sunsets had always been our favorite—those long, golden moments where the world seemed to hold its breath. After we married, we had shared so many of them, marveling at the shifting colors, tracing patterns in the clouds like they were messages written just for us.

I brushed a strand of hair from her face, my fingers lingering longer than necessary, and smiled softly. "If you think these sunsets are beautiful from an earthly view," I said, my voice low, almost a whisper, "just wait until you see the lights in heaven."

Her eyes lifted to mine, shining in the dimming light, and I felt a small thrill of joy at the awe there, the same delight she always carried when I spoke of things beyond this world. She had never ceased to be amazed, and I never ceased to love her wonder.

"I missed you," I murmured in her hair. "I know I have no right to say that now. But I did."

She hesitated, then let her hands rest lightly against my chest. Her shirt had ridden up just a little with the breeze, revealing the soft small swell of her stomach, and she tugged it down quickly. That small motion, so instinctive, so vulnerable. It cut through me deeper than anything else could have. I took a breath and leaned back, just enough to look at her. "Eva," I said, keeping my voice gentle. "You don't have to hide from me."

She looked away, her cheeks becoming red. Even after we had been married, she would blush at any compliment to her body or just her— period. "I know your body's changing. I know you're changing. But it's all beautiful to me. You're beautiful to me."

Her shoulders relaxed as I brushed her hair back again, so I could see her face. "You are my wife. And you're carrying our child. You don't have to be anything more than exactly what you are, right now."

She exhaled slowly. Her eyes met mine, still guarded, but there was a flicker of softness behind them. I saw the woman I loved, the one who had always tried to be strong even when she was breaking. Slowly, deliberately, I slipped my fingers beneath the hem of her shirt, pausing there, giving her time to change her mind. When she nodded—just once—I eased the fabric upward, my touch slow and unhurried. I drew the shirt over her head and set it aside, my gaze never leaving hers.

I guided her back gently, lowering her onto the cool grass beneath us. The earth cradled her, the night air brushing her skin, the sky above painted in the last traces of fading gold and violet.

I followed her down, bracing myself on one elbow, and let my lips trail softly along her shoulder, her collarbone, down—slow, intentional— until I reached her stomach.

My breath caught as I pressed a kiss there, tender and lingering, not fueled by hunger but by awe. By gratitude. By love. My hands moved softly over her abdomen, warm and steady, as if memorizing the shape of her, as if grounding us both in the reality of this moment.

"This," I murmured against her skin, "is life. And you are beautiful."

Her fingers slid into my hair, not gripping, just resting there. I kissed her again, and again—each touch a promise, each breath shared a quiet vow.

The crickets sang around us, the wind whispered through the grass, and for that moment the world felt perfectly aligned—heaven and earth brushing close, love and faith entwined. There was no rush. No fear. Only the quiet certainty that this—*this*—was exactly where we were meant to be.

Eva

When he pulled me into his arms, I didn't resist, but there was a feeling that I could not shake. Something had changed in him. It was almost as if there was a shadow of darkness lingering on him. A shadow that I could not see physically but I knew it was there. Even though his words and actions were that of my Remiel, something lingered there.

His lips brushed my forehead. I let my hands rest against his chest, not holding, just... touching. His heart beat steady beneath my palms, a rhythm that had replaced his once steady heavenly hum.

The breeze tugged at my shirt, lifting the hem just enough to expose the curve of my stomach. Reflexively, I tugged it back down. I didn't want him to see me like this, changed, starting to stretch, unfamiliar even to myself. I didn't want to see the look in his eyes that said I wasn't attractive anymore. But that look never came.

"Eva," he said, his voice softer than I expected, "you don't have to hide from me."

I turned my head slightly, unable to meet his gaze. I wanted to believe him. His eyes stayed on me, steady and open. No pressure. No expectation. Just him, seeing me. Really seeing me.

"You are my wife," he said. "And you're carrying our child. You don't have to be anything more than exactly what you are, right now."

Tears stung the back of my eyes not from sadness, but from the unexpected beauty in his words. I had braced for an ugly silence. But not this. This was different. So when I leaned in again, he gently pulled my hair to one side, and his lips traced down my neck trailing off.

I hesitated, my hands resting lightly against his chest, as if testing whether this moment was real. He drew in a breath, leaning back just enough to look at me, and his voice, soft and steady, cut through the swirl of my fear. "Eva," he said, gently, "you don't have to hide from me."

My eyes flicked up to his, searching for any sign of judgment, but there was none. Only warmth. Only love. Only his raw, quiet devotion that had always made my heart ache.

Slowly, carefully, he lifted his hand and brushed his thumb along my jaw. I felt the electricity in that simple touch, my pulse stuttering. Then his fingers slipped beneath the hem of my shirt. I froze for a heartbeat, then, meeting his gaze, I nodded. And with the gentlest care, he lifted the shirt over my head and set it aside. I felt exposed, yes—but also seen, cherished in a way that left me trembling.

He guided me back gently, lowering me onto the cool grass. The earth beneath me was steady, grounding, but my entire body was alight, every nerve attuned to him. He followed me down, bracing himself on one elbow, his lips brushing my shoulder, my collarbone... and then—my stomach. He pressed a kiss there, slow as his hands moved softly, memorizing the curves and warmth of me. I felt cherished, honored, held in a way I had never known.

"This is life," he whispered against my skin. "And you are beautiful."

I let my fingers drift into his hair, feeling the rhythm of him, the certainty in his touch. Even though uncertainty lingered in my mind. The crickets sang around us, the evening breeze brushing against my skin, and for a moment, the world shrank to this—the two of us, the sky above, the warmth of his hands, the certainty of his love. I had never felt more seen. More treasured. Or more completely his.

When the dew started to fall on the grass around us, we finally went inside. We made small talk about the baby, I could tell it still bothered Remiel that he had been the last to find out. When I tried to talk to him about what had happened and the mission, I was automatically shut down. He wouldn't open up, not even the least bit, about his mission. There was no debating about it. The subject was off limits. I tried not to let it bother me as I cooked supper.

He had gone to shower but he was taking such a long time. I decided to go check on him, when I entered the bedroom, I could see directly into our bathroom. He was putting his clothes on, with his back to me. Remiel hadn't seen or heard me come in.

He was bending down picking up the towel that had fallen, when he stood up, I gasped, covering my mouth with my hands. His back was covered with scars, it looked as if someone had mutilated his entire back. Where his back was healing, the scars were raised and still an ugly bright red and pink. His back shouted of torture.

Hearing me gasp, he quickly turned around and pulled his blue shirt on quickly, "Eva?" I knew he was wondering how long I had been standing there. I walked toward him, my hand instinctively reaching for his back.

"What happened? Remiel, what happened to your back?" I reached for him, but he stepped back.

"Eva, please, it is not something that I want to talk about." His voice was calm but the type of calm that could be deadly. The type of calm and tone that made me stop immediately. I knew if I pressed the issue, he would pull further away from me.

Letting my hand drop, I simply nodded, "Supper is ready, I have your plate ready." He nodded, waiting to see if I was going to turn to go, when I didn't, he walked by me, giving me a simple kiss on the head. As if nothing was wrong, as if I hadn't seen the scars on his back.

At supper, he asked about church and how the young women's group was going. "It is great, we had so many to join, that we had to move it to the church. Annie is actually helping out a lot. We swap up every month, she has this month. Next month Ryta will have it. Each month, each woman brings their own story to the group and some relate to different stories in the Bible. Then we usually do a month-long Bible study on that biblical person or that book of the Bible."

He smiled, "I am so proud of you and them. It takes courage to be vulnerable in front of others and share your story." He reached over and picked up my hand, kissing it. His passionate yet soft gaze, made my heart skip. I swallowed hard, trying not to drown in the overwhelming emotions that I felt for him. I was so happy just to have him home.

We spoke of many things, even while we cleaned up the kitchen and put away dishes. What we did not speak of was *him* and the question of *what had happened to him,* and it gnawed at me.

When we were getting ready for bed, he did not take his shirt off. He laid there in his blue plaid pjs and his t-shirt. He never slept in a t-shirt before and barely slept in pjs or boxers. He said that he always felt confined by them when he tried to sleep. I laid down in the bed beside him, unsure of what to say or do. There was an ugly and awkward silence. Finally, I turned over on my side, away from him.

It was only when he thought I was asleep, that he moved closer and wrapped his arm around me. His hand instinctively went to my stomach, and our baby began moving around. I had not felt the baby move until tonight. It was almost as if the baby knew its father's touch. I wanted to tell Remiel this, but he thought I was asleep. So I let him continue with his hand on our child as he began humming a low melody.

When he stopped, it was because he had finally drifted off to sleep. I turned over to face him, gently tracing his face. My Remiel, he had returned to me as he had promised. Yet, something was wrong, something had happened while he was over there. Something that he refused to share with me. "My Remiel."

I finally dozed off to sleep only to be woken sometime later, Remiel was moving around in the bed as if he was fighting with someone. I turned on the lamp, hoping the light would wake him, but it didn't. He started calling my name, the way he cried out tore through me.

I could not let the nightmare continue, I cautiously shook his shoulder, remembering the last time that I tried to wake him from a nightmare. "Remiel, love, it's okay. Remiel, you are here now. Shhh." Over and over again, I reassured him.

Finally opening his eyes, it took him a second to realize where he was. Then Remiel looked straight up at the ceiling for a very long moment, before he finally rolled over and wrapped his arms around my waist burying his head in my side.

Nothing was said, nothing was asked. I sat there gently, stroking his hair. I knew this giant of a mortal faced unseen demons.

I continued to stroke his hair and face until I saw the steady rise and fall of his chest, letting me know that he was once more asleep. I finally sunk down in the bed beside him. "Oh, my Remiel, when will those demons ever leave you alone?"

Chapter Two

Remiel

I sat there beside Eva. Trying to ignore the chaos of everyone talking at one time. The cookout at Mariana's was a whirlwind of noise and activity, a far cry from the solitude and quietness that I craved. Her backyard, usually a peaceful place, now felt like a crowded cage. I kept stealing glances at Eva, who seemed to be thriving amidst the happy chaos, her laughter and radiant smile was a complete opposite of what I felt inside. I wanted to leave, no, I wanted to run. I didn't like being around a lot of people. It felt suffocating.

Every time our eyes met, she squeezed my hand, a silent assurance that she was okay. Watching her, I was in silent awe. Her transformation from the depths of darkness to the vibrant, glowing woman before me was nothing short of miraculous. Nobody around us had seen the emotional or spiritual hell she had walked through. The strength she had shown. The joy that lit up her eyes as she spoke about the baby's gender and nursery, it was all breathtaking. I was lost in thoughts of her when my phone buzzed with a notification.

I glanced at the screen: **Stables-Lisa.** I sighed, feeling a pang of relief mixed with guilt. I needed an excuse to escape, but I also knew how much this event meant to Eva. I slipped away to a quieter corner of the yard, answered the call, and listened as Lisa explained the issue with the stables.

"Lisa, just tell the owners I'll be there in thirty minutes," I said, my voice steady as I tried not to let the relief come through. "I'll sort it out. It's probably something minor." I hung up, shaking my head. As glad as I was for an excuse to leave, I was somewhat agitated that Lisa was becoming more dependent on me-to the point that she would call me at all hours to talk about a horse.

"Do you have to leave, Remiel?" Her voice came softly, almost as if she feared the answer. I turned to find her standing behind me, her presence sent a wave of peace over me. Her pale green sundress flowed around her, and I couldn't resist reaching out to adjust a strap, letting my fingers graze her shoulder, a touch that spoke of everything I felt.

"I'm not leaving just yet," I murmured, my voice low and intimate. "I'll stay for another half hour. Mariana went through all this trouble for us, and I don't want to seem rude by disappearing." I wanted to leave but I also wanted to be there for her.

Eva's smile was gentle, but her eyes held a knowing glint. She took my hand, her touch sending a warmth to my restless soul. "But I know you're not fond of crowds either."

I raised her hand to my lips, placing a soft kiss on her palm. "For you, my love, I would face all of hell itself just to see you smile."

Her cheeks flushed a delicate pink, a sight that made my heart race. I drew her into my arms, holding her close. The sensation of her against me was a reminder of how much I had missed her touch during my absence. Public displays of affection were new to her, and sometimes she seemed unsure. I could feel her impulse to move away but I wanted her to feel, to understand how essential she was to me. So I continued to hold her just a little longer.

"Why don't I head out—in about thirty minutes," I finally suggested, "and you can stay here and enjoy yourself. I'll come back to get you once I've sorted things at the stables. I doubt it's anything major, just need to observe the horse and rider."

Eva leaned back slightly, searching my face with a mix of concern and love. "Are you okay with that?" Her hesitation spoke volumes.

She knew about my nightmares, my compulsive need to keep tabs on her. Since my return, I had been overly cautious, constantly checking her location and calling her, driven by a fear of losing her that gripped me tightly and would not let go, no matter how hard I prayed.

I nodded, leaning forward to place a soft kiss on her forehead. "Yeah, you should enjoy your time with your friends. I know I haven't given you much space lately."

Her fingers stroked my arm gently, her touch soothing. "But Remiel, I'm not complaining. I promise." Her sincerity, so soft and gentle, made my heart swell with love. Amid my struggles to find my place among mortals and to reconcile with who I am, she has been my anchor.

I traced the curve of her face with my finger. "I know you're not complaining, but I don't want to suffocate you either."

She gazed at me, her eyes shining with emotions that made me catch my breath. Then in a teasing tone, she asked me. "Remiel, do you know how much I love you?" I pulled her closer, wanting to hold her forever. Yes, I knew exactly how much she loved me and all of Heaven knew how much I loved her.

Eva

I had stayed back to help Mariana clean after the party. Matthew had taken little Carlos inside to lay him down for a nap. I watched as my friend's gaze followed them inside, her expression a mixture of love and longing. I cleared my throat, "Matthew is very good with little Carlos, isn't he?"

Mariana nodded, her movements a little uncertain as she started picking up paper plates and cups, shoving them into the garbage bag she was holding. "Yes, he is," she replied shortly, moving down the picnic table.

"Mariana, does he know you love him?" My question stopped her dead in her tracks. She slowly finished putting the plate in the bag before looking up at me, her eyes wide with a mix of fear and confusion.

"It's not fair, Eva. It's not fair to Carlos that I'm already falling in love with someone else, not after the hell I put us both through. I can't love someone else." She shook her beautiful blonde hair as she slowly picked up another styrofoam cup.

When her eyes met mine again, they were brimming with tears. "What kind of person…wife does that make me?"

Reaching over to console my friend, I softly squeezed her hand. "That makes you human. Carlos wouldn't want you grieving your entire life away. He loved you and wanted you to be loved and happy."

She shook her head, tears spilling over. "I can't, Eva. I don't know if he even feels the same, and I don't want little Carlos to never know how great of a person his father was. If I loved another man—"

"If you loved another man, if you loved Matthew and Matthew loved you, he would understand your grief and respect your wishes about Carlos knowing his father. He would never try to replace him. Mariana, you can't love him and never tell him."

"What if he doesn't feel the same?" She said, crumbling napkins and putting them in the bag. "I don't want to take a risk. I'm not sure my heart could handle it."

I wanted to tell her that the way Matthew looked at her, reminded me so much of a love struck person, but I knew that I needed to talk to him first before saying anything. There might be a reason why he was not telling Mariana what everyone else could clearly see.

We finished cleaning in silence. As we were putting the last bags in the garbage can, she turned to me. "Eva, you are my best friend, and I never thanked you for being there for me after I lost him."

"Oh, Mariana, you know you didn't need to. That's what we do; that's what friends are for." I took her hand and squeezed it.

She shook her head as if trying to shake away the memories. "I know, Eva, but I feel like after Gabriel died, I wasn't there for you. Not like I should have been. I feel like I left you alone too much. I felt like *we all* left you alone too much."

Regret poured out along with her words. "I think we all did," she repeated, barely above a whisper. "We thought giving you space was helping…but sometimes I wonder if we just abandoned you in your grief because it was easier than watching you drown in it."

The truth of her words broke my heart. I bit my lip, knowing she would never truly understand the darkness I had fallen into at that point in my life, but something deeper that had reached for me inside the grief. "Mariana, you did what a great friend should have done. You loved me and let me have space."

She nodded slowly and closed the lid to the garbage. Just then, Matthew emerged from the backdoor. "Hey, I'm sorry. Carlos took a little bit longer to get to sleep than I thought. Do you need any help?"

"No, Matthew, we are done. Thank you, though. And thank you for taking care of Carlos." Her words were sincere and grateful, but the tone of affection was not hidden from me or from Matthew.

Matthew's gaze softened as he looked at her. "Anytime, Mariana."

I looked down at my watch, wondering where Remiel was. It had been well over half an hour. But I did not want to call him, especially if he was in the arena with a rider.

"Mariana, I hate to ask but you would mind driving me to the stables?" The stables were about fifteen minutes from her house. She could drop me off there and then I could wait for Remiel to finish.

"I will take you, Eva. I have to go into town anyway. I will take you there." Matthew offered, holding the backdoor open for us to pass through.

"Thank you Matthew, I appreciate that." I said gratefully.

Matthew and Mariana helped load the baby gifts into Matthew's truck. I gave Mariana a quick hug goodbye and headed back out the front door.

Matthew was walking out behind me with his truck keys. He held open the door for me, he and Remiel were always doing that. It was so hard to get used to but I loved it just the same.

On the drive to the stables I had dozed off while talking to Matthew. I woke up, when he was opening the truck door for me. He had parked us on the slope beside the barn so I held onto his hand as I climbed down. "Thank you." I said as I started to walk off to find Remiel.

But I turned back to him, suddenly remembering what I had needed to talk to him about. "Matthew, I know it is none of my business but do you care for Mariana?"

I could tell that my question had caught him off guard as he tried to control his expression. The muscles tensed in his face. "Why? Has she mentioned anything to you?"

"Matthew, I am asking you." I said pointing at him. "Matthew, we are friends, you can be honest with me."

Leaning against the truck door and running his hand through his now short wavy blonde hair, in an agitated manner, he shook his head. "Eva, I can't compete with a ghost. I love her but I will never be Carlos and I don't want to be a replacement to him. I need her to love me for me."

"Matthew, she doesn't want to replace Carlos. It is the total opposite. You need to speak with her and tell her the truth." I said, wondering what if I should tell him about my earlier conversation with Mariana but I stopped myself.

He shook his head. "What about my secret, Eva? Soon enough she will realize I don't age as fast as everyone else does. I can't hide my curse forever about knowing or sensing things."

He became agitated as he spoke and I understood why. Nephilim were often looked at as the evil offspring of the Fallen angels. But many of them weren't, there were actually ones that chose to be good and work for the kingdom of God. Matthew was one of the good ones, the Others, as Remiels called them, were pure evil and gladly did the devil's work.

"Matthew, what you have is not a curse but a gift. You need to realize that and you have used it to help many." I squeezed his hand. "Please talk to her."

He nodded and then reached down and hugged me. I returned his hug, Matthew had become like a true brother to me. I cared about how he felt, especially if it meant his and Mariana's happiness.

Remiel

I had just finished putting Zeus, a bay gelding, in his stall, when I heard Matthew's truck. I latched the door and headed out to meet him, I was sure he had brought Eva. It had taken me longer to finish with the horse and rider than I originally thought. I knew it had been over an hour. I walked toward the front door and was going around the corner to parking spots, when I stopped in my tracks.

The scene before me was Matthew and Eva talking. I saw Matthew say something then run his hand through his hair as if he was really worried about something or someone. Then he turned to Eva, who had taken his hand in hers.

I felt my heart start beating faster, I knew this feeling and I had to control it. It was jealousy, a human emotion that I did not like. I found it annoying and wondered how Beloveds had lived with it all these centuries. No wonder there had been battles and wars started. Jealousy was an emotion that could ruin not only a marriage, but a country and one's very soul.

I watched as they continued talking and then he leaned to hug her. I don't know when I actually took leave of all my senses. My body was no longer one that I controlled as I felt myself moving forward. I could hear a voice telling me that I should stop, but at that moment, I could not.

It was almost as if I was watching myself in slow motion, when I ripped Matthew from Eva's grasp and then punched him. "Don't touch her again!" I could hear myself shouting at him.

I could feel this rage building inside of me threatening to explode, I moved toward him. Why, I didn't know. Then I felt like I was suddenly sucked back into my body as I watched Eva kneeling beside him. "Remiel, Stop!!" She had screamed at me as she knelt down where Matthew was slowly getting to his knees, wiping the blood from his busted lip.

She stood up as she turned to confront me. "What is your problem?!!!" She shoved against my chest. I swayed back, not from her push but from the surprise that I had actually hit Matthew.

I felt my breath coming shallow, like I could barely breathe. "My problem is every time he is around you, he is trying to touch you." I glared at Matthew, daring him to say otherwise.

"Touch me? Remiel, he was giving me a hug. An innocent hug. He is my friend, *our* friend. Or have you forgotten so quickly who helped to find you?" Her words brought me back to reality.

What was I doing?

I shook my head trying to focus on the situation at hand. This was not me, what I had let come over me, or control me? I moved forward and offered Matthew my hand to get up, he looked at a minute before taking and standing up, I watched as he brushed the dust off his jeans and his shirt. "Matthew, I apologize, I don't know where that came from. I am sorry."

Matthew stood there for a moment studying me before he finally spoke. "You still haven't mastered the emotions and senses of being a mortal."

He touched his lips and winced. "I understand, you barely had any time with your wife before you had to leave her. Remiel, I am a friend not a threat. Believe that."

I did but I also remembered the words he had spoken at Sarah's, I knew that he had been in love with Eva at one point. I pushed those thoughts away. No, he was not an enemy. I repeated that in my head, several times.

I nodded, "It is harder than I thought it would be." I sighed, hard was an understatement. It was like being in a tornado of emotions and trying to control them was like trying to tell the storm to stop.

Matthew, understandably put his hand on my shoulder, before touching his lip and winching with a little pain. "Remiel, it doesn't get easier, it just becomes more manageable. Praying, lots of praying, will do a world of help."

I gave a half chuckle before turning around to face Eva's fury. I knew that was not going to be good. She was standing there, just staring at me. Her face was void of any expression, she suddenly turned on her heels and turned to Matthew's truck to unpack the gifts.

Matthew and I looked at each other, he shook his head before we moved forward to help her, not saying anything. Matthew gave me a "good luck" look before we left. Once in the truck with her, I tried to talk to her, but her answers were short, not leaving any room to elaborate or develop conversation. I got it, I had messed up. She was mad, probably the first time she had ever really been mad at me, not including the day I came back.

We were fighting again… I could fight with demons and evil, but with Eva, I could not. I didn't like it either. I wanted to fix this and fast.

Once we made it home, I opened the truck door to help her out. She ignored my hand completely. Instead she started unpacking the gifts and taking them to the nursery that she had created in my absence.

In silence I helped her, hoping that she would be less angry, but I don't think it helped. She remained in the nursery hanging clothes up and rearranging toys and blankets. When she finally emerged, she simply stated that she was going for a walk in the woods, down the path and she would be back later.

I let her go because I knew I had sincerely messed this up. The need to protect her, to keep her close, was driving a wedge between us, and I was lost on how to mend it. I didn't like her walking in the woods by herself, but I knew where she was going. To her tree, probably to pray, cry or complain to God about how stupid I was. I watched her walk away, I would give her a little while, and if she didn't come back, I would go look for her.

I sat on the back door steps with my head in my hands, my mind a whirlwind of conflicting emotions. How could I separate my intense feelings for her from the person she needed me to be? The fear of losing her gnawed at my insides, and the guilt of pushing her away was like a knife twisting in my heart. My actions were replaying in my mind constantly, making it hard to think. Being mortal and trying to understand and control these human feelings was difficult and challenged me. I feared that they would be the undoing between Eva and I.

Time dragged on, each minute feeling like an eternity. Then, finally, I heard the rustling of leaves and looked up to see her emerging from the edge of the woods. My heart leaped at the sight of her, but I stayed where I was, knowing I couldn't rush her. She approached slowly, her hands clasped in front of her, a sign that this was serious.

"Remiel, I think I am going to visit my mother for a few days." Her voice was calm, but I could read the underlying message. I nodded in agreement, carefully choosing my next words.

"I understand." But I didn't. I didn't understand anything that was happening.

She reached out tentatively, her fingers grazing my arm, sending a shiver through me. "Remiel, I do... I do love you. I just need......"

She sighed trying to figure out how to continue. "The last couple weeks have been emotionally confusing. You won't talk about the baby much, you worry when I go to see my friends or go to work. You won't tell me anything about where you went or what you did while fighting...your nightmares…Remiel, I am your wife and you keep secrets from me. I want to help you, but how can I… if you refuse to let me in?"

Her words cut deep, each one a reminder of how I had failed her. The horrors I had witnessed were not something I could or would share with her. The remote village where I had been assigned was a nightmare, a place steeped in witchcraft and black magic. I had been tasked with rescuing a young boy and his sister, ensuring they reached the safety of a pastor's home. But I had failed. I couldn't save the girl, and the boy had to endure the terror of seeing his village burned, his people slaughtered. The screams of the mothers as their children were killed in front of them still haunted me. Then the orphanage, there had been none left to save. That had felt like a defeat and that had only been one of the missions that I had completed. The blood, the smell of burning bodies, the screams... they were all etched into my memory, mingling with the fear of losing her, driving me to the brink of insanity. The demons that haunted me every night, the images of them dragging her away from me as I tried desperately to hold on to her. Her screams and their dark evil laughs......

"Eva, you don't want to know, please don't ask me again." My voice was strained, my body tense with the effort of holding back the flood of memories. I wanted to hold her, to find comfort in her embrace, but I was terrified of her rejection.

She reached up, cupping my face in her hands. "Remiel, please. I know you are trying to protect me, but let me help you." Her eyes were filled with a desperate plea, and it tore at me.

I took her hands, kissing each one gently before looking into her sunflower eyes. "Eva, I will always protect you, even from my own stupidity." My voice was barely above a whisper as I laid my hand on her abdomen, feeling the life growing inside her. The thought of our child brought a surge of love and fear.

She took a deep, shuddering breath. "But you won't tell me what is driving you away from me?" Her voice quivered as she took a step back, her eyes brimming with unshed tears, before walking past me into the house. I watched her retreat. Why couldn't she understand that I didn't want her to carry that burden? It was just too heavy.

That night, after she had fallen asleep, I moved closer behind her. I wrapped my arms around her, and she instinctively cuddled closer, sighing with contentment in her sleep. I pressed a kiss to her shoulder, careful not to wake her. "Eva, my everything," I whispered, my voice barely audible. "You don't understand how much I need you."

When I woke up, the sun was already streaming through the window, casting a golden glow over the room. I turned over, reaching for her, but she wasn't there. Panic rushed through me, until I saw her leaning against the bedroom door frame with a cup of coffee in her hand. She held up the coffee, her eyes softening when she saw me.

"I didn't wake you. You were actually sleeping…peacefully." She walked over and sat on the edge of the bed. "I have coffee and breakfast in the kitchen." She offered the coffee to me. I took it, sitting up in bed and watching her over the brim of the cup as she looked down, nervously tracing the hem of the sheet.

I leaned over and placed the coffee on the nightstand. "Eva, come here." I motioned for her while reaching out, and she straddled me on the bed, her blue cotton nightgown riding up slightly. I let my hands rest on her hips as I positioned her a little more comfortably for me. She chuckled when she realized what I had done.

Letting her arms rest on my shoulders, she ran her fingers through my hair, a gesture that always soothed me but turned me on at the same time. She leaned her forehead against mine. "Remiel, you know I love you, right?"

Running my hands under her nightgown and up her back, feeling the smoothness of her skin, I nodded. "I know, Eva. I don't like to fight, and I'm sorry about yesterday. What happened was completely uncalled for and my fault. I just don't like anyone to touch what is mine."

Her eyes sparkled with amusement and something deeper. "Remiel, when did you become so possessive?"

Giving her a mischievous grin, I quickly changed our positions, flipping her under me but making sure not to hurt her. She laughed out loud, her curls bouncing around her face. "Remiel!"

Reaching down, I brought one of her legs around my waist, and she quickly wrapped the other around me. "You will always be mine," I growled playfully, leaning down to kiss her deeply, my lips lingering on hers before moving to her neck. "Tell me, Eva, tell me that you don't want to be mine."

She opened her eyes and gave me a sideways grin before reaching up to trace my face, then her hand moved slowly down, teasingly, sending a shudder through me. "Remiel, I will always be yours."

Rolling over on my side, I motioned for her to come closer. I held her as we talked about the baby and names. I was still explaining the different meanings of the angel names, when I heard her deep breathing. She had fallen asleep.

I lay there for the longest time, just watching her sleep and running my fingers through her hair. I loved her with everything that was in me and my enemies knew how to use that against me. I was not scared of dying in a mission, I was scared of what would happen to her and our child if I did.

As a mortal, my walk with God was different now. I couldn't hear or feel him as before and that scared me. Sometimes I felt like I had been left in the dark. Learning to pray and have faith like a Beloved was hard. When I couldn't hear or feel him the first time that I prayed, or given an answer…my first instinct was to give up.

Eva

I am not sure how long I had been asleep, but when I woke up, he was watching me. His gaze was intense, filled with a mixture of love and something else. I chuckled softly, pulling the sheet over my body and my head.

Remiel immediately jerked it away, his touch firm yet gentle. "No, my love. I know you are not covering up, not from me." He pulled the cover all the way down and started moving his hand up my leg, causing a ticklish sensation.

"Remiel, stop!" I said, laughing. He laughed too, as he moved to lay beside me. I turned on my side, looking at him, trying to memorize the lines of his face. "That is the second time I have heard you laugh since you have been back."

He ran his hand back and forth on my shoulder, his expression becoming somber once more. "Do you still want to go to your mother's?"

I took his face in my hands, making him look at me. "Remiel, I am not leaving you. I just think a day or two would help. I need to go see Mom anyway. You know how my mother is. She gets so wrapped up in life and forgets she even has a daughter."

"Let me drive you there, Eva. Please." At first, I thought he was joking, but his eyes told a different story.

I propped up on my elbow. "Remiel, I will be okay, but if it means that much to you…"

He nodded. "It does."

His hand went under the cover and rested on my abdomen. For a moment neither one of us spoke. "Eva, I am not sure about being a father when I am not even good at being a mortal husband. I…" His words were unsure.

"Remiel, I don't expect you to be a perfect parent. Nobody is." I said, reaching out to touch him, but he grabbed my wrist and gently put my hand on his chest.

"Eva, you don't understand." He rolled over, sitting up on the bed, beginning to put his pants on.

Sitting up, I pulled the sheet around me, as suddenly my nightgown was not enough to keep me warm. I was trying to hold myself together. "Remiel, I can't understand if you won't talk to me."

He didn't answer me but instead stood up and headed toward the door. "Remiel, I thought you were happy about the baby? Are you going to leave me to raise our child by myself?"

He stopped and slowly turned to face me. "I never said that I was leaving you, Eva. I am here." His look was one of confusion.

"You are leaving, emotionally." I swallowed hard as he walked up to me. Facing this giant of a man, I felt no fear as he placed both of his hands on my shoulders. The fear came from the unknown and this unimaginable space between us.

"No, Remiel, you are not here. You are still over there in that battle and in the realms, battling the demons that haunt you at night." I stepped up to him, daring him to walk away, clutching the sheet tighter around me as I shuddered from an unseen coldness.

"I hear you, Remiel... at night. I hear you as you scream in your dreams. I hear you call for me and I am there for you, Remiel. And I am right here. Every night since you have been back, I hear you and I pray for you. Then you wake up in the morning as if nothing has happened. You put on a mask and put up a wall. I know you are still battling something, but I can't help you fight against them if you won't let me in." I knew I was pleading with him, begging him to let me in.

"You have barely picked up your Bible, you won't go to church with me. What has happened that you have suddenly shunned God?" I knew my question had hit a nerve, his entire expression changed.

He stepped back, putting his head in his hands before looking at me again. "I can't, Eva. I can't... the things that I have seen and done. Even as an angel…"

"Remiel, please let me help you. Let me in." I begged him, my voice breaking, searching his face for any sign of hope, of willingness to let me be his strength. "Remiel, you were the one that taught me about forgiveness, especially to oneself."

He stared at me, his eyes filled with anguish. Then, as if unable to bear it any longer, he closed the short distance between us, his lips capturing mine in a desperate, searing kiss. His hands roamed my body, trembling with the immense pressure of his emotions building from both of us. I responded with equal desire, wanting to pour all my love into that one connection. We broke apart, breathless, as I let my fingers trace his face.

Taking my hands away and stepping back, Remiel's voice was strained, "Eva, I am trying to protect you."

His words echoed the memories of Dagon's voice, vibrating through my mind, a painful reminder of the past. He had said the very same words to me before Gabriel was born. I had heard Remiel say these words but somehow in this moment, it was like reliving it with Dagon. It was almost as if I could feel Dagon there.

I suddenly felt lightheaded and nauseated. Remiel's hand steadied me, guiding me back to the bed. "Eva?"

I placed my hand on his shoulder, trying to brace myself, hoping the room would stop spinning. Suddenly I felt worse. I stood up, moving as quickly as I could to the bathroom. After several moments, he helped me slowly stand. I rested my head against his chest. I had suddenly become very sweaty and there was a clammy feeling all over my skin. "I think I want to bathe and then lie down again."

This pregnancy was taking a toll on me, morning sickness seemed to come and go whenever pleased. Anything could set it off. Especially emotions, it was like this child could sense every emotion in my body.

Remiel moved just enough that I could keep my balance. I heard the water turning on, the sound both soothing and infuriating. A shower didn't seem safe right now. A few moments later, he offered me his hand. He had already laid out fresh towels and bath clothes.

Everything was arranged neatly by the tub, ensuring I wouldn't have to reach for anything. My clothes were neatly folded on the counter. Slowly he undressed me so I didn't have to bend over. He then helped me into the bath.

When he finished, he calmly said. "I will leave you to get your bath. I believe breakfast is cold now, so I will get lunch going." His tone was distant, his demeanor suddenly cold.

My heart felt crushed. What was happening to us? We had endured so much just to be together. Now it seemed as if we were being torn apart by some invisible force.

I lay in the tub, letting the water cover my body, the warmth drowning out the constant hum of the noise called life. I laid there for a long time before finally closing my eyes and allowing myself to slowly sink under the water. Trying to block out the sound of my racing thoughts.

When I opened my eyes under the water, I nearly screamed. A shadowy figure seemed to loom over the tub, watching me. I sat up, wiping the water from my eyes, my heart pounding. "Remiel!" I called out, instantly regretting it but it was too late, within seconds he was already there.

"What is wrong?" He asked, kneeling beside the tub, his eyes filled with concern.

I looked past him in the corner where I had seen the shadow, but it was gone. Had it been Dagon? Or my imagination? I shook my head, trying to appear calm. "I just don't feel steady yet. Will you please help me?" I couldn't mention the figure, but it had to be Dagon. He frowned as he reached for the towel, I knew he didn't quite believe my lie. He held the towel up, wrapping it around me. Once he helped me out, he unwrapped the towel and began to dry me off with slow, deliberate movements.

"Remiel, I can do that." I reached for the towel, but he quickly moved it out of my reach. "Turn around," he commanded softly. When I didn't move quickly enough, he turned me around until my back was facing him.

"I am very capable of drying myself without your assistance." I said, my tone somewhat flirtatious.

The towel stopped, and I felt his hands on my hips, pulling me close to him. His lips brushed against my ear, his warm breath sending a shiver down my spine. "Perhaps you are, but this is my pleasure. Do you dare deny your husband?"

I grinned as I turned around to face him, wrapping my arms around his neck. "No, husband, I would not." I pressed my body closer to his as he lightly traced my ribcage with his fingertips, a touch both tender and electrifying.

"Mmmm, husband… what else would be your pleasure?" I asked as he tightened his grip, pulling my hips closer to his.

He leaned down and kissed me softly, "For you to join me for a very late lunch." He murmured against my lips before giving me a quick peck on the lips before turning away, leaving a cold emptiness in the space he had just occupied. I watched him as he walked back into the bedroom and down the hall. My heart, feeling the ache of all the unanswered questions.

I dressed slowly, taking my time to avoid facing the chill of his sudden detachment. As I looked in the mirror, my somewhat bulging stomach caught my attention. I placed my hand over it, caressing it soothingly. I know I had my doubts, but deep down I had to believe Remiel would be a fantastic father. I sighed and continued to get dressed.

When I entered the kitchen, he motioned to the bar where a plate of grilled ham and cheese and a bowl of fruit waited for me. I sat on the stool, pulling the plate closer. "Thank you." I watched as he nodded curtly from where he stood at the stove.

Unable to stay away from him, I stood up, walked around the bar, and wrapped my arms around his torso. I leaned my head on his back, gently kissing his back. "Remiel, will you please tell me wha—"

"No, Eva." He unwrapped my arms from around him, turning to face me with a stern look and another softer but still firm. "No."

He walked away and sat at the bar, motioning to my plate and bowl. "You need to eat, Eva." Watching him and hearing the indifference in his tone, my appetite suddenly vanished.

"I am not hungry. I'm just going to lie down again." He didn't protest but sat down and looked at his plate. Once in the room, I didn't lie down. Instead, I started packing a small overnight bag. I needed to escape the confusion, the emotional storm that had engulfed us both.

Chapter Three

Eva

I am not sure how long I had been asleep, but when I woke up, he was watching me. His gaze was intense, filled with a mixture of love and something else. I chuckled softly, pulling the sheet over my body and my head.

Remiel immediately jerked it away, his touch firm yet gentle. "No, my love. I know you are not covering up, not from me." He pulled the cover all the way down and started moving his hand up my leg, causing a ticklish sensation.

"Remiel, stop!" I said, laughing. He laughed too, as he moved to lay beside me. I turned on my side, looking at him, trying to memorize the lines of his face. "That is the second time I have heard you laugh since you have been back."

He ran his hand back and forth on my shoulder, his expression becoming somber once more. "Do you still want to go to your mother's?"

I took his face in my hands, making him look at me. "Remiel, I am not leaving you. I just think a day or two would help. I need to go see Mom anyway. You know how my mother is. She gets so wrapped up in life and forgets she even has a daughter."

"Let me drive you there, Eva. Please." At first, I thought he was joking, but his eyes told a different story.

I propped up on my elbow. "Remiel, I will be okay, but if it means that much to you…"

He nodded. "It does."

His hand went under the cover and rested on my abdomen. For a moment neither one of us spoke. "Eva, I am not sure about being a father when I am not even good at being a mortal husband. I…" His words were unsure.

"Remiel, I don't expect you to be a perfect parent. Nobody is." I said, reaching out to touch him, but he grabbed my wrist and gently put my hand on his chest.

"Eva, you don't understand." He rolled over, sitting up on the bed, beginning to put his pants on.

Sitting up, I pulled the sheet around me, as suddenly my nightgown was not enough to keep me warm. I was trying to hold myself together. "Remiel, I can't understand if you won't talk to me."

He didn't answer me but instead stood up and headed toward the door. "Remiel, I thought you were happy about the baby? Are you going to leave me to raise our child by myself?"

He stopped and slowly turned to face me. "I never said that I was leaving you, Eva. I am here." His look was one of confusion.

"You are leaving, emotionally." I swallowed hard as he walked up to me. Facing this giant of a man, I felt no fear as he placed both of his hands on my shoulders. The fear came from the unknown and this unimaginable space between us.

"No, Remiel, you are not here. You are still over there in that battle and in the realms, battling the demons that haunt you at night." I stepped up to him, daring him to walk away, clutching the sheet tighter around me as I shuddered from an unseen coldness.

"I hear you, Remiel... at night. I hear you as you scream in your dreams. I hear you call for me and I am there for you, Remiel. And I am right here. Every night since you have been back, I hear you and I pray for you.

Then you wake up in the morning as if nothing has happened. You put on a mask and put up a wall. I know you are still battling something, but I can't help you fight against them if you won't let me in." I knew I was pleading with him, begging him to let me in.

"You have barely picked up your Bible, you won't go to church with me. What has happened that you have suddenly shunned God?" I knew my question had hit a nerve, his entire expression changed.

He stepped back, putting his head in his hands before looking at me again. "I can't, Eva. I can't... the things that I have seen and done. Even as an angel…"

"Remiel, please let me help you. Let me in." I begged him, my voice breaking, searching his face for any sign of hope, of willingness to let me be his strength. "Remiel, you were the one that taught me about forgiveness, especially to oneself."

He stared at me, his eyes filled with anguish. Then, as if unable to bear it any longer, he closed the short distance between us, his lips capturing mine in a desperate, searing kiss. His hands roamed my body, trembling with the immense pressure of his emotions building from both of us. I responded with equal desire, wanting to pour all my love into that one connection. We broke apart, breathless, as I let my fingers trace his face.

Taking my hands away and stepping back, Remiel's voice was strained, "Eva, I am trying to protect you."

His words echoed the memories of Dagon's voice, vibrating through my mind, a painful reminder of the past. He had said the very same words to me before Gabriel was born. I had heard Remiel say these words but somehow in this moment, it was like reliving it with Dagon. It was almost as if I could feel Dagon there.

I suddenly felt lightheaded and nauseated. Remiel's hand steadied me, guiding me back to the bed. "Eva?"

I placed my hand on his shoulder, trying to brace myself, hoping the room would stop spinning. Suddenly I felt worse. I stood up, moving as quickly as I could to the bathroom. After several moments, he helped me slowly stand. I rested my head against his chest. I had suddenly become very sweaty and there was a clammy feeling all over my skin. "I think I want to bathe and then lie down again."

This pregnancy was taking a toll on me, morning sickness seemed to come and go whenever pleased. Anything could set it off. Especially emotions, it was like this child could sense every emotion in my body.

Remiel moved just enough that I could keep my balance. I heard the water turning on, the sound both soothing and infuriating. A shower didn't seem safe right now. A few moments later, he offered me his hand. He had already laid out fresh towels and bath clothes.

Everything was arranged neatly by the tub, ensuring I wouldn't have to reach for anything. My clothes were neatly folded on the counter. Slowly he undressed me so I didn't have to bend over. He then helped me into the bath.

When he finished, he calmly said. "I will leave you to get your bath. I believe breakfast is cold now, so I will get lunch going." His tone was distant, his demeanor suddenly cold.

My heart felt crushed. What was happening to us? We had endured so much just to be together. Now it seemed as if we were being torn apart by some invisible force.

I lay in the tub, letting the water cover my body, the warmth drowning out the constant hum of the noise called life. I laid there for a long time before finally closing my eyes and allowing myself to slowly sink under the water. Trying to block out the sound of my racing thoughts.

When I opened my eyes under the water, I nearly screamed. A shadowy figure seemed to loom over the tub, watching me. I sat up, wiping the water from my eyes, my heart pounding. "Remiel!" I called out, instantly regretting it but it was too late, within seconds he was already there.

"What is wrong?" He asked, kneeling beside the tub, his eyes filled with concern.

I looked past him in the corner where I had seen the shadow, but it was gone. Had it been Dagon? Or my imagination? I shook my head, trying to appear calm. "I just don't feel steady yet. Will you please help me?" I couldn't mention the figure, but it had to be Dagon. He frowned as he reached for the towel, I knew he didn't quite believe my lie. He held the towel up, wrapping it around me. Once he helped me out, he unwrapped the towel and began to dry me off with slow, deliberate movements.

"Remiel, I can do that." I reached for the towel, but he quickly moved it out of my reach. "Turn around," he commanded softly. When I didn't move quickly enough, he turned me around until my back was facing him.

"I am very capable of drying myself without your assistance." I said, my tone somewhat flirtatious.

The towel stopped, and I felt his hands on my hips, pulling me close to him. His lips brushed against my ear, his warm breath sending a shiver down my spine. "Perhaps you are, but this is my pleasure. Do you dare deny your husband?"

I grinned as I turned around to face him, wrapping my arms around his neck. "No, husband, I would not." I pressed my body closer to his as he lightly traced my ribcage with his fingertips, a touch both tender and electrifying.

"Mmmm, husband… what else would be your pleasure?" I asked as he tightened his grip, pulling my hips closer to his.

He leaned down and kissed me softly, "For you to join me for a very late lunch." He murmured against my lips before giving me a quick peck on the lips before turning away, leaving a cold emptiness in the space he had just occupied. I watched him as he walked back into the bedroom and down the hall. My heart, feeling the ache of all the unanswered questions.

I dressed slowly, taking my time to avoid facing the chill of his sudden detachment. As I looked in the mirror, my somewhat bulging stomach caught my attention. I placed my hand over it, caressing it soothingly. I know I had my doubts, but deep down I had to believe Remiel would be a fantastic father. I sighed and continued to get dressed.

When I entered the kitchen, he motioned to the bar where a plate of grilled ham and cheese and a bowl of fruit waited for me. I sat on the stool, pulling the plate closer. "Thank you." I watched as he nodded curtly from where he stood at the stove.

Unable to stay away from him, I stood up, walked around the bar, and wrapped my arms around his torso. I leaned my head on his back, gently kissing his back. "Remiel, will you please tell me wha—"

"No, Eva." He unwrapped my arms from around him, turning to face me with a stern look and another softer but still firm. "No."

He walked away and sat at the bar, motioning to my plate and bowl. "You need to eat, Eva." Watching him and hearing the indifference in his tone, my appetite suddenly vanished.

"I am not hungry. I'm just going to lie down again." He didn't protest but sat down and looked at his plate. Once in the room, I didn't lie down. Instead, I started packing a small overnight bag. I needed to escape the confusion, the emotional storm that had engulfed us both.

Chapter Four

Eva

Moments later, Remiel walked in to find me packing. Confusion etched on his face, he picked up the bag and held it out of my reach. "What are you doing?"

"Remiel, put the bag down please. I told you I was going to my mother's. Don't act like this." I reached for the bag again, and this time he let it go.

"Yes, but I didn't think you meant today." He watched as I continued to pack.

I didn't offer much conversation as he drove me to my mother's new home. The silence between us was thick with growing, unresolved problems. My thoughts were a chaotic whirlpool, each one pulling me deeper into confusion and heartache. And he continued to remain silent. Unreachable.

Mom and James had recently purchased an older white plantation house near Red Springs, surrounded by a pecan orchard. The house was set back from the road, with a woodshop behind it where James could work on his projects. Mom finally had her long front porch and white picket fence that she always dreamed about.

As we pulled up, I saw her coming down the steps to meet me. She had let her peppered gray strands grow out, and she looked amazing. "Oh, baby, look at you! I have missed you so much!" She exclaimed, wrapping me in a warm hug and kissing my cheek. She turned to Remiel, hugging him and patting his cheek. She acted as if she had not seen me in years when in reality it had only been a few weeks.

"Thank you for bringing her." My mother acted as if we lived three hours away from each other and in reality it was only twenty minutes.

Remiel's face remained unmoving, but his eyes flickered with a mix of emotions—pain, regret, and a hint of desperation. "Of course, Grace. Take good care of her."

His voice was controlled, but I could hear the strain beneath it. Turning to me, his face became expressionless once more. "Call me when you are ready to come home." His voice sounded hard like stone. I stood there a moment, trying to make sense of it all. Mom acted as if she did not notice the tone of his voice, but I saw her eyes. She knew.

As she was leading me inside when I glanced back at Remiel, standing there by the truck. His shoulders were tense with uncertainty. I wanted to run back to him, to soothe the hurt I saw in his eyes, but everything about us was off. The balance that we once had.

Inside, Mom fussed over me, making sure I was comfortable. The house was cozy and inviting, a deep contrast to the emotional storm brewing inside me that I was managing to keep under control. "How are you feeling, honey?" she asked, concern etched on her face.

I forced a smile, trying to ease her worry. "I'm okay, Mom. Just tired. You know how pregnancies can be."

She nodded, understandingly. I didn't want to put too much more out there. I didn't want her to worry or get upset.

"I am glad you came to see us…" I had not said a word to her about my uncertainties but she could read between the lines, there was no reason to believe that she was naive to the problems between a married couple.

"Well, I leave you to get settled in. I am so glad you are staying a few days. We can go fishing at the pond if you want to. I think there are some fish in there. James and I haven't tried our luck yet." She said, while putting my bag on the bed.

Laughing, I unzipped the bag. "Mom, you know I never could hold my mouth right to get the fish to bite."

That made her smile. "Grammy always did say that about you." I saw the wistful look come across her face.

I reached out and touched her arm. "I miss her too, Mom."

She nodded and sighed. "Well you go ahead and get settled in, come down when you are ready."

As I settled into the guest room, I couldn't shake the image of Remiel's eyes, the way he looked at me before I walked inside. The words of our last conversation were still playing in my mind, and I felt tears prick at the corners of my eyes. I just wanted my Remiel back, the warmth, the bond, the being that loved and was open with me. I closed my eyes and memories of before came rushing in. His gentleness and openness. Now I was left with a rugged and cold version of the being that once loved me. I loved him still, with every beat of my heart I loved him. But was that enough to break through his wall of nightmares and past horrors?

Lying on the bed, I thought about his emotional distance and coldness, they were tearing me apart. He was hot and then cold, we were like fire and ice. I needed him to open up, to let me in, but every time I tried, he pushed me away. I knew it was like living in a constant state of emotional turmoil. I placed my hand on my stomach as I drifted off to sleep.

"Eva," The voice was so loud it ripped through me, jerking me from my sleep. I bolted upright in bed, gasping as I fumbled for the lamp switch. The room was in darkness but small shadows danced on the walls from the moonlight that showed in. My heart pounded in my chest as I scanned the room, expecting to see him. Expecting to see Dagon standing in the corner

with his malicious, evil grin. I knew I had heard his voice, clear and unmistakable, as if he were standing over me, watching me.

I swung my legs over the edge of the bed, my feet hitting the cold floor, bringing me to the reality of the moment. The house was silent except for the soft ticking of a distant clock. I stood up, my movements hesitant and cautious, and made my way out of the room into the dimly lit hallway. The shadows seemed to stretch out for me ringing with the sense of dread that clung to me like a dead weight.

Finding the bathroom, I splashed cold water on my face, trying to erase the haunting sound of his voice from my mind. The water droplets trickled down my cheeks, mingling with the trickles of fear-induced sweat. I gripped the edge of the sink, my knuckles turning white as I stared at my reflection in the mirror. My eyes were wide, haunted by the echo of his words. I squeezed my eyes shut before opening them again. Why was he back? It had been months since I last saw him and commanded him to leave. How was he able to reappear?

I dried my face and took a deep breath, trying to gather myself before heading into the den. Grace and James were sitting there, watching the evening news. The soft glow of the television cast an almost haunting light over the room.

"Hey, Honey," James greeted me as he stood up, his smile genuine and welcoming. He pulled me into a hug, his warmth so sincere. "So good to see you. We were waiting for you to see if you would like to go out to dinner with us? They are having dinner for the Cattleman Association. We don't have any cattle, but we were invited to attend." He chuckled as he reached his hand out to my mother. I could just see my mom taking care of cattle. She was afraid of chickens, so I knew cows were a no go.

I looked at them both, dressed in their elegant evening attire. Mom's dress shimmered a deep satin blue. While James's suit was impeccably tailored, it was darker navy blue. They looked ready for an evening at

Wieldmans, the sophisticated restaurant where one bottle of wine cost as much as my entire week's pay.

I forced a smile, "No, thank you. I believe I will stay in this evening and catch the late news. You all go and enjoy yourselves."

Mom's eyes searched mine, her brow furrowing with concern. "Are you sure, sweetheart? You look a bit pale. Maybe getting out would help?"

"I'm sure," I reassured her, trying to steady my voice. "Just a bit tired, that's all. You two go and have a wonderful evening."

Mom gave me a quick kiss on the cheek and one last worried glance before they left. She turned back to me, "There are some salads and ham sandwiches in the fridge, if you get hungry."

I nodded as the door closed behind them with a soft click, leaving me alone in the quiet house. I sank into the sofa, the silence and the shadows seemed to grow longer. The memory of Dagon's voice lingered like a ghost in the corners of my mind.

I picked up the remote and turned on the television channel, hoping the noise and light would chase away the nagging fear. But as the evening news played on the screen, my mind kept drifting back to his voice. Why now? Why was he back? What trick did he have to play? Whatever Dagon's return meant, it could not be good.

As the news anchor droned on about the day's events, I wrapped myself in a blanket, seeking comfort in its warmth. The flickering light of the television was a small shield against the darkness. Hearing my phone vibrate, I checked my cellphone and there was a message from Remiel, **"Know that I love you**." I sighed not knowing how to reply.

I knew he did and I knew that I loved him. What I did not know or understand, was the force tearing us apart. I decided to walk outside onto the porch. Sitting on the swing, I closed my eyes, listening to the sounds of the night. The soft rustling of the trees in the night wind. Just then another message chimed, it was from Matthew. *"**Are you ok**?"*

A sense of dread went down my spine, Matthew knew, he had sensed Dagon. My heart started racing as I pressed the dial button to call him, when suddenly a cold hand grasped mine. I gasped as I looked up and saw Dagon standing in front of me. His amber eyes glistened in the porch light.

"What are you doing here?" I tried to jerk my hand away from him but his grip was like steel and unrelenting. He pulled me till I was standing in front of him. He reached out tracing my face with his cold hand. I pulled away but he tightened his grip which only brought me closer to him. His hand reached out again this time playing in my hair as he leaned forward, inhaling.

I heard his quick intake of breath and I struggled, trying to move away but he held me still. "Eva, my beautiful Eva, you were supposed to be mine always." His voice came out in a very deep and seductive whisper, bringing back dark memories.

"I don't belong to you, Dagon. Let me go." My voice trembled but once more, I tried to pull away but his grip was steady. I heard my phone vibrating again and again. I knew it was either Remiel or Matthew.

Dagon looked down where my phone had fallen, shaking his head, he looked back at me. Slowly he traced my shoulder down between my breasts, causing me to shudder. His hand stopped every so lightly on my abdomen.

He looked down and then looked back at me, "You're?" His eyes were now a golden brown and I could hear the shock in his voice. Biting my lip nervously, not knowing how to answer or what would set him off, I slowly nodded my head.

"Remiel?" The hurt edged into his voice as he said the name. I swallowed, suddenly feeling very nauseated.

I could feel it rising. "Dagon, please I feel sick, please let me go." He released his grip and I ran into the house trying to make it to the nearest bathroom. I bent over, coughing, I hated being sick. I was trying to keep the hair out of my face when I felt Dagon's hands pulling my hair back away from my face.

I heard the water in the sink running and suddenly there was cold bath cloth pressed against my neck. When I felt like I could stand up, I reached out and braced against the sink. He took the cloth and gently pressed it against my face. "Eva, what have you done to me?" He asked as he continued to pat my face with the cloth.

"Dagon, please." My voice trembled, barely steady, and I knew he heard me. His amber eyes searched my face, the familiar warmth in them stirring something I tried desperately to bury. He reached up, brushing the stray strand of hair from my forehead, and I closed my eyes. Memories came rushing back, laughter, quiet moments, the way he had once made me feel safe before his lies and betrayal.

"Eva, I can't hurt you anymore," he whispered, his voice low and raw. Leaning in, he brushed his lips gently against my cheek then his lips softly brushed against mine. The touch should have made my skin crawl; it should have made me recoil. But instead, a strange ache weaved its way through me, something tender that I had no right to feel.

My heart betrayed me with a flutter, and I felt it—the weakness of being human, the vulnerability that made us Beloveds so painfully and emotionally fragile.

I... I should rebuke him, I thought, but the words wouldn't come. My throat tightened as if the air itself was holding me back. The truth was, even in my devotion to Remiel, even in the fire of my loyalty, part of me longed for the comfort of his closeness, the warmth of a connection that existed before I knew the truth.

I pulled away, shaking my head in confusion. "Then please don't, Dagon. Please… let me go."

I looked into his eyes, searching for any flicker of hope or gentleness that could justify the tangle of feelings inside me.

He backed away slowly, releasing my face, but not without tucking the hair behind my ear. I shivered, caught between relief and something far more dangerous, a recognition that despite myself, I still felt.

My pulse raced, my chest tightened. "Please, Dagon… just leave." I shook my head, panic lacing my words. The darkness around us had shifted; it wasn't from him, but it had followed him, heavy and suffocating.

"Eva, I… I—" His words faltered, incomplete, and I knew he struggled as much as I did.

"No, Dagon. Just go. Leave me." My voice hardened, but inside, a storm raged, fear, guilt, longing, and the bitter ache of forbidden emotion.

Then, in a swirl of dark smoke, he was gone. The air smelled of sulfar and ash, a reminder of what lingered even in his absence. And yet, even as my body trembled and my heart screamed for Remiel, I felt the ghost of Dagon's presence. It was almost tender mixed in with danger, and it echoed through me.

When I finally drifted off to sleep that night, I found myself in a realm, which one, I wasn't sure, but I knew this was not just a dream. I was dressed in a long blue flowing dress with short sleeves. I was among the stars, walking trying to find my way. I could feel a slight breeze blowing.

Then I heard a voice, "Come to me and I will give you all that you desire. All the riches of the world and so much more." I knew that it wasn't

Dagon or Remiel's voice. I turned around looking for a direction that it might have come from. I could see shooting stars and I could hear wishes being made.

It was then I remembered what Remiel had said about the falling stars….and the Fallen. "Come to me and I will give you anything you ask for." I turned around and then I saw a figure emerging from the shadows.

Shaking my head, I backed up. "I do not desire things of this world. What I want you can not give."

The shadow came closer till a human form was present. He had the bluest eyes that I had seen, made even more prominent by his black hair. His skin was deathly pale and he had a sinister smile. He was dressed in all black just like Dagon and for a moment, I was drawn to him. He made a wide motion with his hand and images of grand houses and cars appeared, there was laughter and music.

"This could be yours." His voice was low and seductive. "Just surrender to me."

I shook my head, "That is not yours to give."

He took a step towards me, "What is that you truly desire?" He moved his hand again, this time revealing children playing and laughing. Amongst them was Gabriel.

I immediately put my hand on my stomach. I shook my head. "Gabriel is home in heaven, you have no control over him."

The being waved his hand again and I could hear all of the voices of the broken women in our women's ministry. The ones who thought God didn't love or that he had abandoned them. The ones who didn't still didn't know who God was. "They will never receive salvation, your weakness can never give them strength."

Shaking my head, "It is not my strength that will save them. Only by the power of Jesus Christ." The being hissed at the name of Jesus.

He waved his hand once more and there was Remiel and I, we were arguing. It hurt to hear the words again, I cringed at the sound of them. The being let out a low chuckle, "He is falling, even now. His faith will not last much longer. His mortal insecurities and pains will destroy him. He will become like a Fallen,"

The realization of who the being was finally hit me. I shook my head with even more determination."That's not true, he will not." I clenched my fist. "He only needs time, he knows that God loves him."

The being hissed at the mention of God's name. "You can not have him, I tell you, in Jesus name."

The being hissed once more and I felt wind swirl around me, there was a smell of death and then I was waking up. I sat up, looking out the window into the deep night. "You can not become one of them, Remiel. You are still my angel. Somewhere in there is my Remiel." I whispered into the night.

Remiel

I had awakened to Eva still asleep and curled up next to me. I had come to get her but James and Grace had invited me to stay the night. A big football game was playing and they wanted us to stay and watch.

I watched, as the light played across her face through the window. I gently eased my arm out from under her and eased off the bed. In the kitchen, I found James was already cooking. "Morning, I thought I would let the women sleep and get started on breakfast." He greeted me, his cheerful attitude was one to be envious of so early in the mornings.

I nodded as I reached around for a cup and poured some coffee. "Do you need some help?" I sipped some of the wonderful black brew. Coffee and sweet tea have become my favorite beverages since becoming mortal.

"No, sir. I am good. I have become an expert at cooking." He grinned as he flipped the egg. "Grace is a good woman but cooking is not her speciality."

I chuckled, thinking about Eva and what an amazing cook she was. I never had much time to talk with James but there were things that were curious about him that I had questions about. James passed a saucer with some bacon and toast. Then he let a hot egg slide off the spatula on top of the toast.

There was silence before he started talking again. "I know what you are thinking, Remiel," he said quietly. "Yes… I am. But I intend to take care of Grace. If necessary, Eva too."

I nodded slowly. I knew what he meant. If I didn't return from one of the missions, he would step in. He would help Eva carry what was coming.

For a moment neither of us spoke.

I leaned forward slightly, studying him. "Are you like him? Like Matthew? Can you sense things?"

James shook his head slowly. "Yes…and no," he answered. "Sometimes I can see things before they happen. It comes as a vision. But it doesn't happen with everyone. Only with those I am close to… or when I am near them long enough."

His gaze drifted toward the kitchen window, thoughtful. "Before you ask," he continued, "I didn't know about Dagon until we returned the other night. As we were coming into the house, I saw him in the vision."

His jaw tightened. "I'm not sure why it came to me so late. If I had known earlier, I would never have left her." A quiet tension settled between us.

After a moment I asked the question that had been sitting in my mind since the beginning of this conversation. "What exactly are you, James and what was your assignment?" I knew my question was blunt, but I figured that I needed a direct answer.

His eyes lifted slowly to meet mine. A faint, humorless smile crossed his face. "That," he said softly, "is not a complicated answer."

"You already know the first part," he continued. "Nephilim. The offspring of angels and humans. That's what the old texts call us."

He paused, his expression darkening. "But the texts leave out the parts the realms would rather forget."

I said nothing, waiting. James rubbed the back of his neck, clearly debating how much he should say. "When the Fallen first came to this world, they didn't just corrupt humans," he said. "They built bloodlines. Some of those lines became powerful… dangerous. Too dangerous."

His eyes flicked back to mine. "So the realms and guardians made a decision."

"What decision?" I asked quietly.

"They created a place," he said. "A realm where the unwanted ones could be sent."

The air in the kitchen felt suddenly cold, as I tried to digest what he was saying. "A prison?" I asked.

James shook his head slowly. "No," he said. "Not a prison exactly." He leaned forward now, his voice lower. "An exile."

"A world where the abandoned Nephilim live. The Fallen stopped claiming them, and the realms refused to accept them."

My brow furrowed. "You're saying there's an entire realm… full of Nephilim?"

"Yes." The single word shook me. Even as an angel this had been hidden from me.

"Most people or beings– don't know it exists," James continued. "Those who do pretend it doesn't."

His gaze darkened slightly. "I came very close to being sent there once."

That caught my attention immediately. "What happened?"

He gave a small, bitter laugh and looked away. "I refused an order."

"What order?" I asked as his eyes returned to mine. "The kind that tests what you really are." He rubbed his hand across the back of his neck. "After the rebellion, there were… cleanup operations. Some of the Nephilim bloodlines escaped and existed even centuries later."

The way he said the words made my stomach tighten. "Bloodlines that needed to be erased. Children who were considered too dangerous to exist on Earth and were considered too weak for the Fallen to want."

He paused, his expression darkening. "I was supposed to make sure two of them disappeared."

A long silence stretched between us. "But you didn't," I said.

"No." The word was quiet, but absolute.

"I was told they would grow into something the Fallen wouldn't be able to control or fight," he continued. "That their existence could shift things that had been stable for centuries ...but the Fallen lied to me. They said they were of Nephilim blood but they weren't, they were Beloveds."

I studied him carefully. "So they tried to send you away."

"Yes." His voice carried a hint of old bitterness. "Refusing that order made me… inconvenient."

"And the exile realm was their solution?" I stated, knowing his answer.

He nodded once. "For a while, it looked like that's exactly where I was going."

"What changed?" I asked, curious to know how he escaped the Fallen.

James let out a slow breath as he pointed up. "Someone higher up decided I was still useful but not to the dark but to the light."

The words were simple, but I could hear the meaning underneath them. Useful. Controlled. Watched. Meaning if he messed up redemption would not come easy for him.

"And those two?" I asked quietly.

A faint shadow of a smile touched his face. "They lived."

The room fell quiet again. After a moment he added, almost thoughtfully,

"The funny thing about the Fallen and the realms, Remiel… is that they think they can control destiny by removing the pieces they don't like."

He turned back to the stove, "But sometimes the pieces they try the hardest to erase… are the ones that change everything."

For a moment neither of us spoke. Then he looked at me again, more serious now. "That's why I protect Grace," he said. "And Eva."

I understood his meaning. I sat there wondering about Eva and the information that I had just been dealt. I wondered what else she was keeping from me. Finally shaking my head, I decided that I would deal with that later. "Does Grace know about your abilities?"

The spatula he held, stopped in midair. "Grace will never know. She is a delicate soul, one that can not handle the reality of the supernatural, even though she is surrounded by it."

He started to say something else but stopped mid sentence, just as Eva walked in. She had showered and dressed. As I looked her over, amazed at how gorgeous she looked. Her curly hair was pulled into a high pony tail but still managed to flow to her waist. I noticed that she had on a pair of cut off denim shorts that came mid-thigh, and she wore an oversized blue cotton T-Shirt, that was my shirt.

Watching her, I knew a stop that we were making on the way home. We were on our way home. Eva had barely said two words to me since this morning but she never let go of my hand once we were in the truck. I squeezed her hand, she looked over and smiled at me. "Love you too. You know that?"

Smiling at her, "I am sure you can show me once we get home, but first we are making a stop."

She looked surprised as I pulled into the shopping square. Looking back at me, she shook her head. "Remiel, I don't need new clothes. I have plenty."

She then pointed to the store. "Liztan's is a very expensive clothing store and I can just order my clothes online."

"Eva, you are wearing my shirt.You have been wearing my shirts. They aren't just big on you, they swallow you." I knew how much she hated shopping for herself. She could always shop for everyone else but she would never just go shopping-not for herself.

I got out, walked around and opened her door. "Come on, you are going   to   get   some   clothes."
Once in the store, she walked around the racks and shelves looking but not really picking anything out. I caught her glancing at the price tags and it irritated me. Finally, I motioned to one of the sales ladies and pointed to Eva. Explaining the situation and handing her my card, the lady smiled.

Patting me on the arm, "Don't worry we will take care of her." She motioned to another lady. They both walked toward Eva as she gave me a deer in the headlight look. I calmly walked over and sat down on the sofa in the corner.

I stretched my arms across the back of the couch and leaned my head back. Staring at the ceiling, I wondered when the next assignment was coming and then how long I would be away from her? Just then I heard a little laugh coming through the door of the store. I looked around as a couple came through, the woman was clearly expecting, and handed her purse to the husband who was also holding their baby girl. The little girl looked to be about two years old, with big brown eyes and red pigtails that bounced when she moved.

The man sat down in a chair opposite from me and settled in to wait. He was bouncing the little girl and trying to keep her entertained. I watched, amazed how quickly he was able to grab her attention time after time. After a while she curled up against his chest and was soon fast asleep. He continued to rub and pat her back, humming softly. He smiled up at me, "Daddy's little princess."

I nodded and looked over to find Eva, she was walking toward me with bags upon bags. She shook her head as I got up to help her. "Here let me get those."

"Remiel, why did you do that?" Her voice was somewhat concerned but more aggravated than anything. I placed the bags in the back and then opened the door for her.

"What are you talking about, Eva?" I closed the door before she could answer and walked around to get in. After buckling my seat belt, I looked at her.

"Remiel, why would you do that?" She asked again. I noticed that she didn't have her seat belt on, so I reached over and buckled her in. "Remiel, answer me. Do you know how much you just spent in that store?"

Getting frustrated with the conversation, I started the truck. "Eva, you are my wife, my child's mother. There is no reason why you should walk around in my shirts when I am perfectly able to buy you more clothes."

"But Remiel, I know Lisa doesn't pay that much, I am capable of buyin–"

"Eva, can we just stop this conversation?" I snapped before realizing how sharp I sounded. Guilt hit me, sudden and hard.

I never wanted to talk to her like that again. I ran a hand through my hair and looked at her. "Eva, I am a mercenary. A paid mercenary. I suppose that is one perk, as you Beloveds say—that I would not be left without a means to support you."

She blinked at me, confused. Of course she didn't understand. How could she?

The first memories of my missions were still so fresh and painful that it slammed into me like a blade in the dark. My back stung and pulsed with the memory. I remembered…I could never forget the first mission. The Council's command had been clear-eliminate the possessed, destroy the portal seed she carried. No negotiations. No redemption. Her time was out.

Her name had once been Ashley, a teacher, a mother of two. But after the grief became a fire that even the strongest prayers couldn't be put out, something from below stepped through and made her body its home.

She was then called Ashtara, and in whispers, they named her "The Weeper." She wore sorrow like a perfume, and the Council feared not just what she had become…but what she might still become and what she might do. What portal she might open to allow others through.

I had tracked her to a crumbling and burnt orphanage. The demon inside her had grown clever. It wore her face like a mask and smiled with her lips as it carved symbols into the floor of the orphanage she once worked in.

She was singing when I arrived. A soft lullaby but the children were gone. Taken. As I had stepped through shattered doors. Candlelight flickered, warped. She had stood at an altar she had built, still humming the lullaby in tongues not meant for the human ear.

"You're late, angel," she whispered, standing barefoot in a circle of ash. Her eyes were black from edge to edge. No whites. No soul.

"I know," I replied. "But I don't get paid to be early."

"I was waiting for you," she said without turning back around. Her voice layered–hers and something else. A whisper underneath. A promise of death.

"I'm not here to save you," I replied, blade in hand, holy mark burning in my palm.

She dropped the candle. The circle ignited. That's when I moved. I never saw her leap. I only felt it. A sudden weight crashing into my back, talons like bone hooks sinking into my flesh, raking down hard.

The scream was mine. The fire in my spine. The smell of burning skin and blood. She laughed. A high and unholy laugh all while she tore into me.

I hit the ground. Blade spinning from my hand. Pain blurred everything. She whispered in my ear, "You're not divine anymore. Just meat with a memory."

I fought blind. I fought bleeding. And when it was over……when the room was bathed in silence…I had killed her. Not because I wanted to, but because I was the only one who could. And when it was done, when her body burned into smoke and the ground cracked under the force of her expulsion from this world… I had stood alone in the silence. Blood dripping. Heart pounding. My first tally…but a once beautiful soul had been lost. Lost to the demonic power that had overtaken her.

I stood with smoke curling from my back, and the Council's payment was already loaded into my ledger. No words. No comfort. Just numbers. A contract was fulfilled. Cold. Calculated. Necessary.

It had taken the angel several visits to completely heal my back…and even then I had waited before going onto the next mission to track the children and return them home. Home to parents who had worried and prayed. Even then when my team and I had finished, I stalled my return home to Eva. For fear she would see the demonic scars on my back.

Shaking my head, trying to forget the scent of the memory. I reached into the glove compartment and pulled out the worn leather wallet Matthew had crafted to pass for human wallet. Slid behind the forged ID was my card, thin as glass, edged in silver. I held it out to her. It was something that I despised and I would not carry with me unless it was to the mission field.

My name was encoded into it in a celestial dialect only certain beings could read, but I knew what it said even without looking:**777 / Death-Soldier-Angel / Contracted by the Council.**

She took it with hesitant fingers and stared at it for a long time. The card shimmered faintly in the sunlight, pulsing like a heartbeat. A living reminder of what I really was.

"Eva," I murmured, watching her expression shift, "the Council of Dominions pay me. Not a government, not your world's idea of warlords or kingdoms. The Council governs the *between* realms and the earthly realm. When humans become possessed and twisted, someone has to handle it."

Her lips parted, but no sound came out. Slowly, she handed the card back to me, her eyes distant. She turned away and stared out the window, her fingers curling against her lap.

"Eva, please… look at me. Talk to me." I practically begged her.

She turned, and her tears hurt more than the memory of the orphanage. "Did you kill people?" she whispered. "While you were… over there, wherever *there* is… is that how you got the scars? Is that why you don't talk about it?"

Her voice was trembling, fragile with grief and……horror? I reached for her, but she pulled her hand back like I was something venomous. As if I was the one who was evil.

I didn't answer at first. The silence stretched, weighted and raw. Finally, I said, "Not people. Not always. Sometimes they look like people. Sometimes they used to be. But by the time I get to them, they've already become something else. And yes… that's how I got the scars."

"Tell me Remiel, what has happened to you– to us? Did you become a mortal just so you could become a murderer?" The accusation in her voice stung, but it was the truth.

Shaking my head, "No, I became a mortal so I could be with you. You are the reason that my heart beats… because of you."

"Because of me you left your heavenly realms and came to hell on earth. I never wanted you to become something you weren't. I would have rather you stayed an angel then become a human and kill other humans. That is not who you were, that is not who you are Remiel. I knew this would happen! Is this any better than being a Fallen?" Her words stung.

"Eva, that is not fair." I could feel her pain penetrating within me.

"Fair, Remiel, you just bought my wardrobe with *blood money*." Her voice strained as she tried to keep it under control. She looked at me, eyes glistening with tears that she was trying not to let fall.

She leaned back against the seat, closing her eyes. "Please let's just go home. Please." Her words meant the finality of the conversation.

We drove the rest of the way in silence. Once at the cottage, I went around and opened her door. I helped her down, but instead of letting her walk around, I held her in place as I cupped her face. "Eva, you trusted me before, can't you trust me now? When I tell you, this won't be forever–"

Jerking away, she crossed her arms. "But this is because of me. This is my fault, Remiel. I did this to you, to us. I was a human and you were an angel."

She was no longer trying to control her tears or emotions. "I should have let you go the first time." Her breathing was shaky and she kept looking down. "But I loved you…"

I took a deep breath and stepped towards her and then took her by the elbows. "Eva, this is what I wanted, was to be with you. You understand that our bond, our connection would never have been broken."

She jerked away again, "But look what is happening to us! To you!"

Chapter Five

Eva

Standing there, staring at the man who had once been my guardian angel, so many conflicting emotions ran through me. Realizing what Remiel had become—what he had done, nearly knocked me to my knees. When he reached for me again, I clung to him, closing my eyes as a wave of nausea rolled through me. He noticed immediately.

"Eva?" His voice dropped, gentle but full of concern. He moved without hesitation, steady hands guiding me onto the porch steps and then into the living room, I didn't object.

Once I was sitting on the couch, I tried to relax, but my back screamed against it. The nausea twisted deeper, coiling like a snake in my gut. I groaned softly and rolled onto my side, curling slightly, my hand automatically pressing to my stomach.

Remiel's voice was quiet. "Eva, here lay back. Let me help you."

"I can't," I whispered. "My back…it makes it worse. I think the baby doesn't like it when I'm upset... it feels like everything gets turned inside out."

He stilled beside me for a moment, like the puzzle pieces were clicking into place. "You think... the baby's feeling what you feel?"

"I don't think…I *know*," I muttered, eyes shut tight against another wave of nausea. "The more upset I get, the sicker I feel. It's like the baby is... reacting to me."

He said nothing for a moment, then he stood and walked to the kitchen. He came back with a cold bottle of ginger ale and a sleeve of saltine crackers, handing them to me wordlessly.

"I keep them stocked," I murmured as I took the drink. "I've learned... the baby settles a bit with ginger."

He knelt on the floor beside me and reached for me slowly, carefully. One hand settled on my stomach. So gently it felt like a wisp of warm air. Then he leaned forward and pressed a kiss just above where our child lay, growing, listening. And the strangest thing happened.

The moment his lips touched my skin, the fluttering kicks started. Soft at first, then stronger. The nausea eased back like a tide receding. It wasn't instant relief, but it was undeniable, she moved when she heard him. I don't know why I continued to think of the baby as a girl, I had chosen not to find out what the gender was but in my heart, I knew it was a girl.

"She knows you," I said, stunned. "Remiel… she knows you."

He glanced up at me with something unreadable in his gaze. Awe. Fear. Maybe love, tangled with guilt.

A tear slipped down my cheek before I realized it. I blinked hard. "Remiel?"

"Yes, love?" His hand was still resting protectively over our daughter.

"I like your shirts," I said softly. "I like wearing them. Their scent reminds me of you, and I pretend you're holding me. That's why I started wearing them... and now it's just out of habit."

I braced myself for a laugh, a joke, anything to dismiss it. But he didn't. He just looked at me like he was memorizing everything.

"I wish you didn't have to pretend," he said finally. "I wish I'd been here. Holding you."

As I lay there I felt the baby's movements begin to settle. She was responding to the calm between us. It made my heart ache. Not just for what was happening now…but for what never had. Gabriel.

My first pregnancy had been different. Softer, somehow. Quieter. I had felt the shifts in my body, but they were distant, like someone else's story unfolding inside me. I loved him, *of course I did*…but I hadn't understood how to listen back then. I hadn't known how to feel for two. I didn't know how to speak without words, or to recognize emotions that weren't mine. But this child? This child felt *everything*.

I could barely hold my sadness for a moment before she would stir, unsettled. I would wake in the middle of the night gripped with unease, only to realize it wasn't mine…it was hers, reflecting back what I tried so hard to bury.

She was like a mirror to my soul, and I wondered if it was because of who she was going to be or because of who I was *now*. Older. Wiser. Maybe a little more broken and a little more healed. I blinked up at the ceiling, brushing a tear from the corner of my eye.

"Are you okay?" Remiel asked softly, his hand still on my stomach like he wasn't ready to let go.

I nodded, but it wasn't really an answer. "Gabriel never reacted like this,"

I admitted after a moment. "Not like... her. He didn't kick at voices or stir when I cried. He was peaceful. Still. It's not that I didn't love him. I did, more than anything… but I think... I think I didn't know how to open myself then."

Remiel watched me quietly and with no judgement.

"With her," I continued, "it's like I don't have a choice. She feels everything. My fear. My anger. My... love. It scares me sometimes."

"Why?" he asked.

"Because what if I can't protect her from me?" I whispered. "What if everything I carry is too much for her little heart?"

He reached for my hand, threading his fingers through mine. "She's strong," he said. "Just like her mother."

I didn't speak. I just let that sit with me. He continued to talk in a deep soothing voice to the baby, before long I drifted off to sleep. I wasn't sure what time it was when I woke, but the living room was in shadows. The only light came from the faint glow of the porch, casting long, silent beams through the window. The couch beside me was empty. I stood, nerves tightening. The kitchen was dark. So was the hallway. I felt it, a feeling of dread.

"Remiel?" I called softly yet desperately, but there was no answer.

I made my way to the bedroom, still no sign of him. My heart began to beat faster, heavier. I moved toward the back porch, drawn by a hum…something quiet but pulsing, like a deep vibration I once heard come from him.

There he was. Bathed in the soft glow of the porch light, standing completely still, shoulders squared, eyes fixed on the edge of the forest.

I took a step closer. "Remiel?" He didn't turn. I followed his gaze and froze. There, at the tree line, stood a being unlike anything I had ever seen.

Taller than Remiel by nearly a foot, it wore silver and gold armor that shimmered without light. The body was that of a warrior, but its face… its face was sharp, majestic. An eagle's countenance. And its wings were that of biblical description. There were four of them, unfurled like a warning. At the bend of each wing sat another eagle's head, alive, watching me, as if they'd always known me.

A gasp escaped without permission. One I didn't know that I had been holding. In that instant, all five eagle heads turned to face me, their piercing eyes burning into my soul. Not cruel. Not cold. Just... *knowing.*

Remiel finally looked over his shoulder. There was hesitation in his eyes, almost like regret. Then he motioned me to come closer. I hesitated only a heartbeat before stepping toward him. My legs shook beneath me, but I kept moving until his arm slid around my shoulders and pulled me into the warmth of his side. His lips brushed against my ear. "His name is Seraphiel."

Seraphiel tilted his head slightly, and though his beak never moved, I heard his voice. It echoed not in my ears but inside me. *"Beloved, do not fear me."* The vibration of his voice thrummed like thunder beneath still water. I gripped Remiel's hand.

"There are things you have yet to remember," Seraphiel said. *"what was sealed away cannot remain hidden much longer."* His wings shifted, graceful and vast, like they brushed through unseen layers of air. The eagle heads on his wings never looked away.

"Yours was a memory forged in the between." Something in my chest throbbed.....an ache like old grief trying to wake.

Seraphiel's eyes narrowed, not cruelly, but with a kind of ancient knowing. *"The child inside you will carry pieces of that."* I looked at Remiel, startled.

He didn't speak....but he was pale. Still. His eyes wide like he'd heard something too, something meant only for him. Something completely different...something taking him away again.

Seraphiel's wings arched higher. *"The time is near. Do not fear what you are to face, Eva."*

Then, with a rustle that didn't touch the trees, Seraphiel vanished. Not vanished like a man walking away but like a ripple in time smoothing itself out. I blinked to make sure I was awake and not dreaming because even the stars and the air seemed too still.

Remiel turned to me slowly. "Are you okay?"

"I... I think so," I whispered.

He took my hand gently and pulled me to him. I leaned into his chest, curling against him like the world had just cracked open and I wasn't sure what was about to spill out.

I listened to the rhythm of his heart, steady and strong. "Remiel?" I asked softly. "You have to go again, don't you?"

 I didn't need his answer. I could feel it in his silence. And I had felt it the moment I had woken up.

"Take me with you," I whispered. "Please?" I looked up into his face, pleading. His eyes widened in surprise, and then slowly, he began to shake his head.

"No, Eva. What I see... what I *do*….I don't want you to carry that part of me."

His voice cracked a little, and I saw something flicker behind his eyes. Not fear. Guilt maybe? And something else….

He had taken my hand as we had walked back into the house, he didn't speak about it again, till later when he saw me reading the scripture. He gazed down at me as if he was trying to remember every detail and etch it into his mind. And as if he could read my mind, he shook his head.
"No, Eva, the answer is no. Eva you will not go to that place with me. These places are opening portals that allow demons to travel back and forth. Sometimes the people, the others that I have to —" When he could not finish his sentence, I did.

"The people that you kill?" I said, touching his face gently, trying to let him know that I wasn't judging him. His face carried two day's worth of a five o'clock shadow. "Remiel, please tell me."

He shook his head and grabbing my hand he gently placed a kiss in my palm before looking at me again. "One more time, Eva, just wait for me one more time."

"One more time, Remiel?" I could see that my words struck a chord because he started clenching his jaws and his eyes darkened. He knew that I understood…..this might not be the last time.

The one more time came five weeks later. I watched him pack up and leave. Taking my heart with him. Why? I wanted to cry out to God, why allow him to become mortal if he was only going to be taken away from me and put in danger?

I stood there watching him leave, a dull ache in my chest. It seemed to never truly go away. It was part of the connection, knowing that he was far away from me. I gently rubbed my chest but the pain was still there.

After he left, I stayed up cleaning, which there wasn't much to clean, both of us were pretty tidy and didn't like a mess. I sat up reading some of the Bible, highlighting parts that I was still unfamiliar with. The one verse stood out to me…I took and tucked it away in my heart. It gave me peace for a little while……but it didn't last long.

My nights were not filled with peace. The dreams of the realms had returned, each one deeper and darker than the last, like falling through layers of shadows I could never climb out of. The air in the realms was thick and filled with voices I didn't understand, visions that blurred the line between memory and reality. I woke each time breathless, heart pounding, drenched in sweat and confusion. Calling for Remiel.

It all began to affect my body. The dreams, the pregnancy, the constant ache in my heart, it began to take a toll I could no longer ignore. My body no longer belonged to me, and neither did my mind. I was carrying something heavy, and it was starting to show.

I finally took early maternity leave, even though I didn't want to. But my doctor's eyes had been serious, concerned about my weight loss, the stress levels, my blood pressure, the exhaustion I tried so hard to hide. She didn't give me a choice.

Now, with the house quiet around me, I sat at the kitchen bar surrounded by scattered envelopes, unopened bills, and reminders of a reality I had been trying to push aside. I rubbed the side of my swollen belly, hoping for a soft kick, anything that might settle the nausea..

How was I supposed to do this? How was I supposed to keep a roof over our heads while Remiel was off fighting something I couldn't even name?

I stared at our online bank account, feeling the tightness in my chest grow. The checking account wasn't going to cut it. We had a separate savings account, but I didn't remember the login information. It was under both of our names, though. With trembling fingers, I picked up my phone and called the bank.

"Thank you for calling First Sun Bank, this is Donna. How can I help you today?"

I cleared my throat. "Hi Donna. I need to check the balance of our savings account and transfer funds to checking."

"Sure thing, ma'am. Can I have your name and the last four of the primary account holder's number?" I gave the information as I readied my pen to write the balance down.

There was a pause. "Okay, I have it here. Just confirming, you'd like the current balance of the joint savings account?"

"Yes," I said, nervously, dreading the number that was coming. "Please."

She read the number aloud, but I didn't understand it at first. I blinked, my ears ringing slightly. "I'm sorry, can you repeat that?" She did.

"Again?" I asked one more time.

The third time, I finally wrote it down just to see if I was hallucinating. I transferred a portion over to checking, quietly thanked her, and ended the call.

I sat there staring at the phone in my hand like it might change its answer if I blinked enough. The number echoed in my mind and quickly I did the math. Remiel had left enough money to pay the bills for the next year and then some.

I didn't cry. I didn't scream. I just sat there in silence, a quiet storm of gratitude and dread rolling over me. Because it felt like a goodbye. Like he knew. I put my head in my hands, elbows pressed to the cluttered bar top, and let the tears fall in silence.

Not because of the money. Not because of the exhaustion. But because I could feel him slipping away from this mortal life.

I wanted to laugh–I wanted to scream–I wanted to cry…. I wanted my Remiel.

Chapter Six

Eva

That night I dreamed of him. It wasn't the kind of dream you wake from and dismiss with a hand wave and a sigh. It was vivid, almost too vivid. I could smell and feel the earth under my feet, feel the chill of the air in my lungs. I was standing just outside an opened tent, dimly lit by flickering lanterns that cast shifting shadows on the canvas walls. Remiel was inside, surrounded by a few other men, soldiers, I assumed by the way they stood.

Their voices were low, serious. They hovered over a worn leather-bound book spread across a wooden table. I couldn't make out all the words, but it looked like a map of some kind, tattered pages inked with symbols and old script that almost looked like scripture. I knew the dream had carried me through the realms to Remiel.

I leaned forward, trying to hear. But the edges of the scene became blurry, distorted, like oil smeared across glass. I pressed my hand out, trying to push through the haze, but something invisible stopped me. It was soft and firm at the same time. The air around my fingers rippled, humming with power. I pulled my hand back instinctively, examining it as if I expected to see a burn or a mark of some sort. There was nothing.

Remiel's brow was furrowed as he pointed to something in the book, and I could see the others nodding. The conversation grew more intense, but I couldn't make out the words. I didn't care about the conversation anymore. I just needed him to see me. I needed him to know I was there.

"Remiel," I whispered. Nothing. I tried again, louder. "Remiel."

Still nothing.

"Remiel!" I cried.

This time, he stopped. He lifted his head slowly, as if unsure of what he'd just heard. His eyes scanned the air and then locked in my direction. His expression changed as he stood up suddenly, stepping away from the table.

I could see the alertness in the soldiers around him, but Remiel didn't stop. He held up a hand and motioned them to stay. He walked toward me, his eyes narrowed in confusion.

"Remiel, do you hear me?" My voice cracked. The invisible wall between us pulsed, and I leaned against it, desperate to break through.

I could almost smell him, warm and familiar. I pressed my forehead against the barrier. "Please," I whispered to the void. "If this is a dream, let me wake up. If I can't touch him, if I can't speak to him. Please let me go back."

But something changed. I felt it in the air….but I stayed rooted in place. Remiel was only inches away now, reaching forward. I needed him, the urgency in me. I just needed to touch him and know that he was ok.

"Eva?" he said, almost under his breath. He didn't seem to be speaking to me, more like speaking *toward* something he sensed but didn't fully understand. His hand extended close, but not close enough.

I lifted mine to meet it, just a breath apart… But then the pull began. Not physical. Spiritual. Something was pulling me away back through a tunnel.

I felt the presence before I heard it. A being I couldn't see, but could feel something that was powerful and urgent. "You, Beloved… you can't be here. How did you get here? You have to leave."

The voice didn't sound angry, just… alarmed. As if I had stumbled into a place I was never meant to find. I shook my head, clinging to the last thread of hope. "No…please. Let me talk to him. Just for a moment."

"You *can't* be here," the being repeated, this time with more urgency. The voice was not human. It echoed from within itself, it sounded both beautiful and yet terrifying.

The pull became stronger. The space was distorted. I saw Remiel's face one last time…confused, searching….and then it all collapsed.

I woke up with a gasp. Darkness surrounded me, and the sheets were tangled around my legs. I reached for the lamp and flicked it on. The room glowed in the soft and warm lamplight. But it was all too real but somehow I was back in my bed, back in the cottage, and alone. The baby began moving and put my hand to try to soothe the uneasiness that we both felt. But I knew I hadn't been dreaming, I had *been there*. Wherever *there* was.

I didn't sleep again. Not really. I must have dozed off eventually, but the rest of the night was blank. When I finally opened my eyes again, sunlight streamed through the curtains and my phone showed that it was nearly noon.

I got dressed slowly, choosing Remiel's shirt and a pair of jeans that barely fit over my growing belly. I still did not like wearing the clothes he had bought me, they reminded me too much of why he was gone.

I needed to get out of the house, shake off the pain of the night. So I grabbed my keys and decided to go to the bookstore. Maybe even the library afterward. I wasn't sure what I was looking for but something in me felt pulled, like a thread being gently tugged by an unseen hand.

The bookstore smelled of paper and worn leather mixed with new pages. I wandered the aisles aimlessly at first, letting my fingers graze across the spines of novels, journals, and forgotten memoirs. But then, without thinking, I turned toward the psychic section, the part I used to avoid because it made me uncomfortable. This time, I let myself walk straight into it.

Books about portals. There were texts on realms and spiritual dimensions. Some were too modern, too performative, but others... others felt older. Wiser and heavier. I found one that had no title on the spine, just a faded cover and a symbol etched into the leather. A circle within a triangle, lines running through it like veins.

I opened it. The first page read: *"The space between realms is thinner than most believe. Some Beloveds have always known this."* I immediately slammed the book shut. I clutched the book to my chest like it might disappear. This was what I came for. Or maybe... what had called me?

I held the book close and walked slowly toward the register, my fingers still resting on the worn leather cover as though afraid it might vanish before I made it to the counter. The bookstore was mostly quiet. A faint melody played in the background, something instrumental and old, like it belonged to another century. Then someone laughed softly a few aisles over.

Low. Feminine. It wasn't the kind of laugh meant for humor... but recognition. I glanced up briefly and caught sight of two women standing near the far end of the metaphysical section.

One of them—tall, wore glasses and dark curly hair pulled into a loose knot at the base of her neck—was flipping through a book on herbal correspondences. The other leaned against the shelf beside her, long braids draped over one shoulder of her overalls, as she watched the room with idle curiosity.

Or maybe... not the room.

Maybe me.

I looked away quickly, shaking off the strange prickle crawling up the back of my neck.

Behind me—

A book fell.

The sound echoed loudly in the quiet space of the bookstore. I turned instinctively without being able to stop myself. The braided woman had dropped it. Her gaze wasn't on the floor where the book had landed. It was on my hands. Our eyes met briefly before she bent to retrieve it.

"Sorry," she murmured. But the apology didn't feel like she really meant it.

Somewhere behind me I heard another voice. "Jona…" the curly-haired one whispered quietly. A breath caught sharply behind me.

I held the book close and walked slowly toward the register, my fingers still resting on the worn leather cover as though afraid it might vanish before I made it to the counter.

As I passed them—The braided one stepped aside to let me through. Up close, her voice was softer. "You felt it too, didn't you?" she asked quietly.

I frowned slightly, unsure what she meant. Before I could respond.

The other woman smiled politely. "Ignore my little sister," she said lightly. "She thinks every old book is cursed." But her eyes flicked down to the one in my hands...and didn't leave it.

Behind the register sat an older woman with a long silver braid and thin glasses perched halfway down her nose. She looked up as I approached, her eyes flicking to the book in my hands. And then she stilled. The smile she'd worn faded, not out of rudeness but recognition.

She stared at the book, then back at me. "Where did you find that?"

"Just…back there," I said, turning slightly to point toward the far end of the aisle. "It was tucked in with some older editions. It didn't have a label or barcode, but I thought I'd take a look–"

"It shouldn't have been there," she interrupted softly. "That book hasn't been touched or brought out in years."

I blinked. "It was on the lower part, right next to a copy of *The Keys of Enoch*."

Her eyes sharpened with something unreadable. "That's even stranger."

I offered a half-smile, trying to keep things light. "Well, it kind of found me, I guess."

She didn't return the smile. Instead, she reached out and gently turned the book in my hands, her fingers hovering for a moment above the etched triangle symbol. She didn't touch it. She just looked at it with a gaze that made my skin prickle.

"You're not just curious," she said, finally meeting my gaze. "You've seen something, haven't you?"

The question pulled the breath right out of me. "What do you mean?"

She tilted her head slightly, her voice quiet. "Most people come in here wanting crystals or self-help books. Not you. You walked in like you were listening for something. And that book" she tapped it once, gently, "only shows itself to people who are meant to read it."

I didn't know what to say. My heart thudded against my ribs, as if trying to speak for me. "I had a dream," I admitted, my voice barely above a whisper. "About someone I know. And a place I shouldn't have been able to reach."

She watched me carefully. "Did you cross?"

I felt the other two women walk up behind me, I was getting a very uneasy feeling about this. I hesitated before I said very low, "No… not exactly. There was a wall. Something kept me from getting closer. But I heard him. He heard *me*. And someone pulled me out. Someone said I wasn't supposed to be there." I had no idea why I was telling her this.

She leaned back slowly, folding her arms, her gaze unreadable now, guarded, but not unkind. "There are layers to this world," she said, "and not all of them can be walked with flesh and blood. Some are only meant for spirit, the guardians and guides. But once you know and your body and mind *remember* how to move between them…"

Her voice softened again. "It's like the veil stops caring who you are."

"I have nothing to remember," I whispered.

"Not yet," she said. "But you will. That book…it's not going to give you answers. Not right away. It's a mirror. It'll show you only what you're ready to see. Much like the Bible, it only reveals when you are truly ready."

I looked down at the book again, tracing the symbol with my thumb. "What's this symbol mean?"

She glanced around watching the others in the store before she leaned forward slightly. "Some say it represents the three thresholds…the physical, the celestial, and the shadow realm. The circle is what binds them." I swallowed hard. The air around us seemed heavier now, like the moment was suspended in something thicker than time. "I'll ring it up," she said quietly, finally taking the book. "No charge."

"What? No, I can…." I let my words fade as she shook her head, cutting me off with a soft look. "If the book called to you, it's not mine to sell."

I opened my mouth to thank her, but something in her expression told me to just take it and go. Then suddenly something whispered in my ear, *"Put it down and leave."*

I blinked for a moment, staring at her and then suddenly knowing what I should do, I put the book down on the counter. She opened her mouth to say something but I turned and practically ran out of the store.

As I stepped outside, the sunlight blinded me momentarily. I didn't know what any of this meant. I stared out across the town square at the bustling shops before I climbed into the car. I no longer had any desire to shop or buy a book. I cranked the car, I didn't know where I was going, but I suddenly knew I couldn't go home. Not yet.....

When I turned to look back at the store, there the two sisters stood, Shondra's hand was closed around Jona's wrist and she was shaking her head once. I could have sworn, she said *"Not here,"* as they both continued to watch me back out and leave.

The Church

I hadn't planned on driving to the church. I was not sure Matthew would even be there. But my hands knew the way, even if my mind didn't. Matthew was at the front, adjusting the cloth over the altar.

He turned when he heard the door, his face softening in recognition."Eva," he said, his voice calm and steady....almost too steady.

"I didn't know where else to go," I admitted.

He didn't answer right away. Instead, he reached out and took my wrist. Not gently but not harshly. His thumb pressed into the inside of my pulse point as his eyes closed.

And then, his entire body went still. Completely still. Like he was listening to something I couldn't hear. Or feeling something I couldn't see.

When his eyes opened again, they weren't calm anymore. They were alert. Sharp and afraid.

"You weren't alone," he said quietly.

The words made my stomach drop. "I know. There was a woman working the register—I was at the bookstore. There was a book, it was like it was calling me. I had it in my arms and was going to buy it. It spoke about the Beloveds and realms."

"No," he interrupted softly. His grip tightened slightly around my wrist. "There were others near you."

My mouth opened to answer but no words came. I thought of the two women in the aisle. The way one of them had dropped the book. The way the other had stopped her from speaking when I put the book down.

Matthew's jaw clenched. "Did either of them speak to you?" he asked.

"One of them asked if I felt it," I admitted slowly. "But I didn't know what she meant."

He released my wrist immediately. Like he'd been burned. "Eva," he said, his voice low now, urgent in a way I had never heard before, "you need to be careful."

A chill ran down my spine. "Careful of what?"

"I don't know what they are yet," he admitted. "But whatever stood near you in that place, whatever touched your aura while you were reaching for that book, it wasn't drawn to the book."

His eyes met mine. "It was drawn to you."

My breath caught. "I didn't feel anything," I whispered.

"You wouldn't," he said gently. "Not yet. The Beloved rarely recognize danger until it's already inside the gates."

A knot formed in my chest. "Matthew…what does that mean?"

"It means you need to pray," he replied immediately. "Not for answers. For discernment. For guidance. For protection."

"From what?" I pressed.

But he shook his head. "I am not sure about this that I sense."

Frustration sparked in my chest. "Matthew—"

"Eva." My name wasn't spoken sharply. But it stopped me anyway. "Some doors are best left closed."

Silence stretched between us. And then— he stepped closer. "May I?"

I didn't know what he meant until his hand lifted toward my head. I nodded. He placed his palm gently against my hair, bowing his head as his voice dropped into quiet prayer.

"Father," he began softly, "in the name of the Most High, I ask that You surround Your daughter with Your protection. Guard her mind from deception, her spirit from intrusion, and her body from harm."

My throat tightened.

"Send Your angels to stand watch at every threshold she walks through. Let no spirit speak into her ear that has not been sent by You. Let no darkness come against and defeat what You have called holy." His voice wavered slightly. "Give her discernment where memory fails her. Give her wisdom where fear rises. And if anything unclean has marked her path—"

His jaw tightened as he continued. "Break its claim now." A warmth spread through my chest, chasing away something I hadn't even realized was there.

"In your son Jesus Christ's Holy name," he finished quietly. "Amen." When he pulled his hand away, I realized I had been holding my breath.

"Matthew…" I whispered.

But his expression had already closed again. Guarded and distant.

"You're not going to tell me, are you?"

"About the book with the veil, the realms… the Beloved?" I tried to control the urgency in my voice.

He finally looked at me, a long, sad stare. Like he was seeing someone else…something else. He shook his head. "What's written in that book… is dangerous. And unfinished. You're not ready for it. And even if you were, I wouldn't be the one to tell you."

Frustrated, I almost stomped my foot in protest. "Then who will?"

He didn't answer. The air itself held its breath as Matthew's silence was like a stone, cold and unmoving. I took a breath, trying to steady the tremble in my voice. "You're not going to tell me, are you?"

"You've already stepped into something that most Beloveds do not believe exists. You're drawn to the supernatural. The spiritual realms are hard for people to believe, Eva."

He looked at me, eyes that looked tired, not tired of life, but tired of the fight. He shook his head. "Eva, some things you do not need to search for. That is not a holy book and one that is best forgotten."

"Why would it call me then?" I asked, pressing for answers.

"Why does sin call to any believer? To disrupt the path they are on. To steer them away from the path of righteousness. Sin does not come clothed as sin, it comes as wolf in sheep's clothing. Just as Lucifer doesn't come with a red cape and pitchfork. He comes as something more soft and seductive. Something that doesn't feel like it's forbidden. It isn't until you have realized how far off the path you have gone, that you see sin for what it truly is." His words stuck with me and so did his refusal to explain things to me.

The sky was beginning to show the evening shadows by the time I reached the stables. The book was still turning over and over in my mind. Nevada neighed softly when she saw me, the red of her coat glistening with the rays of sunlight that peeked in. Her head lifted over the stall door, and I stepped into her space without thinking, pressing my forehead gently to her neck. Inhaling the horse scent that always seemed to calm me.

"I don't know what's happening," I whispered.

She exhaled a warm breath, as she turned, her whiskers rubbed against my neck. Almost as if she was trying to understand.

But the peace didn't last. Something changed and my vision blurred….not with tears, but with light. Gold and blue, rippling like reflections on water. Then there was a bright flash. Not harsh or blinding, but shimmering with gold and blue, rippling like reflections on water.

I blinked, and the barn was still there. But not *quite*. The hay beneath my feet shimmered like reeds at the edge of a lake. My mare, once solid and warm, stood unmoving almost as if she was frozen. I turned slowly. There beyond the far wall of the barn, where there had only been weathered boards and shadows, a light had formed. Not a door, but a seam? Like the world had split open just slightly, and something behind it was waiting.

Then suddenly a ripple stirred around me, soft and silver like mist, but too still. Too heavy. I reached out without meaning to, the air humming against my skin. What I saw next felt like a long forgotten memory. The shimmer widened and deepened. A field stretched in front me, waving not quite steady. Almost like the heat wave that you could see on the pavement on a hot July day. The sky above me rippled like a pond. And then, without sound, something moved, something in the sky. There was no warning, not any thunder or lightning.

I watched as five shapes fell through the cracked sky, glowing and soundless, like stars slipping from their places. They didn't plummet….they descended slowly, almost gently, as if guided by their own choice.

"If you remain in your seat, souls will be lost….go, intervene, and you can save them." It was a dark voice that whispered to them, one by one, planting doubt, fear, and urgency in hearts that had only ever sought to serve. I could feel this even when I could not hear it.

Then a smaller voice came that pleaded. As if trying to rectify what they had done wrong. ***"They acted with the best of intentions, thinking they could save what they were sworn to protect. But in doing so, they abandoned their posts."***

They landed in a single, vast valley. The ground seemed to hum beneath their arrival, echoing the power they had once held. They were together yet separated by a few paces, each struggling against the invisible bindings that the dark being had left behind.

"His trick had worked, he had manipulated their fears, made them believe they were needed elsewhere, and in that single moment of obedience, they had fallen." The frail voice came once more, desperate to explain.

They were broken, waiting to be remembered. And then he came. A figure, who lingered behind the broken sky. Cloaked in a brilliance that was dimmed by a shadow. His wings were vast and on fire. Yet, he did not fall from the sky. He hovered there above the breach. His dark presence sent a chill through me. This being was beautiful in a way that felt like betrayal. The being lifted a hand and spoke but it was not to me, not to the world below, but to them.

"Let them forget. Let them all forget. Let the realms mourn what it cannot recall."

And then a wave. But not of water or of heat but one of *forgetting*. I saw it, like mist rolling over a field, swallowing light. Each figure that had descended, their glow dimmed and disappeared. Suddenly everything went quiet and even the stars stilled one split second.

"No one will remember. Not even them." The dark voice whispered.

I didn't understand what I'd just seen as the ripple shifted and disappeared. Time began to move again, Nevada moved and snorted beside me as if nothing had happened but something had happened. I had seen something that I could not understand.

There is a difference between what is holy...
and what only feels powerful.

Darkness rarely introduces itself as evil.
It comes cloaked in understanding.
In comfort.
In things that feel familiar enough to trust.

It speaks in gentle tones.
Offers knowledge.
Promises protection.
Sometimes even love.

But holiness has never needed to persuade.

The holy does not beg to be followed.
It does not twist truth into something easier to swallow.
It does not whisper in secret or isolate you from the light.

The holy waits.

Because what comes from God does not need urgency to be obeyed,
only discernment.

Scripture warns that the line between the two is not always easy to
see

"For Satan himself masquerades as an angel of light."
— 2 Corinthian

Chapter Seven

Eva

I tried to call Remiel but his phone went straight to voicemail, which had been the ongoing norm for the last month. Frustrated, I paced in the barn, not knowing what to do but knowing I needed to do something. I knew I would not get any more answers from Matthew.

I found myself driving once more but this time I went to my mother's house. Mom had been sitting on the porch when I arrived, her face showed some surprise, especially since I usually called when I was going to visit.

She met me in the yard with arms open to embrace me. "Sweetie, I am so glad to see you." For one split second, I could hear Grammy's voice echoing in hers, as she squeezed me tightly. "Come on, let's go in."

I followed her in and to the kitchen where she immediately handed me a glass of sweet tea. She sat down across from me at the table. Neither one of us said anything until I finally spoke up. "Mom, I need answers." I saw her tighten her grip around her glass.

"What do you mean, Sweeti?" Her voice was suddenly too calm.

"Mom, you know what I mean. There are things that I see.....that I dream....I don't understand." My voice cracked under the pressure and strain that I felt.

There was silence and she tapped her nails on her glass, we didn't speak at first.

Finally—

"Mom," I said, my voice already beginning to shake, "Please, I need answers."

My throat tightened painfully. "Places I've never been. Voices I shouldn't recognize. I hear things in my sleep that don't sound like dreams. They sound like… memories."

Silence. Then her nails continued tapping softly against the glass. Then she stood. "Come on," she said quietly. "Follow me outside. I want to show you something."

I followed her outside and down the porch. She stopped just outside the ring of the porchlight. She looked up at the sky where the stars were now dancing and shining.

And when she spoke her voice was almost a whisper. "When you were little, you would always look up at the sky. It didn't matter if it was daylight or dark…..and you would say strange things."

She went silent for a moment before taking a deep breath. "Things like the river under the sky is too loud or the sky behind the mountain isn't sleeping. It hurt your ears and you would cover them and cry. You said words and mumbled things that a child your age should not have known or said."

I could feel my chest tightening as I looked up at the stars before looking back at her. "Mom, why would I say that?" I saw her close her eyes and exhale slowly. She turned to me, tears brimming her eyes.

"You ask me a question….. that I can not answer." Her voice was filled with so much emotion that I could feel my heart breaking with it.

"Mom, what do you mean? Please tell me." I could feel panic starting to rise in me.

She took my hands in hers and took another deep breath. "I think it's time you know…" She took a deep breath before continuing. "Grammy and Papa aren't my biological parents. They adopted me."

I looked at her in shock. "So that means, Grammy was not my real grandmother?"

Mom shook her head, "No, she is your real grandmother…"

"Mom, I'm confused. What are you trying to say?" I dreaded her answer. Somehow I knew it would change my life.

She wiped the now visible tears away and I could tell she was thinking hard on how to phrase what she needed to say. "Eva, I can't tell you where you were born or anything about your birth…because I am not your real mother…."

There, those words shattered my world. The truth that maybe somehow I had felt all of my life. "What do you mean? Did you adopt me?"

She smiled faintly and squeezed my hands in hers. "Yes and no, not in the traditional sense. When Grammy and Papa adopted me, they had a daughter already. She was much older than me."

I frowned, "Mom, wait if you were adopted? Grammy is not your mother. How old were you when they adopted you?" I was trying to put the puzzle pieces together but it didn't make sense."

She shrugged, "I really don't know and neither did they. They said they adopted me when I was young, maybe four or five, but I really don't remember anything till I was around sixteen, it was like all the years before that were erased. Grammy would not talk about where they adopted me. She was very hush hush about it."

Mom motioned to the porch, "Let's go sit down."

Sitting in the rocking chair, I slowly rocked back and forth, waiting for her to continue. "Your real mother's name is Faith. Grammy named me Grace so that we both would have proper names. Faith–because Grammy had faith that God would bless her with a child."

She pointed to herself. "Grace, because he had graced her with another one in her later years."

"What happened to my biological mother….what happened to Faith?" I asked, not knowing if I wanted the real answer or not. Mom stopped rocking her chair.

"I don't know. …I wish I could tell you. All I have are the pieces that I remember and what Grammy told me. I know she came to visit one weekend. Grammy thought something might be wrong because she had brought so much of your stuff. Grammy told me that several times. She always regretted not asking Faith what was wrong."

She started rocking again. "We were both so wrong to think she was ok. Sunday morning when we woke up, you were crying and she was gone. You were barely three years old." She took a ragged breath before continuing. "You cried for her every single day for three months. We searched for her and could not find her. Your dad would not answer calls and when Papa went to see him, that man had the nerve to laugh at Papa. To actually tell him that Faith was on drugs. We all knew he was lying. Grammy and Papa filed a petition for abandonment and adopted you. As they got older, they knew someone else needed to take over raising you. So they allowed me to take over. I was so young and had no idea what I was doing. But I tried. Papa died….and then Grammy."

A deep sadness filled her voice and she tried to make light of it, "And we survived." She gave a little chuckle.

I returned her chuckle, remembering now how it felt that Mom had always been more like a sister instead of a mother figure to me, "But Moma what happened to him…to my father?"

"He drank himself to the grave. After your mother left, he drank until he died from it. I believe that it was his drinking that partly drove her away."

She paused for a moment. " But I just never could understand, how could she leave you?"

"Mom, I have dreams and visions that I don't understand….." I watched as her face went still, sort of staring straight ahead. Almost as if she was scared to ask. Finally turning to me, she nodded as if knowing already.

"What are they about?" Her voice carried a very eerie calm.

"Realms, other people, the sky, angels….demons." I had stopped my rocker too.

Grace inhaled sharply. "What do you mean, realms and demons?" She had given her full attention to me.

"Eva, what do you mean? What have you seen?" It was almost as if she expected it.

"I …in my dreams I can travel to different places, to different realms. Then today, I saw a vision of beings falling from the sky."

Grace started shaking her head, she stood up and started pacing around on the porch. I stood up too, just watching her trying to figure out what was going on. Rubbing her forehead as if trying to make the thoughts go away.

"Eva, dreams…do you remember the very first dream you ever had……like the one that has stuck in your mind since you were a child?" She took a deep breath. "I know this is crazy, because we often forget our dreams, but is there any particular dream that has—you have never forgotten?"

"What…what do you mean?" I asked, not certain on what she was asking. I looked at Grace, now realizing for the first time in my twenty nine years, that I looked absolutely nothing like her. It had never occurred to me to ask who I looked like.

I tried to bring myself back to the reality of the moment. "Dream, the first dream that I can recall." I closed my eyes. Dreams passed through my memory, some I could barely remember, and then suddenly I opened my eyes. "Your dream."

My voice shook as I continued. Pieces of the dream flew through my mind and were beginning to fit together. Things that made no—sense. "The dream I remember the most…it is the man in the shadows and you."

Memories of the supposed dream ran fresh through my mind as if it had just happened. I closed my eyes but it wasn't to shut out the memory of the dream but remember, to embrace it. Because I knew it held answers that I needed.

I couldn't remember how old I was when I had the dream, I knew it was young because I could barely reach the door knobs to open the doors in the cottage. I remember going to Grammy's room but she was still asleep. I could remember the cold hard wood floor as I walked barefoot down the hallway to Grace's room.

At the time, I had never thought it odd that I would go to the Grammy's room first. I then made my way to Grace. She was awake and sitting on the side of the bed, she was staring out the window as the winter wind blew the bare limbs across the tin roof. For a moment she did not see me, when she did…she motioned for me to sit with her. "What's wrong, Eva? You can't sleep, either?" Her voice was not the voice of Grace, my mother, that I knew now. Something was different. She was so young.

I could see Grace holding me and gently rubbing my back. I was holding a little baby doll. "Come on, we won't wake Grammy, you can sleep with me." I remember drifting off to sleep as she hummed a song to me. It was in that sleep the man in black had come.

I opened my eyes, staring up at Grace. "It wasn't a dream, it was real. You traveled a realm that night."

She stared as if trying to force herself to remember but she was only met with emptiness. Mom shook her head, "I don't know Eva, I can't remember everything. That seems to be the same weekend that Faith brought you. After that night, I could only remember bits and pieces of my life before. I think I was searching for something but I don't know what or why. I barely remember that night…it was like whatever happened erased everything important. I didn't know you remembered that night. I had always wanted to ask but I was worried that it would upset you and I didn't want to hurt you anymore than life had already done." She squeezed my hand, her memories were gone but mine remained, and they could possibly give us both the answers we needed.

I squeezed my eyes shut. It came like breath on cold glass, its edges soft, colors blurred, too vivid to be real and too strange to be forgotten, but I remember waking in the middle of somewhere else. Somewhere that was alive and breathing. I could barely see Grace ahead of me, I could remember clutching my doll close to my chest.

Suddenly I wasn't just remembering but the dream was alive again. I was there. The ground beneath my feet was soft like moss but glowed faintly blue. The trees rose tall and bone-pale, and they shimmered in the moonlight. The sky above me churned with clouds that didn't belong to any sky I knew.

They pulsed with light, like a heartbeat. It scared me and I whimpered, calling out for Grace. Then my hand was in hers, "Shhh Eva, shhh don't cry. Come here." She looked scared as she was picking me up and cuddling me close to her. "Eva, how did you get here?" I buried my face in her neck as I started to cry.

"Ssh, don't cry, be brave. Okay? I need you to not cry, so we can go home. Come on, let's go home." She had started walking with me, leaving the churning clouds behind.

"Go home?" I asked, though my small voice sounded far away.

She didn't answer. Her eyes were fixed on something up ahead, a shape that didn't belong in the forest. A gate. Thin and glittering like folded light. It stood between two crooked trees that bent toward each other, like they were trying to keep it hidden. The air around it buzzed, like a bell that had just been struck. Something inside me told me that we had to go through that gate to get home. But then I *felt it.*

I turned my head, and there, just in front of the gate, stood a figure. A man cloaked in black shadows. Still as stone. Watching. He didn't move, but I could feel his gaze crawl beneath my skin. His eyes were sharp, burning gold, like sunlight reflecting off glass just before it shatters.

Even as a child, I knew he wasn't supposed to be there. Something in the realm twisted. The ground beneath us shuddered. The trees groaned as if they were bearing the weight of some enormous dark secret. Grace stumbled forward, but caught herself in time, so that she didn't drop me.

Voice shaking, she whispered. "Eva, don't look at him. Close your eyes and stay with me." I clung to her, my little arms wrapping around her neck. I heard his voice, deep, dark and evil.

"You refuse to stay away." His voice echoed around us. "How many times do I have to send you away?" His voice betrayed his anger and frustration.

Grace tightened her hold on me. "I remember....I know what you have done. Sha–"

He let out an ungodly screech, "Do not say my name!"

Grace stepped back from him, protectively placing her hand on my head. "Let us go and I will not speak your name again. I will not speak your names, so that the realms and heavens will not remember what you have done. But, please, this child has no part of this war. Let me take her back."

"It is too late for that. You will not go away." he said.

I could feel his cold presence as he moved closer to us. "I have to make you forget once and for all."

His voice held a promise of what he was going to do. He raised his hand as if to draw something from her but nothing came forth. In his frustration he screamed an unholy sound. I didn't know what was happening and I didn't understand, but my chest burned.

I looked down and saw something. Grace held one of her hands to my chest and something was moving from it. It wasn't light…. it was something deeper. *Her memories.* It rushed into my chest and filled me until I couldn't breathe. I had woken up crying, clinging to my doll and I wasn't in Grace's bed anymore.

Down the hallway, I could remember hearing a soft thud. Grace had woken too. I remember hearing her footsteps pause. She had come in, holding me so that I could stop crying. But I could tell something was wrong with her. I couldn't see it then but I could see now. There was confusion and worry. Almost as if she didn't know where she was or where she belonged.

And that was the dream that I remembered, a dream that somehow surpassed all memories of my biological mother. Something had changed in Grace after that. I now understand that the dream or whatever had taken place in that realm was to blame.

Bringing myself back to reality, I knew I had to tell Grace. When I had finished, her eyes went wide for a moment as she paced back and forth. Frustration evident on her face.

The inability to remember brought on even more agony. "How can that be, how could you have had that same dream?" She began to rub her chest, not knowingly just instinctively. I reached out and put my hand on her chest, "Mom, how often do you rub your chest……does it feel empty?"

She stopped and looked down at our hands, swallowing as she looked back up at me. "I have felt empty ever since that night. The day after the dream, I couldn't remember anything previous to that night. I mean…I could vaguely remember the dream…the realm. But I can't remember what happened. But I felt it. My life before that night was totally erased, I could remember only Grammy, Faith, Papa and you. Even that was blurred. Grammy took me to see so many doctors and not one of them understood how I had just suddenly lost my memory overnight. They chalked it up to a traumatic childhood that had affected my memory. But I knew that wasn't it. Grammy knew that wasn't it either."

We walked back inside and sat on the couch. "Eva, everything is so confusing. These realms that you travel…the dreams. I think they are a part of my past. But I don't know or remember my past…so I can't tell you why."

I was trying to put the pieces together but the puzzle was so large. I felt like I was reaching into different and vast spaces, trying to pull pieces together. Then a thought clicked, as if someone had switched the light on. "Mom, the weekend that Faith left me, you said it was the same time you had the dream?" I could see her thinking, trying to remember.

"Eva, I am not sure. I can't remember for sure. I sort of remember it as such." I could tell she was telling the truth.

We sat there in silence, just thinking, trying to piece it together. Suddenly Grace stood up and pulled me up, "Come on, There is something. Maybe it will give you more details."

I followed her to the bedroom that she shared with James. He was off on a trip, purchasing some Cypress and Cedar wood to make more furniture. I was glad that Grace had decided to stay back.

I watched as Grace went to a chest at the end of the bed. She removed blankets, shawls and dresses. Finally she reached into the bottom and retrieved a book. It was leather bound and had the same symbol as the book that I found in the bookstore, just a different size, this one was smaller. Matthew's words echoed in my mind as she turned to me, offering the book to me. I took a step back as if the book would burn me.

"Eva, this Faith's journal. She left it here. I would see Grammy read it from time to time. I tried to read it after Grammy passed, but her writing didn't make sense to me."

I hesitantly reached for the journal, wondering if I needed to? I flipped the journal open, the first few pages were blank. Then letters began to stand out. Faith, my real mother wrote about her marriage and my father. Everything blurred together, then she mentioned a friend…one that she confided in. Then the pages were blank, then she picked up writing sometime later after she had me. Her entry spoke of her broken relationship with her husband, dangerous things were starting to take place and she was scared. *I don't know what to do, Eva is in danger. I don't know how to protect her. This is all my fault! They are going to come for her and he will let them take her. They will take her away from me forever. I know the only place to take her and then I will have to leave so they will follow me. I will lose her either way. If I stay they take her, if I leave….Grace can protect her.* I read the last passage out loud.

Mom sat on the edge of the bed. "What did she know, what did Faith know? And who were *they*? How could I protect you?"

I flipped through the journal and a photo fell out, I picked it up. There was a young woman holding a baby, a young man who did not look happy, and another woman, a beautiful redhead. She looked exactly like Alysson, that had to be her mother. Alysson's mother had to be the new friend my mother wrote about!

Alysson's mother had been rumored to be a witch. This didn't make sense though, if this was Faith holding me, then where was Alysson? We were the same age, not even a year apart. From what I knew, I was just a little older than her. But this woman did not look like she was even expecting.

The puzzle had started to fall into place only now to be strewed apart again. I turned to Grace, "This journal was written in English, I could read this......why couldn't you?"

Grace bent her head for a moment, taking a deep breath. "I don't know why, Eva. I can read if it was things or books that I had read previous to the vision-the dream. If it was anything after that…it was like looking at another language. I couldn't—can't read it. No matter how hard I tried. Even if it was words that I had read before, if it was something different, a different book or a sequel… I can't read it."

"And you had never read her journal before so therefore you couldn't read after. But you can't remember your life from before?" I let out a sigh of exasperation. The truth continued to remain hidden from me and somehow I carried Grace's memories inside of me, memories of a dark figure and realms. But which ones were her memories and which ones were truly mine?

Chapter Eight

Remiel

On the seventh night, as the watch fires burned low, Eli found me. I was sitting on the hilltop looking out into the deep desert night. He didn't speak at first. Just stood beside me, shifting awkwardly as if unsure whether to interrupt grief. "They've seen her," he finally said.

I turned sharply. "What?" I stood up immediately.

"The prayer warriors. Every night since her Bible was found, during evening watch, they gather. They say her voice comes during prayer."

He swallowed. "But tonight was different."

I stood as he continued, "They didn't just hear her. They *saw* her." He looked shaken. "All of them. At once. They all described the same thing."

"A tunnel. And your Eva, kneeling. Praying." His voice dropped. "And then… she looks up. As if she heard someone. As if she was trying to reach someone."

I didn't speak. I couldn't. The air had thickened around me and I felt as if I could not breathe. I felt as Eli laid a hand on my arm. "She's alive, Remiel."

I knew his words were meant to be comforting but they did nothing but tear me apart. I couldn't do anything but walk away. Away from him, away from the camp, away from the pain that had settled on my shoulders from the weight of the trials.

We had just stopped a portal from being opened near the Mount, during the fight, I could hear Eva praying. Then once, just briefly, I saw her. When everything was done and the Others camp had been burnt down, two of my soldiers had brought a Bible to me. They said that they had found it just outside the circle. It was Eva's Bible. We had searched the surrounding areas, the destroyed camp of the Others, the local caves…we could not find any trace of Eva. I knew that she had traveled the realms, that was the only way her Bible could have gotten there. I just prayed she was able to travel back.

I had prayed. No, I had begged and I still did not hear from God, Michael, Gabriel, not even Serephiel. I was angry, so angry. I wanted to leave but could not. Why would God not let me leave? Did he find me wanting? Was I not good enough? Had I not obeyed his every command once I had become mortal? These thoughts haunted me all through the night…..

The following morning, Hunter came to me, his jaw tense, eyes shadowed from too many nights of too little sleep. He sat down across from me. "The messenger spoke to me," he said simply.

"What did he say?" I asked, I really didn't care if it did not involve me going home.I stood up from my chair, getting ready to exit the tent.

He hesitated. "He said… it's time." I stared at him. Was this what I had been praying for? Was I really allowed to leave now?

"He said, *'Tell him he can return.'"* Hunter's gaze didn't waver. *"And you'll go with him."*

I did not ask why Hunter was being sent with me, there was a reason I was sure. It was yet to be revealed.

Homecoming

Anxiety crawled over me as the truck tires crunched over the gravel as I pulled into the yard. It was almost dark and the porch light was off. That was strange because Eva always left the porch light on. Her car was here. I cut the engine and stayed there for a moment. For a second, I could see her, such a clear memory. Standing on the porch steps, damp hair sticking to her cheeks, coffee mug in her hand.

I blinked and the steps were empty.

Hunter climbed out of the passenger side without a word. He followed me to the front door, shoulders tense, eyes scanning the quiet yard like it might still hold answers. I opened the door slowly. The house greeted us   with   silence.
Everything was still in place. The framed photo of Gabriel on the entry table, the blanket folded over the back of the couch. I could almost feel her presence here, but not fully. Something was wrong, something was very wrong.

"Eva?" I called out. My voice barely rose above the hum of the refrigerator. No response.

I moved to the hallway, eyes catching little details….her mug still in the sink, her shoes by the door, one of her scarves draped on the coat hook. I turned into the bathroom and found her towel was still damp. Still hanging on the shower rod. She had taken a shower sometime today which meant she had not been gone long. I returned to the living room slowly, heart pounding with a strange combination of dread and hope.

Hunter was there, pacing now. "She's not here," I said.

He nodded. "I figured. Where do you think your Eva is?"

I didn't answer. Before either of us could speak again, the front door opened. We both turned. Mariana stood in the doorway, she looked exhausted. She stopped short when she saw us. Her eyes widened.

"Remiel?" she said, breathless. She stepped inside slowly. "I didn't know you were back." She looked Hunter up and down, as if trying to decide whether he was a friend or enemy.

"We got in about ten minutes ago," I answered. "Where's Eva?" I didn't bother to introduce her to Hunter. That was not as important as finding Eva at this moment.

Mariana's expression changed. A ripple of guilt and pain passed through her eyes. "I just came to pick up a few things for her." Her voice held a hesitation.

I stepped forward. "She's not here. Where is she?" I heard myself practically growling at her.

She flinched as she hesitated. "She's at the General. They admitted her two hours ago."

My mouth went dry and I tried to breathe. "For what?"

Mariana swallowed and she looked quickly from Hunter then back to me. "She collapsed and started bleeding. They think it was stress maybe. They're running tests…Matthew and I were coming to visit…we found her on the back porch. I don't know how long she had been there. "

I stared at her, there was something else she was not telling me. Mariana's eyes blinked with unshed tears. Her next words were quiet. "It's the baby. Remiel…the baby didn't make it."

Eva

The day felt so nice and fresh as I stepped onto the back porch to breathe the air, hoping it might settle the ache that was in my chest and hadn't left.

It had been *seven days*. Days that I spent praying and asking. Crying out. Whispering Remiel's name. Each night, I'd see the tunnel again. I never could get to the end of it. Something was always keeping one step away from him. The tunnel was cold and silent. But outside of it I could hear fighting,

I could hear Remiel commanding his soldiers. I could smell smoke from fires and screams of victory and cries of defeat.

Each prayer felt like it echoed through a hallway that swallowed it whole. And still, I kept praying. *Protect him, Lord. Let him return. Don't let him die where I cannot reach him.*

I hadn't eaten. Sleep came in short spells. Each time I closed my eyes, I felt myself drifting back to that place between…..*neither realm nor Earth.* A suspended place of prayer and silence. At one point, I was beginning to question my sanity. Then it just stopped.

I was getting ready to sit down and that's when I felt it and then came the voice, his voice. Smooth. Familiar. Wrong…..

"He didn't make it." The voice was so confident and certain.

I turned as a cold waved over my body. There Dagon stood in my doorway, impossibly tall, his features too perfect, like he'd been carved by something that hated imperfection and his eyes…they were too cold. Too still. Too knowing.

"Remiel fell," he said. "He was cast down, broken in the battle. I came to tell you because no one else would. None of his so-called soldiers. None of your prayer warriors. Not even Matthew. Remiel will not be coming back to you."

I opened my mouth, but no sound came. It felt like the world had tilted, just slightly, just enough to make standing feel unnatural. I grabbed onto the post to keep from falling.

"You asked for him," he continued. "You prayed. Sometimes Heaven chooses silence. God likes to play games with you, his precious Beloveds. You should know that by now." He smiled. Not with his lips, but with something behind his eyes.

A storm of emotions rolled over me, each wave forcing me to steady myself. "You lie, Dagon. I would have known. I would have felt it. If Remiel died, I would know." My hand immediately went to my chest.

He let out an evil laugh, "Do you really believe that? After all he had put you through and you still believe that you are connected to him? That was a lie! Eva, wake up! It was a lie he created to keep you waiting for him." He took a step toward, reaching out to touch my face but I moved away.

"Why do you come here? To only torment me?!" I moved further away from him. I felt like I couldn't breathe.

I felt Dagon's hand on my arm as he turned me around. "Don't touch me!" I said, jerking my arm away from him. This couldn't be happening. This was all happening too fast.

Dagon ignored me and reached out and pulled me to him. His touch, his smell, it had all once made me desire him. Now it made me physically sick.

"Eva," His voice came out soft and desperate. "Eva, you will not leave me alone. Your memory haunts me." He pressed his forehead against mine and suddenly there was a scene being played in my head. I had no control to stop it.

A version of me, younger and wild. There were bars, alcohol, drugs and dancing. But there was no church, there was no God. Just a downward spiral into sin. And a huge emptiness. The vision suddenly stopped. Dagon did not immediately move away. He pulled me even closer as he placed his lips next to my ear. He inhaled, as if my scent was life to him. "I was supposed to do that to you. And I didn't. I couldn't because I loved you."

He didn't move away. Instead, he pulled me closer, lips near my ear, inhaling as though my scent were life itself. "From the first moment I saw you—I loved you. I loved everything you were, because you were everything I was not. I… I never stopped…"

His eyes shifted, golden brown now, warm and haunted. His eyes—warm golden brown now—locked onto mine, and he kissed me. Deeply. Passionately.

Every inch of him radiated longing and regret, love and betrayal intertwined in a single, suffocating wave. I could feel the weight of every command he had been given to destroy me, and yet the tenderness of a love that had never truly left him.

And then, just as suddenly, the kiss broke—but he held me close, forehead pressed to mine. "And then… I was commanded. Ordered to destroy you, to undo everything you were. And I…I disobeyed for a time. Then I had no choice. I tried to let it go, tried to follow the mission…but every command, every dark order, twisted me. For the first time since the descent, I hated what I had become… and all I could see was you."

I wanted to scream, to tell him that loving him was impossible. But he pressed on. "I watched you from the shadows," he whispered, "as if my very soul were chained to your steps. Every smile, every tear…it tore me apart that I couldn't protect you, that I had to pretend the mission mattered more than you. I…I hated myself for it. And I hated myself more because every time I thought I could walk away, I couldn't. I was tethered to you, even when all I wanted was to disappear."

My hands clutched his shoulders. My heart raced. I could feel the pulse of his pain, like fire in my chest, like a memory not my own.

"And when I…when I lost our son," he whispered, voice breaking, "I thought it would destroy me. But it didn't…because even in that moment of despair, all I could feel was you. Your grief. Your loss. Your life, and the impossible weight of it. And I… I loved you through it. Even as I hated myself for what I had to do, I loved you. I still do."

He kissed me again. Long, searing, desperate. Every second of it spoke of longing and remorse, of desire and guilt, of betrayal and devotion all at once. I pushed him away, stepping back. Needing air to breathe.

He looked at me, almost sorrowfully. "And now? I came to finish what I delayed. Because love, Eva…it isn't always salvation. Sometimes it's the knife that waits. What you prayed so hard for and believed in, is no longer."

"You *tormented* me," I whispered. "Every dream. Every fear. Every nightmare. You took my son."

"Our son and because I couldn't have you if you were saved," he said softly, reaching out and pulling me closer to him.

"You had me once," I stated, raising my face where I could look him fully in the face.

"But you will never have me again." Shaking my head, I stepped back, voice trembling.

"You lie about Remiel. I don't believe you." My voice was weak and I felt like I was going to pass out. I shook my head as I pointed at him.

My voice was low but I commanded it to speak. "I rebuke you in the name of Jesus, you can not stay here. Be gone you worker of iniquity. I cast out your powers over me and bind you by the blood of Jesus, you shall not torment me anymore."

A storm of ash and heat coiled around his feet and climbed his legs like smoke made of shadow. Then the stench of burnt metal and sulfur.

"As you wish," he said, voice now warped. "But before I go... let me leave you with one truth." He lifted one hand, fingers curled like claws and the world blurred. And in its place…a battlefield. Charred earth. Ash falling like snow.

Remiel stood in the center, bloodied, staggering, blade cracked and shoulders bent beneath the weight of too many wounds. A creature loomed behind him. It was massive, faceless, its wings made of flames and dead hanging leather.
Remiel turned his head, just slightly, his eyes finding mine. "Eva…" His mouth formed my name. Then the beast struck. Remiel's body folded. He crumpled to the ground….still. Lifeless. Gone.

"This is the truth," Dagon whispered in my ear. "You prayed for him. But your God was silent...and your name was the last word he called." And then the vision shattered into black smoke.

I heard the screaming before I realized it was me. I gasped as my stomach twisted. A sharp pain, so sudden it stole my breath again and again. The baby! But no, this was something else. Something was tearing inside of me…not just my body. A tearing that started in my soul. My connection to Remiel, my grip on faith, it all began to slip.

Then everything dropped away. My entire world was torn apart. I felt myself falling into the great gaping hole and was completely helpless to stop it. "Oh, God no!" And the last of my strength unraveled.

"When you pass through the waters, I will be with you." I didn't know if it was a memory… a whisper… or God Himself. I heard it once more as I fell to my knees.

"Weeping may endure for a night, but joy cometh in the morning."- *Psalm 30:5 (KJV)*

Often God will break you to heal you completely, he will take you to a place– to kneel alone. So that he will become your only strength.

I floated in the dark, cradled by wires, machines, and that never-ending annoying beeping. I didn't want to open my eyes. I wanted to stay there in the dark. Away from reality. Away from death. The lights of the room were too bright even though Mariana had dimmed them. The vampires called nurses continuously came back and forth to take my blood. As if they expected the results to change and it would tell them something different.

I couldn't—wouldn't speak to anyone, there was nothing left to say. I heard the hospital door open. I looked over and saw Stacy, my nurse coming back in. She quietly rolled the ultrasound machine in with her. She gave me a sad, knowing smile as she started setting up beside me. "Dr. Nelson wants to get one more ultrasound before the surgery."

I simply nodded and looked away. I stared out the window as she pulled back the blanket, applied the cold gel to my stomach. She then moved the probe with careful circles for five minutes or more. No thump. No flutter. Just silence. I never looked. I didn't need to.

When she finished, she wiped my stomach clean and gently covered me again. She hesitated, then touched my shoulder briefly before walking out. When I heard the door shut behind her, I let the tears slide slowly out…I could not do this again. Not anymore.

There was no Gabriel, no Remiel and now our baby was gone. All that was left was just me. Hollowed out and empty. How much did God think that I could endure before finally breaking?

I closed my eyes when I heard the door open, I could hear Grace telling James to be quiet that I was asleep. She leaned over and kissed my forehead but I kept my eyes closed because speaking took too much energy. That was something that I no longer had. I faded off to sleep as their whispering voices began to fade.

In my mind, in the silence…I prayed that God would turn this around. That this would be an ugly nightmare and I would wake up. And in that dream-like space, he came. Remiel. He didn't speak. Just sat beside me on the edge of the bed, his weight warm, familiar. He leaned forward and pressed a kiss to my forehead.

His lips lingered, as if afraid I'd disappear if he pulled away too soon. He took my hand, lifted it gently to his mouth, and kissed the center of my palm. I felt him. His warmth. His love. His sorrow. I wanted to reach for him, to say his name, but this was a dream. It *had* to be. He couldn't really be here.

Tears broke again, hot and new. *Please don't be a dream.* And somewhere in that delicate space between sleep and waking, I whispered into the dark, "Remiel… don't leave me again." Some part of me *knew* this wasn't real. Couldn't be real. He was gone.

And yet…

The moment didn't fade. His hand didn't vanish. His forehead still rested gently against mine. My tears now streamed down the side of my face and into my hair. I felt the back of his hand gently wiping my tears away. "My Eva," he whispered. "My love. I am here." His voice cracked on the last word, and I heard it for what it was. He kissed my cheeks, like he could undo the grief with his lips.

"Please," he said softly, the edge of desperation creeping in. "Eva… look at me."

Something in me clenched, the part that wanted to stay in the dark…stay curled in silence. That part warred with the part that had been waiting for his voice since the moment I knew I loved him. I wanted to believe. I *ached* to believe. But I had seen him fall. Dagon's scene still haunted my vision.

My lashes fluttered, but I didn't open my eyes yet. What if this wasn't him? What if this was the last kindness before insanity took over and I lost all touch with reality?

He took a shaky breath and pressed my hand against his chest. His heart beat strong beneath it, steady. Real. "You're not alone anymore," he said. "I came back." And this time, something moved inside me. Not just in my mind, but in the place that remembered him long before the missions. The memory of the first touch, first kiss, his first heartbeat under my hand. *My heart knew his.* "Eva… look at me."

I let out a breath I hadn't realized I'd been holding. My eyes fluttered again, slower this time. No longer fear. Just weariness. And ache. And then…I opened my eyes.

The hospital room blurred around the edges, lights too bright, the walls too white. But his face…that was all I could focus on.

His eyes were tired, rimmed red, full of something more than sorrow. His eyes searched mine like a man who had been lost too long. His face was unshaven, a small cut ran along his cheekbone, and he looked like he hadn't slept in days. But he was here. Alive. Real.

I blinked slowly, trying to form words, but my throat burned with silence. He smiled, faintly…"Hey," he whispered. "There you are."

I could only look at him. There were no words, no explanation. I reached up to touch his face and he cupped his hand over mine. "You came back to me," he said, more breath than sound.

I tried to speak. My lips parted. The name tasted dry. "Remiel…" It came out like a gasp. He bowed his head against my hand again and exhaled hard, like that one word had resurrected something in him.

"Remiel, our baby…" I started to cry, unable to stop it. Remiel leaned forward taking me in his arms. He held me, no promises of *it would be okay.* We sat there and we grieved together for a life that had never been lived.

"I'm here, you aren't alone in this." His voice sent warmth through me. I didn't have the strength to smile, but my eyes told him everything.

Chapter Nine

Eva

The silence between us was held together with something painful and something unspoken. Remiel moved away and reached toward the edge of the bed where the dirt-stained Bible lay. He picked it up gently, holding it like something fragile. *My Bible.*

He ran his thumb across the bent edge, over the pages stained by battle and earth. Then he looked at me. "Agon and Masaungo found this," he said quietly. "On the battlefield." He paused for a moment. "Why did you leave it?"

The question wasn't an accusation. It was filled with ache. Like he was asking where I went and if he had failed me. I looked at him….not just at his face, but at the shadow in his eyes. This wasn't about the Bible. It was about *him.*

"I didn't leave it," I whispered. "I placed it." He waited, eyes searching mine. My voice trembled, but I forced it forward. "It was a reminder. For you."

He blinked. "Of what?"

I turned my face toward the window, thinking of how I could explain it to him, then back to him. "Of who you were and still are. You were the one who led me to faith." His breath caught…just barely…but I saw it.

"You were the one who showed me light when I didn't know how to ask for it. You pointed me to salvation long before I even believed it was meant for me. You were the one who taught me how to forgive myself. You wanted to protect me from your pain,

Remiel…but I wanted to help you. I didn't want you to drown in the darkness of the earthly hell you came to."

A tear slid down his cheek, but he didn't look away.

"I left it to remind you of who you still are." I reached and gently wiped his tear away, placing my palm against his cheek. "Even if you didn't make it back to me...I wanted you to remember who you were. That God loves you and I love you."

He lowered his head, forehead resting against the leather cover. "I don't deserve that." He took a deep breath before exhaling slowly.

He looked at me once more. "I have been so angry and doubted my Lord. I questioned everything, my duty, the commands, the vow, my purpose, even my own existence. The only thing I never questioned was my love for you." He said, voice raw with emotions. "Even in my worst doubts, when I stood in the battle, you were the one constant. The one truth I could still hold."

"I don't know what I am anymore," he whispered. *"But I know what you are to me."*

The ache in his voice struck something deep inside me. I saw it all in his eyes. The war he carried in his bones, the centuries of silence, and the guilt. He battled the spirits of hell to protect people's souls that knew nothing about him or the war that was waged for them. He had fought for heaven and he had descended for me.

I reached out and took his hand. His fingers were calloused, warm, trembling ever so slightly beneath mine. "You say you don't know what you are anymore," I said softly, "But I do."

His eyes lifted to mine, searching, like a man who dared not hope.

"You are the one who still believes even though your soul is full of doubt. You are the one who chose to love me even when we knew it was forbidden. You are a warrior, the memory of mercy in a war that others do not see. You carry that because somewhere inside you, you still believe…..and I believe in you. Because you are my Remiel."

He ran a hand through his hair, "I have argued with God, asking why would he separate us? Why would he allow me to become mortal, if he was only going to break us apart. I have been so angry…I don't deserve his mercy."

I took a deep breath as I closed my eyes and opened them once more. "None of us do." Slowly, he opened the Bible. The pages whispered as he flipped through them…..not searching, just letting them fall where they would. They settled near the back. His eyes scanned the page. His lips moved silently once, twice. Then he read aloud:

"Is anyone among you sick? Let them call the elders of the church to pray over them and anoint them with oil in the name of the Lord. And the prayer offered in faith will make the sick person well… The Lord will raise them up…"
(James 5:14–15)

His voice cracked on that last line. *"The Lord will raise them up…"* The words fell quietly in the room. Not loud. Not shouted. Just spoken in faith.

He looked at me, then almost without thinking, he placed his hand gently on my stomach.There was no expectation….only love. Only faith, trying to reach through grief. "God, if *You* are listening… raise her up."

His voice was barely audible now, a plea more than a prayer. "Heal what's broken. Restore what was lost. Let this be the moment *You* step in."

He closed his eyes, still holding the Bible in one hand and me with the other. "I believe, even if I don't feel worthy." Remiel sat still, his hand resting gently over my stomach, the open Bible in his lap.

He opened his eyes, looking at me he whispered one more time. "I believe... even though I am not worthy. In Jesus name...Amen."

Then the door opened. Soft shoes, hushed voices. The nurse, Stacy, entered first, followed by a younger one with a clipboard. Their faces were kind, but focused. The silent space evaporated in the sound of protocol and procedure. "Ms. Eva," Stacy said gently, "Dr. Nelson wants to move ahead with the surgery."

She glanced at Remiel but didn't question him being there. Something about the way he sat beside me, with his hand on mine, the Bible open in his lap...made it clear he wasn't going anywhere.

I didn't speak. I only nodded. The nurses moved quietly around the room. Checking monitors. Adjusting lines. The lights above me buzzed softly as they prepared me for surgery. "We'll be delivering within the hour," one of them said. "Just rest. We'll take care of everything."

Remiel leaned down again, pressing his lips to my forehead. "I'll be right there," he whispered. They unhooked and hooked different lines. They focused on prepping me for the surgery before finally sliding me gently from bed to bed.

I caught one last glimpse of the Bible. *The prayer offered in faith... will make the sick person well. But could our faith raise our child back from the dead?* As they wheeled me toward the OR, I closed my eyes, not in fear this time, but in surrender. Not to fear. But to hope and belief to the God who was listening.

The lights in the operating room were so bright. I closed my eyes against their glare. Then when I opened them, I saw only him. Remiel stood beside me, gloved and masked, but I could still feel his gaze. He hadn't let go of my hand since the moment they brought him in. I didn't need to see his face…I felt him, steady and warm, my angel. "You're not alone," he whispered. "I'm here." He knew I needed those words. Memories of Gabriel, flashed through my mind. Another child, I would have to bury another baby.

They placed the warm blanket on my chest and over my arms so that I wouldn't move them. There was a low toned conversation between the nurses and doctor. Then everything went silent and I knew.

The doctor's voice was calm, but you could hear the emotions underneath as she placed the baby in the nurse's hands. "We have her." And then…*silence.*

No cry. No sound at all. The nurse walked around from behind the curtain, carefully placing the baby…so small, so still, on my chest. *Blue. Motionless.* Her body limp and blue, there was no breath. Her chest didn't rise. I swallowed back the panic clawing its way up my throat.

Remiel reached out with trembling control and placed his hand gently on her back. His eyes closed. And he prayed. Soft. Simple. Steady. "Lord…You gave her to us. She is Yours before she is ours. I have no right to ask. But I do….You are the breath in all of us. If it is Your will…"

A pause.

And then he whispered, "Thy will be done in Jesus Christ's name, Amen." As he opened his eyes, there were several murmured amens and the room seemed to hold its breath with him.

Then…a flutter. The tiniest rise of her back. And a sound. *A weak, broken cry.* Frail. Trembling. But there. Alive. I gasped and started crying. One of the nurses gasped. "She's crying."

The quiet broke. Suddenly hands were moving. Voices calling for vitals and warming blankets. Another nurse gently lifted the baby from my chest with urgent care, pressing a stethoscope to her chest, calling for oxygen, checking color, checking pulse. *"She was supposed to be stillborn," one whispered. "She's blue but responsive. Get her to the NICU."*

Remiel hadn't moved. His hand was still outstretched from where she had breathed beneath his touch. He looked down at me, eyes wide, mouth barely moving.

"She heard you," I whispered, tears rolling down my cheeks and into my hair. I was helpless to stop them.

"No," he replied, wiping my tears. His voice cracked with the unspoken emotions. "She heard *Him*. She obeyed Him."

Remiel

The walls of the hospital seemed so long as they wheeled Eva back into the room. I walked beside her, my hand still holding hers even as she slept..emotionally drained, yet quiet. Once inside the room, the nurse adjusted Eva's blanket, checked the lines, and dimmed the lights.

The baby, our baby was alive, they were still monitoring her vitals, warming her, confirming what none of them could explain. I didn't speak. I couldn't. I just sat there, watching Eva breathe.

I had begged for seven days then I had let go. Today, I asked again then whispered *thy will be done*, and *He had heard.* When the door opened, I stood immediately. It was Dr. Nelson.

Her face was calm, but there was something in her eyes…disbelief barely contained beneath professionalism. She looked at Eva, then at me, then took a step inside. "She's stable," the doctor said softly. "Your daughter."

I exhaled, so quietly, but it felt like I hadn't breathed since they took her from Eva's chest. "Is she…" I paused. "Will she be all right?"

Dr. Nelson glanced down at the chart in her hands, then back up at me. "We don't know yet. Her oxygen was low, but she's responding now. Her heart rate is strong. APGAR was zero at birth... then six after four minutes. We're calling her condition...." Her words trailed off.

She hesitated, then added, "We were preparing for the worst. There was no reason to expect a live birth, given the vitals earlier today." She looked at me again. Not as a doctor but as a woman who had seen something unexplainable and didn't know how to name it. "Whatever happened in there… whatever brought her back… I don't have medical terminology for it."

I did, I knew exactly what it was. "Can I see her?" I asked.

"Just a few more minutes of monitoring and then one of the nurses will let you go see her." The door closed behind her, and the silence returned. I turned back to Eva, still sleeping. I brushed the hair from her forehead, as I knelt down beside her bed, and rested my hand over her heart.

I had prayed. Not because they weren't capable, not because I doubted the hands working in that room…but because I knew there was something deeper than anything their charts could explain. I had prayed because this wasn't just about life and death. It was about faith.

I knew the team would do everything they could. But what happened in that room went beyond medicine. She was gone….*gone*….and somehow, something pulled her back. I didn't need monitors or numbers. I know what it was. He heard me. God had shown me that he still listened and his timing was perfect.

I stood up and called Mariana, she had been waiting downstairs with Grace and the others. Just as I was hanging up with her, a nurse entered quietly. "You can come meet your daughter."

I looked at Eva once more before rising to my feet. As I turned to follow the nurse, movement drew my eyes, her hand. It twitched. Then her fingers curled lightly against the blanket. I leaned over and kissed her forehead, breathing her in. "Your mother and Mariana are coming to see you."

I stood up quickly and followed the nurse out. I stepped out into the corridor, the soft click of the door behind me echoing louder than it should have. The air was thick with an antiseptic smell and the hum of halogen lights. Just ahead, the nurse motioned for me to follow.

"It's just down this hall." She said, waving to her left.

I nodded, still torn…Something was telling me not to leave Eva, but something about the nurse's calm demeanor reassured me. "She will be alright, we will be back …probably before she wakes."

As we turned the corner, another nurse approached from the opposite direction, a stainless tray balanced in her hands. Small glass vials clinked softly with each step. My gaze passed over her briefly…until one vial caught the light. A pale, ***blue-violet glow*** shimmered inside it, subtle, but almost unnatural.

But the nurse with the tray kept walking, head down, not making eye contact. The other nurse continued speaking, and I forced myself forward, following her toward the nursery viewing window. I looked back once…just once. But the glint of the vial was already gone around the corner with the nurse

I stood at the glass, unmoving. Beyond it, rows of swaddled infants slept beneath soft light and steady rhythms of monitors. I knew which one was ours the moment I saw her. I didn't need a name tag or nurse to point her out. She *pulled* me. My daughter, our daughter.

The nurse beside me finally spoke. "You can come in now."

I didn't answer. I just moved, the door opened with a hush. They led me to a rocking chair near her incubator. I sat down slowly…. Then they placed her in my arms. And just like that…the war, the fallen, the anger…they disappeared. As I held our child in awe.

She was weightless. Her skin, soft and warm, had the gentle flush of rose across her cheeks. When she yawned, her tiny nose wrinkled in a way that made my entire being ache. Not from pain …. but from love too large for words.

I stared at her face and whispered, "You're perfect." She stirred at the sound of my voice. Not startled … but familiar, like she knew me.

"You look like her," I murmured. The nurse behind me said something soft…that she hadn't cried, that she was peaceful. But the words barely reached me.

I was caught in the stillness between us. And then…It started low in my spine…a tremor I couldn't name at first. Not physical. Not of this place. A warning. I blinked as I tried to breathe. Eva. Something had changed. I stood too quickly.

The nurse caught the change in my demeanor. "Is everything alright?" The nurse asked, reaching out for my daughter.

"I have to go," I said, already handing my daughter back. My arms resisted letting go. I took one last look, her eyes just beginning to open. I turned and walked fast…faster than a mortal should. My body stayed contained, but my soul was already ahead of me, stretching down the hall, reaching for the bond I had with Eva …and finding something had gone dim.

She stirred. Slowly. Her eyes blinked open ....bright, but distant. "Eva," I repeated, kneeling beside her. "It's me. Hey, my love." I gently brushed her curls away. "Eva, can you hear me?"

Just then Mariana and Grace came in followed by James and Matthew. There was a concerned look on Matthew's face and it only reaffirmed my fears.

Her eyes fluttered open again. For a moment, they were unfocused. She blinked against the lights, then turned her head weakly toward me. Her eyes darted across the room as if searching for familiarity that wasn't there.

Relief that she was ok, surged through me. I reached for her hand. "You rest a little more." I whispered. "I am here, I met our daughter."

She stared at me...calm, quiet. Then she drew her hand away. I immediately took it once more in mine. "I'm sorry...do I know you?" Her eyes opened fully now, blinking slowly, adjusting to the light above her. And in that moment, I saw it, a blankness behind the sunflowers. She looked down at my hand in hers, and then at her surroundings. "Where am I?"

"You're safe. You gave birth. She's alive...she's beautiful." I swallowed hard, trying to fight the panic. She closed her eyes for a second, wincing like a wave of pain or memory brushed just beneath the surface but didn't break through.

"I believe you," she whispered as tears slipped down her cheeks. "But I don't —"

Just then Grace cried out in pain, as she placed a hand over her chest. Matthew and James help steady her into a chair. Her next words sent a chill over me. "She has forgotten."

Chapter Ten

Deuteronomy 4:9 (NIV)

"Only be careful, and watch yourselves closely so that you do not forget the things your eyes have seen or let them fade from your heart as long as you live."

Eva

I watched Remiel as he gently laid our daughter in her bassinet. A giant of a man but he was so gentle with her. It was hard to believe that Zariah was almost a month old. We had named her from the Bible, her name was fitting. It meant "Yahweh remembers." Because he did…even if I couldn't.

Outside, the trees had already begun shedding their leaves, and the crispness in the air whispered of Thanksgiving's approach. Then too soon, Christmas. I gazed at Remiel. He stood still for a moment, watching Zariah with an expression that shattered me and even though I could remember nothing of our life before, I knew that I cared for him, something in me was drawn to him.

He looked up suddenly and caught my eye. I flushed, heart racing. I quickly turned away. A moment later, the cushion dipped beside me as he sat down beside me. He propped his elbow on the back of the couch as he reached out and gently brushed the curls away from my eye.

"What is it Eva? What are you thinking?" His voice was low but vibrated in my soul. When I didn't look at him, he gently placed his two fingers under my chin. His touch was careful. Knowing. Waiting. "Eva, you can talk to me. Ask me anything…just please talk to me."

He didn't rush me. He never did. That was something I was beginning to notice about Remiel, his stillness. His patience. Like time moved differently around him, or he'd learned long ago how to wait for things worth keeping.

My fingers curled around his without thinking. "I want to remember," I whispered again as I looked down at my lap. "But there's this wall in my mind. I reach for something and it slips away… like it doesn't want to be found."

His brow furrowed slightly, but he masked it well. "Then don't force it," he said softly. "Memories are doors. Not all of them open the way we expect. Some only open when it's time." Something in his voice..something older, more sorrowful…made me turn to him.

"You know why I don't remember, don't you?" I asked. "You won't say it, but you're guarding something. Not just me…the truth."

He looked down for a long moment, then back at me. There it was again. The ache behind his eyes that no warrior could hide. "There are things you carried, Eva," he said quietly. "Things—Your mind… it may be protecting you. Or—" He hesitated… "Or something else may be trying to keep it locked away."

A chill moved through me, though the room was warm. "I keep dreaming of a name," I said slowly. "I hear my mother's name, Grace. And someone else… a presence. I can't see his face, but I feel like I knew him. Deeply. Like I trusted him once."

Remiel's jaw clenched, almost imperceptibly. "Dagon," he said under his breath.

The name went through me like an echo. But that wasn't the name. It sounded different. I turned to him. "'No, Shazamiel. Who is he?"

Remiel didn't answer. The question hung between us, heavy, dangerous, as if saying his name again might tear open the air itself. Instead, his thumb moved in slow circles against my knuckles, steady, grounding.

His silence was not avoidance..it was more like protection. I watched him for a moment, "I just want to know…"

"Eva, if you are told things now…there are things you might not believe." He stopped for a moment, gazing at me. I met his eyes, I felt it. Whatever it was burned between us and made it almost impossible to not touch him, to not want him.

He moved closer, closing the small distance between us. His lips brushed mine with a tenderness that felt like a question and a promise all at once. I answered with a kiss that deepened slowly, arms wrapping around his neck, drawing him into me. There was no rush in his touch. No urgency. Just knowing. Needing.

His hands slid gently along my sides, memorizing me, as if relearning something precious. I breathed him in…earth and fire, wind and something else. He guided me gently back on the couch cushions, his body pressing to mine, careful, never demanding.

Every touch was quiet but filled with desire. As I reached beneath the fabric of his shirt, he paused, watching me with unspoken permission in his eyes. I lifted the cloth slowly, and as it passed over his shoulders, I saw them, the scars. Undeniable. I reached out without a word, fingertips brushing across them. His entire body tensed as he waited. I searched his face. What was he waiting for? Disgust or questions. I ran my hands down his back and over the mountains of scars.

I leaned forward and kissed where the scars crossed on his shoulders. A slow kiss..not because I understood what they meant, but because I *felt* the pain buried in them.

He exhaled, a sound that vibrated through me. I felt his body tense, then soften under my hands. His gaze had changed, full of wonder and yet restraint, like he was holding back the flood. "Eva," he whispered, voice thick with emotions.

Remiel met my eyes and just then a heavy knock sounded on the door. The sound shattered the moment. Remiel bent his head in agitation, groaning as he got up to answer it. Pulling his shirt back on as he went to open the door. In came Hunter, Remiel's friend. Remiel was tall but this man was taller.

A man so large that he literally had to stoop down to come into our cottage. Broad shouldered, he stood there looking less like a man and more like a soldier that had been chiseled from stone. His long red hair was pulled back away from his face, almost in dreads. He was a stern looking man but very handsome, if one could get past the cold expression.

He didn't speak. Just tilted his head slightly, as though hearing something I couldn't. He looked strangely at me before Remiel motioned him back outside. "Come on, I want to show you the work I have done. Tell me what you think."

Hunter's gaze lingered on me before turning to follow Remiel back out the door.

I knew that wasn't the truth. Remiel and Hunter were hiding something from me.

The way Remiel's face changed when I said *Shazamiel*, the flash of recognition he tried to mask, the silence that followed. It all made me believe he knew exactly who it was.

I sat on the couch, cradled in the soft hum of Zariah's breathing, my thoughts tangled in questions with no answers. The quiet was then interrupted by another yet gentler knock at the door. Moments later, my mother stepped inside. She was carrying two canvas bags and smiled as she bent down to kiss my forehead…but the smile never reached her eyes.

"I brought groceries and found the perfect little dedication dress for ZaZa," she said, setting the bags on the counter with deliberate cheer. *ZaZa.* That was her name for Zariah. At first, it grated on my nerves.. But now… it had become familiar. Comforting, even.

I followed her into the kitchen, watching as she began unpacking canned goods and vegetables with practiced grace. "Mom, you didn't have to do this. Remiel was going to make a run later."

She waved her hand dismissively and pulled out a bag of seasoning. "I know. I just wanted to see you both. Thought maybe I'd make some chicken pot pie." She gave me a sideways glance. "Still your favorite?"

I smiled faintly and nodded. "Yeah. I think…."

But something was off. Her movements were too careful, her words flowed naturally but the cheerful tone was forced. "Mom," I said softly, "are you okay?"

She froze for a beat, one hand still in the bag. Her shoulders stiffened, and I could see her weighing her next words like they were heavy stones. She didn't look at me when she finally said, "There are things, Eva. Things that…." She didn't finish her sentence…she just went silent.

I blinked. "What? What things?" Curious to know what she was going to say but before she could answer, the front door creaked open behind us.

Heavy footsteps echoed in the livingroom as Remiel and Hunter entered the kitchen. Grace's entire body went still when she laid eyes on Hunter, almost as if she was seeing a ghost. The color drained from her face. The bag of flour she was holding slid from her hands and hit the counter with a soft thud. Her eyes locked onto Hunter like the past had suddenly returned, wearing flesh. Remiel noticed instantly and instinctively stepped beside me, as if to protect me from something.

"It's you?" Hunter said cautiously, stepping forward. But Grace wasn't listening. Her hand slowly reached toward her chest, not for pain…..but for memory perhaps.

"I know you," she whispered.

Hunter's expression faltered. Something unreadable flickered in his eyes. Was it shock, regret, defiance? Grace took a step forward, her voice shaking with old grief and memories. "I know you." And suddenly she was speaking but it was as if in another voice from another time.

"You were called to lead, not to defy. I warned you... I begged you not to build that tower. You were meant to guide your people to God, not away from Him."

Hunter's jaw tightened. "You think I didn't believe?" he said, barely above a whisper. "I believed. But not in the way you wanted. You came preaching surrender. I was trying to give them strength."

"You were building rebellion," she replied. "And when I told you the truth… you silenced it with your blade."

For a moment, no one spoke.

 "I never forgot what you said before I fell," she added. "That you would rather be god than serve one."

Hunter's hands clenched at his sides. "And you…." he paused, voice raw. "You looked at me with pity. Like I was lost."

"You were," Grace said softly. "And you still are." As she reached up to touch his face…as if trying to understand how he could be there.

Hunter stepped closer to Grace, his face softer now with traces of love. Had he loved my mother?

"You were the beginning of my punishment, why I was forced to live all these years not knowing who or what I was." He reached down gently tracing his finger down Grace's face.

She inhaled sharply like he was burning her face. "Your face haunted me, but I never knew your name or why you came to me night after night, but now...Aurariel...I know. I was sent here so that I could understand my life of punishment and wandering. God finally has allowed me to see my past."

Grace closed her eyes and she breathed in deeply before looking at him once more. "You chose her and power... over the love of our God."

I stood there, watching these beings...two people whose past I didn't remember but whose pain I felt deep in my chest. And though I didn't know all the details...Something in me remembered that tower.

Hunter's expression didn't change, but something flickered in his eyes. A hesitation. A shadow of something long buried. And then a memory surfaced, rolling over me like a wave. Lightning split the sky, rain hammering against the stone walls of a great palace. I stood before him, before Hunter, only he was dressed as a king, I was pleading through the storm.

"Please, listen to me!" My voice was raw, desperate. "Turn back before it's too late! God has not abandoned you. You're the one walking away!" But no, that wasn't my voice, that wasn't me.

Hunter stood tall, his expression hardened with defiance. "I was meant to be more than a man! I was meant to rule! You would rather see me bow than rise!" He walked toward me with a sword in hand.

I stood firm in my stance, "You were meant to serve Him! You were meant to lead people toward the light, not into ruin!" The wind howled around us, but I did not move.

"You still have a choice! You still have time! Destroy this tower that you are building before God destroys you!" His face twisted with something unreadable...pain? Anger? Then, his jaw tightened, and his eyes darkened, the moment before the blade fell. No, not me! It was my mother.

The present slammed back into me. My knees nearly buckled, and my breath shuddered as I looked at Hunter now... the man who had once been Amraphel. His ancient name whispered in the back of my mind. I saw it again, that shadow of something buried too deep for him to face.

"No, it's not, this can't be true." I pressed my hands to my eyes trying to make it stop. Her words came once more as she had laid bleeding on the stone floor.

"Turn to God while you still can. Before you lose everything." The words spoken had killed her. Grace had been sent by God to warn him, and he had killed Grace for it.

"You killed her!" my voice shook as I felt Remiel's arms wrap around me. "Eva, Eva. It's okay."

I clung to him, trying to gather my senses. "How could I have just seen that? What is going on?"

I looked at Grace, my mother, trying to figure out what I had seen. "You were the one who stood before Amraphel...and tried to stop him from building the tower."

Grace's voice shook as she stepped back from Hunter. "I was sent to warn him, to remind him that his purpose was not to build a monument to reach the heavens, but to lead his people back to the God who made them. But pride doesn't bow easily. He killed me for it."

I saw Hunter flinch under her words. He was Amraphel, but how was he still alive? How was he here? I shuddered, and Remiel wrapped his arms tighter around me. "I felt it. The lightning. The storm. Your blood…on the stone floor."

Hunter's eyes dropped in shame. Years of pride, anger, and ambition bound him like chains. "All that power, and yet… I was blind. I killed her. I killed Aurariel." For the first time, the magnitude of his actions…..beyond the memory, beyond the pain….settled fully in him.

Slowly, he lowered his clenched hands. His voice barely a whisper, "I…I see now. The path I chose… was my own ruin. Forgive me Aurariel… if You can." The giant of a man knelt down in front of Grace with his head bowed.

Grace gently touched his head, running her fingers through his auburn hair. "I forgave the moment that your blade ran through me, I had already forgiven you. Now, it is not me you need to ask forgiveness from…."

He looked up at her with heaviness in his eyes as something passed through the air.. It was subtle, but undeniable….a quiet acknowledgment from the one he had long resisted. He was still burdened, still marked by his sins.

I watched him, the man who had been Amraphel. His posture had shifted….not triumphant, not defiant, but honest, carrying the weight of his wrongs with open eyes. And as he looked at Grace, I saw a flicker of hope. I didn't understand it all, but perhaps God's mercy had touched him. As he stood up, the memory of what I had saw, came back to me. "Mom, Remiel, I don't understand….any of this. That…night..how…what?"

Hunter slowly stood up and put a protective arm around my mom, she looked so small compared to him. Grace slowly placed a hand on his chest as if assuring him that everything was alright. She looked at me and exhaled slowly before speaking. "That night, everything changed. When

Amraphel killed me, I was taken before the Throne and offered a seat among the Seven. A place as guardian of the realms."

She paused, her gaze flickering to Hunter. "I accepted. But we were betrayed."

"The Seven Seats," I echoed, and then I felt it ... .something, a recognition stirring behind my ribs. "You said there were guardians?"

Grace nodded. "Each seat was a point of balance between realms...seven guardians, chosen to uphold the order between heaven, earth, and what lies between. But Shazamiel... he fell. He let pride and the ancient darkness twist his purpose. He deceived us. He tricked us and cast us out. He stole one of the seats for himself."

"And the others?" I asked, the question trembling on my lips.

"Fallen. Scattered. Hidden. Forgotten." She looked toward the window, as though seeing something far beyond it. "Only one guardian still holds their post. And the seventh and the highest among them…still belongs to God. Untouched. Unreachable."

I turned slowly toward Hunter. "And you... you killed her."

He didn't deny it. "I was blinded by power," Hunter said quietly. "By the promise that the tower would touch the heavens. I thought I was building something divine. I didn't see what I'd become… until it was too late."

I looked at Grace again…..no, not Grace. *Auraliel.* The name bloomed across my memory like fire through frost.

"You're Auraliel. A guardian? Then you can't possibly be my mother...oh, this is too much." I rubbed my forehead as Remiel gently wrapped his arms around me from behind. I leaned into him, needing that comfort, needing his stability.

She met my eyes, her expression softening. "You, Eva… you carry more than you know. You don't remember it all, but I … when you followed me into the realm… when you saw Shazamiel… my memories passed to you. Not all at once. But he was trying to make me forget what I had started to remember. He wanted the guardians to remain silenced. If we couldn't remember what he had done, we could not return to our seats. It allowed them to open more portals and for evil to travel. I passed my memories to you so they would not be completely erased."

There was silence as I let her words sink in. "And when I lost my own…" I whispered, realization washing over me. "More parts of yours came alive."

Grace-Auraiel,nodded. "My memories are what drew you to the realms."

I looked at Remiel, "Realms….I don't understand.What are you? None of this makes any sense." I knew the question sounded so stupid and naive. I watched as Remiel looked questionably at Grace. She slowly nodded.

Remiel took my hand. "Come, Eva."

He led me to the door that had been locked. The one that I asked him about before and simply explained that it was a storage room. He raised his hand above the doorframe and brought down a key. He unlocked the door and gently pushed it open. He switched the lights on and immediately I could tell we were in a nursery. It had baby clothes folded and the crib and toys. It still smelled like fresh paint, which meant someone had been working on this before Zariah was born. It was her things, I didn't understand. I looked at him, "This is ZaZa's nursery?"

He smiled and nodded. "You did all this while I was gone, this was once a play room and before that a nursery."

Thoughts ran through my mind, a nursery, whose nursery?

"Why did you lie to me about it? Why did you keep it locked?" I did not try to hide the anger or betrayal that I felt.

He walked over to the closet, hesitating before he opened the door. He reached up and brought out a folded blanket and on top of the blanket was a photo frame turned with the front facing down.The blanket, it wasn't pink but blue and gray.

Remiel looked down at the blanket before handing it to me. "Eva when your memories return….I need to remember—you are a child of God. No matter what memories return, you are his and you are redeemed. And I love you."

"Remiel," I said quietly, "you're scaring me."

His shoulders tensed. He didn't look at me. Whatever truth lay behind his silence…it was heavy, and it hurt him. I swallowed hard. "If the past is that bad…" I hesitated, heart hammering, "maybe it's better that I leave those memories asleep."

The blanket slipped from my fingers as I gently pushed it back toward him, not bothering to pick up the photo. "I choose to love you as you are. Now. Not for who you were or where you came from. The past doesn't matter to me…not if it's going to destroy what we have right here."

He opened his mouth as if to speak, but I held up my hand. "I know I am a child of God. I don't need every piece of the past to tell me that. I feel Him when I speak to Him. When I hold Zariah, when I breathe, when I look at you. That will be enough for me right now."

A silence stretched between us, deep and aching. I could feel his war, between the desire to protect me and the truth he carried.

And still, I chose to leave the memories asleep. "I know you want to help me," I whispered. I felt his gaze searching me, but I avoided it, because the truth was…..I was afraid. As much as I yearned to know the past, it also scared me.

What if the woman I was before wouldn't love him the way I do now? What if the memories twisted everything, pulled me away from this fragile peace I've only just begun to feel?

I didn't want to know why there was a storm that lived behind Remiel's eyes. Because if I remembered it all…..then I would no longer be able to pretend that this moment, this little sanctuary we had, could last. And I needed it to last. Even if it was borrowed time.

He looked at me then…eyes shadowed, full of sorrow and awe. "You don't understand what you've forgotten."

"I know," I said. "And maybe I will remember… when I'm ready. But today, I choose this."

Remiel

I waited till Eva had laid down with Zariah to walk outside. Frustration was taken over. She didn't know who I was. Not fully. Not truly. And that terrified me more than any demon I'd ever faced.

I heard Grace step behind me before she spoke. "You can't let her choose forgetfulness, Remiel. Not now."

I didn't turn. I didn't want her to see the uncertainty in my eyes. "She's been through enough, Grace. She's finally breathing without trembling around me. Do you want to rip that away from her? She is beginning to trust that she loves me."

"She will remember eventually," came Hunter's voice ...low and gravelled, still laced with the memories and remnants of who he once was.

His words caught me off guard but for only a moment. "I know who she is." I said. I didn't need to be reminded that she was a Beloved.

"Then act like it," Grace said, her voice stern like that of a mother's.

I turned to face her, running a hand down my face. "She looks at me like I'm the only safe thing in the world, Grace. What happens when she remembers I'm not just the man she loves….but the angel who once wielded judgment? What happens when she remembers that I descended to kill mortals?"

"Mortals used by the Others. Mortals inhabited by demonic spirits." Hunter stated, trying to bring clarity to my indecisiveness.

Grace's voice softened. "Then she remembers *why* she loved you. Why… she chose you."

"She didn't choose me, I chose her. I bound us together without asking her what she wanted. Don't you understand? She doesn't believe or remember the realms," I said, frustrated with the possible circumstances of my actions.

"She speaks of God, of peace…but she won't let herself see the battle. Shazamiel. Gabriel. Dagon…she's locked them away." I shook my head at the possibility of awakening her past. Most Beloveds wandered through life unaware of the realms surrounding them…unaware of the fierce inheritance placed within them. If they ever truly understood it…..if every Beloved remembered who they were in the Spirit, evil would not run rampant. Darkness would tremble. Kingdoms of darkness would fall.

But the enemy's greatest weapon was forgetfulness. If he could make them forget their identity, their authority, their divine adoption through the blood of Christ…he could keep them silent. Powerless. Distracted by flesh and bound by fear.

"And if she stays buried, Shazamiel will find her first." Hunter said. His words were true. I knew that and my stomach twisted at the thought. Shazamiel's voice had already seeped into her dreams once before. She had cried out in her sleep. I'd held her through it. Shazamiel, Dagon, the Others, the demons that haunted us……

"She carries my memories," Grace went on, her voice softer now. "But they aren't just mine, Remiel. They were given…..by the Lord himself. He allowed them to pass from me to her, for a reason."

Grace continued, "You think you're protecting her by letting her forget….but you're weakening her."

 "She's not a weapon," I snapped, the heat rising in my chest. "She's….she's Eva."

Grace met my eyes without flinching. "She's more than Eva. She's a Beloved. A warrior of God." She sighed deeply.

"Remiel, she still carries some of my memories, the important ones of the Guardians. The ones….that are needed to find them. I can't pull that back from her. I don't know why they didn't come back to me, but they didn't."

I looked away, jaw clenched. "No, I will not take her peace away."

 Grace said softly, almost mournfully. "Then you choose to leave her as she is… unguarded."

My breath slowed as I turned my gaze to the cottage. She was in there, curled protectively around our daughter. Zariah. Both so fragile in the flesh.

"She has to remember," Grace continued.

"She's not ready," I said quietly.

"That's what the darkness is counting on." Grace said, her voice pleading with me for understanding.

My hands curled into fists. "She remembers pieces," I whispered. "I see it in the way she watches the rain and the storms. In the way she says certain names. But when the fear comes….she chooses silence. She chooses not to see."

"She's afraid of what remembering will cost her," Grace said.

"She's afraid of losing you," Hunter added. "And that's exactly why the darkness will use *you* to get to her."

I exhaled slowly, pain deepening in my chest. Memories of her falling made my chest tighten. "Then what do I do?"

"You remind her," Grace said gently. "Who she is. Who *you* are. And what you both were created for."

"She might hate me," I said, barely above a whisper. Remembering the connection that I had created and could not undo.

"She might…she might hate us all." Grace agreed. "But with the light of God, she will forgive and love. But if the darkness consumes her? Would you have that possibility? Would you have her and the other Beloveds lost. The ones she is meant to raise in this spiritual battle?"

If Eva remembered. Remembered everything—not just the wars of the realms…not just me as an angel. But the authority that was sealed in her spirit by the sacrifice of Jesus Christ. The inheritance that made her more than just human. She was *Beloved*….marked, redeemed, and would be dangerous to every demon that dared walk near her.

That's why the war wouldn't just find her. It would rise from *within* her. Because one Beloved who remembers is a weapon. Two who know the truth, they are an army. I swallowed hard, a tremor moving through me. "She thinks she's choosing peace… I can't take that away from her."

"But the moment when she remembers who she is," Grace said softly. "Hell will shake."

Hunter stepped forward, placing his hand gently on Grace's shoulder, his voice rough. "She is a Beloved and Heaven will answer her."

Chapter Eleven

Eva

The morning air carried the scent of fallen leaves and distant chimney smoke when I stepped outside with Zariah wrapped gently against my chest. Remiel stood on the porch watching me as I adjusted the blanket around our daughter.

"You sure you're ready for town?" he asked quietly. His voice always carried that careful tone now, like he feared the world itself might break me.

"I'm not made of glass," I said softly, though I smiled so he wouldn't worry. Truthfully, I needed the change. The cottage had begun to feel too quiet. Too full of questions. And Mariana had been asking to see me. Even though I couldn't remember our friendship that well, I was eager to get out.

Remiel hesitated a moment longer before nodding. "Call if you need anything." His hand brushed Zariah's tiny head before I walked down the porch toward the road.

The town square was already alive with the slow rhythm of late morning. A few vendors had set up stands along the sidewalks. Someone was playing soft music near the fountain, and the scent of roasted coffee drifted through the cool air. Normal life. Something I was still trying to remember how to live.

Mariana waved from a small table outside the café when she spotted me. "There she is!" she called brightly. Carlos sat beside her in a booster chair, swinging his little legs while banging a spoon against the table like it was a drum.

Carlos looked up immediately. "Baby!" he announced proudly when he spotted Zariah. I laughed softly and sat down.

"That's right," Mariana said, brushing her son's hair from his eyes. "That's baby Zariah."

Carlos leaned forward to inspect her with serious concentration.

"Tiny," he declared.

Mariana rolled her eyes affectionately. "He's decided he's an expert on babies."

"I can see that." I laughed as he pointed to Zariah again. For a while we talked about simple things. Sleep schedules. Diapers. How quickly toddlers discover they can climb absolutely everything.

Carlos proudly demonstrated this by trying to stand on his chair. "Carlos!" Mariana caught him quickly and sat him back down. He giggled like it was the greatest game in the world.

I smiled, watching them. For a moment the quiet rhythm of ordinary life wrapped around me like a blanket. But something tugged at the back of my mind. A strange sense that I was being watched. I glanced across the street. Nothing. Just people walking along the sidewalks. Cars passing slowly through the intersection. Still, the feeling didn't leave.

Every so often Mariana would glance at me with quiet curiosity. "You seem better," she said finally.

I shrugged slightly. "I feel… calmer." That wasn't exactly true. My mind was still full of fragments that didn't belong together. Storms. Voices. Names. But something about being here helped quiet them.

At least for a moment. I rose to order coffee when something across the street caught my attention. A man stood near the bookstore on the corner. Tall. Dark coat. For a moment the world seemed to narrow. My heart began beating strangely fast. I knew that silhouette. I knew it. A memory tugged hard against the walls in my mind. His head turned slightly. For the briefest second I saw his face. And the name slipped through my thoughts like a whisper. *Dagon.* Remiel had mentioned that name to me.

My breath caught. But when I blinked, the man was already gone. The corner stood empty except for passing cars and pedestrians. I stepped slowly back toward the table.

Mariana looked up. "You okay?"

I forced a small smile. "Yeah." But I turned again toward the street. Still empty. Yet the strange feeling remained. Like someone had been watching me from the edge of memory itself.

By the time Mariana gathered Carlos and headed down the sidewalk, the afternoon had grown quieter. Carlos waved enthusiastically from her hip. "Bye baby!" he shouted toward Zariah.

I laughed softly and waved back. "Bye Carlos."

Mariana smiled warmly. "We'll do this again soon."

"I'd like that." I said as I watched them disappear down the street before turning toward the small parking lot behind the restaurant.

The wind had picked up slightly, pushing dry leaves across the pavement as I walked. Zariah slept peacefully against my chest.

For a moment, the world felt calm. Almost normal. Then I saw him. He was leaning against the driver's side of my car like he had been waiting there for some time. Long black coat moving slightly in the wind. My steps slowed immediately. A strange tension moved through my chest. He straightened when he saw me approach. Something about the way he watched me felt unsettling… and familiar at the same time. I stopped a few feet away from him. "Can I help you?" I asked carefully.

For a moment he simply looked at me. His amber eyes moved across my face slowly, almost searching. Then he spoke. "Eva."

The sound of my name in his voice sent a ripple through me. Not fear but of recognition. But it didn't make sense. I frowned slightly. "How do you know my name?"

He didn't answer right away. Instead his eyes moved briefly to Zariah before returning to mine. "You don't remember me," he said quietly. It wasn't a question. The certainty in his voice unsettled me.

"Should I?" I asked cautiously.

For a moment something painful flickered across his expression. "No."

I studied his face more closely now. There was something about him. Something that made my chest ache in a way I couldn't explain. "I feel like I know you," I admitted slowly. "But I can't place where from."

His jaw tightened slightly. "It's not important."

The answer confused me. "That's not very helpful."

For the first time the faintest hint of something like sadness crossed his face. "No," he said quietly. "It wouldn't be."

Zariah stirred suddenly in my arms. Her small eyes opened, unusually alert. Instead of fussing, she stared at the man standing in front of us with a strange, silent focus.

I shifted her slightly. "That's odd," I murmured.

"What is?" he asked.

"She usually sleeps through everything." I said, shifting her weight around.

For a moment his gaze dropped to the baby. Something unreadable passed across his expression. Then he looked back at me. "Children notice things adults forget how to see."

A chill moved down my spine. I shook my head slightly. "I'm sorry," I said again. "But I really don't remember meeting you."

For a moment the silence between us stretched. "You will," he said quietly. The certainty in his voice made my stomach twist.

"How do you know that?" I asked as he stepped past me, moving toward the far end of the lot.

"Because some memories," he said without looking back, " are not meant to stay buried." And just like that, he walked away. Leaving me standing beside my car with a thousand unanswered questions. When I turned to ask him again, he was gone. There was no trace of him.

That night, as I lay awake in bed, one thought kept returning again and again. I didn't know who the man was. But somewhere deep inside my mind, a name repeated over and over again. *Dagon.*

Chapter Twelve

Eva

I didn't know how to handle or fix what was happening to me. I felt like everything was slipping away. I sat on the back porch swinging, listening to the sounds of Remiel working on the barn. Zariah was sleeping, Mariana and little Carlos had just left.

And as much as I tried, I couldn't remember her but I felt close to her. Matthew had come with them but he had stayed outside with Remiel and had barely spoken two words to me. I rested my chin on my knees as I wrapped my arms around my legs.

I prayed but I prayed tentatively to God. I didn't pray for what I was really afraid of. I prayed for the things like blessings and protection on my family, on my church. Little prayers if you could call them. I read my Bible but only the parts that spoke of happiness and love…I would quickly flip the pages when it spoke of darkness and spiritual wars.

I knew that one day I would need to pray those hard prayers for a revelation….

Thoughts of the blanket and that photo tucked in the closet plagued me constantly almost as if it called me.

I squeezed my eyes shut, what would happen if I remembered everything? Who would I be then? Who would Remiel be to me? The love that we felt or I believed that we felt, would it still exist? Or would it disappear into the deep dark hole of ugly memories?

Because somewhere deep inside me, I knew there were ugly memories…dark memories just waiting to be awakened. The back door was opened with the screen door shut so that I could hear Zariah. Her beautiful baby doll face and curls of blonde hair, brought a smile to my face.

I loved that child, she was my baby. That I felt…but somewhere I felt a disconnection. I couldn't remember my pregnancy or her birth and that felt wrong. I could not remember the pregnancy glow or being excited for her birth.

The blanket called to me. It was tucked high on the shelf in the nursery closet, untouched, folded neatly as though waiting. My chest ached just looking at it, but something deeper inside me pulled….an ache, an urgency.

My hand trembled as I reached for it, brushing my fingers over the soft worn fabric. Slowly, I brought the fabric to my chest and then to my face. I slowly inhaled the scent…and slowly I turned the photo over. The moment I did, the world split open.

Memories I had buried…no, memories that had been *buried for me*— flooded back in a rush so violent I couldn't breathe. My knees buckled, and I clutched the blanket to my chest as the flood came.

His face. Oh God…his face. Gabriel. My son. My baby. My arms holding him, his tiny chest rising and falling, his breath soft against my skin. The warmth of him, the miracle of him. And then…the silence. The weight in my arms without breath. The scream that had torn through me then, echoing now in my bones.

And more came with it..memories that weren't only mine. The realms, shifting like fire behind a curtain. Grace's hand in mine..no, Aurariel's..when Shazamiel struck. The guardians falling. The tower, burning. Amraphel's shadow becoming Nimrod's betrayal. Every loss. Every wound. Every forgotten oath.

And Remiel. Always Remiel. His presence. But now I saw it clearer than ever…his hand binding mine where I couldn't fight, his being entwined with mine, never asking if I wanted it, never letting me *choose*. His comfort and peace had been real, but it had also been chains disguised as light.

The grief was too much to contain. It ripped from me, a scream that tore through the house, through the realms, through the very air. A mother's scream. A broken soul's scream.

The back door slammed open. Footsteps thundered down the hall. "Eva!" Remiel's voice broke as he reached the nursery, finding me crumpled in the center of the floor, rocking with the blanket pressed so tight to my chest I could hardly breathe. My body shook, wracked with sobs that wouldn't stop.

He dropped to his knees beside me, reaching…desperate, helpless. "I'm here—I've got you, Ev—"

"No!" I tore away from his grasp, curling tighter around the blanket, as if my arms could bring my baby back, as if they could shield the memories from his touch. My eyes, blurred with tears, met his….

"You don't touch me," I sobbed. "Not after this."

Remiel froze, pain flashing across his face, but I pressed on, the words spilling out like blood from a wound.

"I remember now. Every time you left me. Every time I begged for you and you chose duty over me. And worse…." My voice broke into a whisper, raw and jagged.

"You tied me to you. You bound me without asking. You made me love you without letting me choose." Silence fell, thick and unbearable.

I buried my face into the blanket, inhaling the faint, lingering scent of a life that ended too soon. My baby. My Gabriel. My heart. Another sob ripped through me, shaking me until I could barely breathe.

"You took my choice," I whispered. "And I had already lost too much."

Remiel, the once great angel who had fought legions, who had never faltered in war, could do nothing but kneel on the floor, helpless, shattered…as I fell apart in front of him.

Across the realms, in the shadows where no light reached, Dagon staggered as if struck. The sound of Eva's scream pierced him, ripping through his spirit, dropping him to his knees. He pressed a hand against his chest, then began clawing at the place where Eva and Gabriel's memory lived like fire.

Her grief. Her fury. Her broken love. He felt it all. And he knew… her memories had awakened once more. "Eva…" His whisper was a curse and a prayer, twisted with torment. He doubled over, gasping as though the scream had hollowed him out, leaving only agony. For the first time, the destroyer of souls understood what it was to be destroyed.

Eva

Remiel didn't move. The silence between us was deafening, broken only by the ragged sound of my sobs and the trembling in my breath as I clutched the blanket tighter.

He was still kneeling in front of me, his face carved with anguish. He looked like he was the one breaking, not me. "Eva…"

His voice cracked, heavy with centuries of battles, of secrets kept, of love buried under obedience. "I didn't want this for you. I would have carried the pain for eternity if it meant sparing you from hurting."

I lifted my head, eyes burning red. "You don't decide that for me." He flinched, like the words were a blade.

"Do you know what it feels like?" I pressed on, "To wake up every day with holes in your life? To rock a child you can't remember birthing? To feel love, but never know why it feels…wrong? You left me in the dark, Remiel. And you call that love?"

His lips parted, but nothing came. The truth hung between us like a blade suspended by a thread. Finally, his shoulders sagged underneath the reality. His voice was barely above a whisper. "I have fought demons and rulers of darkness. But I never feared anything more than the moment you would look at me….and hate me."

Tears streamed down my face, relentless. "I don't hate you." My throat tightened. "But I can't love you either…."

The words shattered something in both of us. Remiel bowed his head, then he slowly looked at me. He reached one hand toward me….but stopped inches away, letting it fall uselessly to his knee. The distance between us was more than the width of the nursery floor. It was a canyon carved by choices that could not be undone.

Remiel didn't try to bridge it. He simply knelt in the quiet, watching me fall apart in the middle of the room, the blanket of my dead son pressed to my chest. My sobs had quieted to tremors, but the heaviness of all the memories still sat down on top of me. I held the blanket tighter, rocking without meaning to, as though my arms could somehow undo what had been stolen.

Remiel hadn't moved. He was still kneeling in front of me, his hands braced against the floor, his eyes fixed on me with a rawness that stripped me bare. He wasn't an angel now, not anymore…just my husband, just a man. "Eva," he whispered, his voice rough, torn. "Let me—"

"No." My answer was trembling but sharp. "Don't touch me. Don't try to make this better. You can't."

He froze, pain flashing across his face, but he didn't move. He stayed there, as though praying for words that would never come. The silence stretched…until Zariah's cry rang through the house, shrill and piercing from down the hall. Remiel's head turned toward the sound. His gaze darted back to me…torn, desperate…caught between the broken woman before him and the child calling for him.

"Go," I whispered hoarsely, clutching the blanket tighter to my chest. "She needs you." He lingered, I could see every muscle in his body fighting to stay. But finally, with a grief that was almost physical, he rose. His steps were heavy, reluctant, carrying him to the door. I didn't look up. Couldn't. The blanket and photo was all I had left, and I buried myself in it, even as his absence opened a deeper wound inside me.

The hall and nursery filled again with Zariah's cries, echoing down the hallway, and then his footsteps faded into the sound. And I was left in silence drowning in memories I couldn't unremember. Some of the memories did not belong to me but I carried them as if they did.

The cottage had gone quiet again, I hadn't moved. The door eased open. His footsteps were soft this time, cautious, as though he feared the very sound of his presence might shatter me further.

"Eva…" Remiel's voice was low, almost reverent, his words unsure. I didn't answer. My eyes were focused, fixed somewhere far beyond him. Memories still spilled through me…..flashes of realms, of wings and fire, of Gabriel's tiny face, and of Dagon's shadowed eyes. When Remiel crouched again, his hand hovered but didn't touch.

He looked at me the way a man looks at someone slipping beneath dark waters….desperate to dive in, terrified to lose them. "Come back to me," he pleaded softly. His voice trembled. "Don't stay there, Eva. Please… don't stay where I can't reach you."

A broken laugh caught in my throat, bitter and jagged. "You left me there many times," I whispered, not looking at him. "Every time you left, I stayed. Alone. Buried in it. Believing that you loved me. You sent Matthew to watch me to make sure that I didn't fall in love with anyone else. So that

I would still be here waiting for you in case you decided to come back to me."

His face tightened as though I'd slapped him. But instead of retreating, he leaned closer, the pain in his eyes raw. "Then let me make it right. Let me stay now. Don't push me away."

For a long moment, I couldn't breathe. I wanted to tell him it was too late, that the memories and pain had already swallowed me. But his voice, steady despite the cracks, reached through the dark fog that threatened to swallow me once more.

Slowly, my body betrayed me….I leaned, just barely, into the warmth of his presence. Not fully, not enough to forgive, but enough to feel the ground beneath me again. Remiel's breath broke out in a quiet exhale. He didn't move closer. He didn't wrap me in his arms. He simply stayed……..waiting, steady, as though his very being was a vow that he would not leave this time.

Three days later

The night air was cool and damp with the scent of earth after sundown. I sat on the back porch again, the old wood creaking beneath me. The stars hung bright above, scattered like broken pieces of promises I could almost reach, almost touch…..but never hold.

The blanket lay folded beside me, the fabric still warm from where my fingers had clutched it until they ached. Every time my gaze drifted toward it, memories surged in waves….Gabriel's face, so small and fragile;the shimmering light of the realms I had once walked; and Remiel's arms around me when I first broke. Then all the other memories that did not belong to me.

In the back of my mind, I could hear Grammy's voice. *"Don't drowned in your sorrow, when you still have life to live."* But it was all too much, and yet too little. For the first time, I could see the whole picture….and it was unbearable.

"I don't know how to live with this," I whispered to the stars, though part of me hoped someone higher was listening. "How am I supposed to breathe when everything I loved has been broken in two?"

The crickets hummed their endless song, a rhythm that should have been soothing but only deepened the silence inside me. Behind me, the door creaked softly, and I stiffened. Footsteps paused in the threshold, and though I didn't turn, I felt his presence…..hesitant, waiting.

Remiel. He didn't try to speak. He just stood there, his silence steady, letting the night fill the space between us. I thought he might leave again. That maybe this was the way it would always be….me on one side of my grief, him on the other. But then, his voice broke through the night, quiet, unpolished, as though he'd rehearsed and failed a thousand times before opening his mouth.

"I don't know how to make this right," he said, the weight in his tone heavier than the night shadows around us. "But I know I can't keep leaving you to carry it alone."

Words caught in my throat. My grip tightened around my knees, and I forced myself to look forward, not back, not at him. I blinked back the tears.

"I can't undo what I was. I can't take away the times I wasn't there. I can't undo breaking your heart. But I'm here now. And if you'll let me…" His voice faltered, raw. "…I'll stay. Even if it means just sitting in the dark with you."

The stars above blurred through the sting in my eyes. For a moment, I hated him for speaking and yet, beneath the ache, something in me called out to him. I didn't answer. Not yet. But I didn't ask him to leave, either. He didn't touch me. He didn't move closer. He only stayed.

And I…unable to give, unable to take…let the silence stretch. It felt almost as if the whole night was holding its breath. Somewhere inside, I wanted to believe him. But I knew belief was a dangerous thing. So I said nothing. And in the dark silence, the war I had tried to outrun rose up inside me….the war of spirit, of mind, of heart. Not a clash of swords or armies, but something far more merciless. The kind of war that leaves only scars…….

Chapter Thirteen

Remiel

The hammer slipped from my hand when I heard her scream. It wasn't a startled cry, not the kind a person makes when they cut their hand or stumble in the dark. No, this was something ripped from the depths, the kind of sound that makes the world stop.

My heart lurched as I forgot to breathe. "Eva." Her name tore out of me before I could stop it. I vaulted off the half-built stall, my boots hitting dirt, every nerve alive with dread. My legs carried me faster than my mind could catch up, faster than my lungs wanted. The barn smelled of sawdust and sweat, but out here in the open, all I could taste was fear.

I had faced danger before, but nothing prepared me for the terror of not knowing if she was safe. If she was breaking. If she was calling out and I couldn't reach her. Every step felt like eternity. When I found her on the nursery floor, she was folded in on herself, her frame shaking beneath the weight of something I couldn't see. My first thought was to run to her, to pull her into my arms and swear I'd never let go. But I froze. And it had cost me.

Here we were three days later, after I had put Zaza to bed, I walked out to the back porch. She would not speak to me, so now I spoke instead, words breaking out raw, stripped of pride; "I can't undo what I was. I can't take away the nights I wasn't there. I can't undo breaking your heart. But I'm here now. And if you'll let me…" My voice faltered. "…I'll stay. Even if it means just sitting in the dark with you."

She didn't answer. Didn't turn. And so I lowered myself onto the swing beside her, the wood groaning under my weight. I kept my hands knotted in my lap, fighting the pull to reach for her. Waiting for her to make a choice. One that could break me in two. She was right there yet she felt farther than the stars scattered above us.

I wanted to tell her that I'd felt her scream like a knife to the chest, that the sound of her breaking had broken me, too. But words were dangerous. Words asked for things. Words opened doors that neither of us might be able to close. So I held my tongue and let the silence swallow me.

Once, I had known power that could tear down kingdoms. I had walked in light that never dimmed. And yet here, beside her, I was only a man, helpless and waiting on the edge of her mercy. I thought I had known fear before. I hadn't. Not until now. Because fear wasn't the threat of death or the shadow of an enemy…..it was sitting here, watching the woman I could never stop loving decide if I was worth letting in.

The wood beneath me groaned as I shifted, trying to steady myself. My jaw ached from holding it tight, my fists from clenching too long. I wanted her to look at me….just once. To see that I wasn't the same being I'd been when I failed her. To see that I wasn't leaving this time.

But she kept her gaze fixed on the dark, as if the night itself had more to offer than I did. I deserved that. I knew I did. Still, the ache of it was unbearable. And so I sat, the swing swaying with every second stretching into eternity, waiting for a word that might undo me completely. She didn't turn. Didn't answer. But she didn't send me away, either. And in that pause, my chest ached with something I couldn't name..hope, fear, love, all tangled into one unbearable truth that I wasn't her guardian anymore. I was just a man. And maybe that was why losing her now would destroy me more than anything ever could.

The silence dragged me backward. I didn't want it to, but memory has no mercy. I remembered the night I tried to leave her. Back when I still carried wings on my back and the law of Heaven on my shoulders. I told myself distance was safer…..that if I stayed away, she'd be spared the weight of my command.

But I hadn't left. Not completely. I lingered, unseen. And I saw her fall apart. Saw the way she crumpled when she thought she was alone, when the strength she wore so fiercely like an armor finally cracked. She pressed her face into her hands and sobbed like her soul was unraveling.

And I…mighty and sworn… had stood there useless. Bound by law, by command, by my own cowardice. I couldn't hold her. Couldn't reach out. Couldn't even whisper her name. The memory burned, a brand I carried still.

Then another memory rose in my chest. The day I returned after too long, too far. I hadn't seen her first. It was Matthew who told me that she was carrying our child. My fury had blinded me. At her. At the world. At myself. Words I can't take back had spilled out, each one crueler than the last.

I had accused. I had judged. I had said things no man…should ever say to the woman he loves. Her face from that day still haunts me…the way she flinched from my words. I hated myself then. I still do. And now, sitting here in the dark with her, I wondered how she could even bear to be near me at all.

Slowly, she moved. She turned, hesitated..and then lowered her head into my lap. I bent my head. For a moment I hovered, afraid of myself, of what my touch might mean, of what it might stir. But then…just once..I let my hand drift through her curls…

And the strangest thing happened. The war inside me, the clash of shame and longing, love and fear…quieted. Not gone, not defeated. But stilled, the way a storm sometimes pauses before it breaks again.

She sighed, unguarded, the sound nearly undoing me. I closed my eyes against it, clutching the moment like something I knew I couldn't keep.

"Eva," I whispered, though I wasn't sure if I wanted her to hear it. For years I had fought battles I could win. Against Hell. Against myself.

Against the memory of her. And still, here I was, undone by the tilt of her head and the quiet of her breath.

Now I sit here, waiting for her to make a choice…..one that could heal me, or break me in two. And I knew, with a certainty that echoed like a never ending drum, that this would be the war that undid me. Her head rested in my lap, her breath soft and uneven, and all I could do was wait. Wait for her silence to turn either into forgiveness…..or the final sentence against me

Chapter Fourteen

Shadows

Grace sat on the park bench, the sound of children's laughter ringing in the distance. Their voices lifted and fell like the wind that stirred the swings and rattled the chains on the monkey bars. Eva's laughter had once joined that chorus. The memory ached sweetly in her chest.

A presence, familiar yet heavy, pressed against her heart before her eyes confirmed what her spirit already knew. She turned but Hunter was already there, sitting beside her as if the years had only been one day between them. They did not speak at first. Only the sound of the wind in the trees filled the space between their shoulders. Finally, he reached out, palm open, a quiet plea.

"Will you walk with me?"

Her hand trembled as it slid into his. Warmth surged through her fingers, too much, too dangerous......and still she did not let go. They walked away from the playset, each step a measured surrender, until the wooden bridge appeared ahead. The water below whispered secrets, carrying them out of earshot from the world behind. She knew that was why he had brought her here.

Hunter leaned on the railing, head bowed. His shoulders rose and fell with a deep, ragged breath.

"Now that I remember," he said, voice raw, "I can't forget. Every night your name runs through my head. And now it's your blood, your body on the floor. It haunts me. Before, it was only your face. But now, Aurariel, I can't unsee what I have done."

The name cut through her. Grace pressed her lips together, the sting of tears sharp in her eyes. Hunter's grip on the railing tightened until his knuckles whitened. "God punished me all these years.....for pride, rebellion, for you, for the tower." His voice cracked as though the confession itself was a wound.

Grace shook her head, stepping closer. "What if He wasn't punishing you, but giving you time? Time to repent, to seek forgiveness?"

His eyes lifted, wild, anguished. "Forgiveness for a sin I couldn't remember?" The words sounded harsh in the quiet air.

She steadied herself, then raised a trembling hand. Her fingers brushed his cheek, hesitant at first, then tender. The warmth of him was too human, too alive, and it made her ache.

"Amraphel," she whispered, "before you saw me, did you ever ask for forgiveness? Or did you believe that fighting darkness was enough? You've walked through centuries. You saw the Savior born. You saw Him crucified. You witnessed him rising. Did it never occur to you that just by asking the Lord, He would have returned what was taken?"

Silence stretched long and heavy. At last, he closed his eyes and caught her hand, pressing it hard against his face. His body shook beneath her touch, as if holding her steadied him against madness.

"What will happen," he whispered, "when the guardians are united again, when they ascend to their seats to continue the war?" His voice was barely sound, yet it carried a weight that struck her to the core.

Her breath faltered. "Hunter... I don't know."

He lifted his hand, brushing her cheek before restraint snapped. He pulled her into his arms, lips crushing against hers. For one shattering heartbeat she resisted, but his desperation was fire, and her arms betrayed her, circling his neck.

They had never kissed when he was a king and she was a prophetess. Then, it had been forbidden, tangled in his marriage to the witch who bound his mind and heart. Yet the longing had always lingered. Now, centuries later, it ignited. But as her lips trembled against his, memories surged…his violence, her death, and the Beloved she had pledged her love to. She gasped and tore away.

"No, Hunter. I can't!" She turned, but his hand caught her arm, grip filled with desperation.

"No, Aurariel. I will not lose you again. Don't turn from me." His embrace tightened, pressing her against the thundering beat of his chest.

Tears burned her eyes. "I can't….we can't."

"Why?" His hand slid under her chin, lifting her gaze to his. "God has allowed us to be together once more."

Her eyes dropped to the hand on her arm, memory colliding with the present. That night. But it wasn't only that which bound her in resistance. Slowly, she freed her arm from his grasp, drawing a steadying breath though her voice quivered from emotions.

"Because," she whispered, "I am married to a Beloved."

Hunter froze. The words struck him harder than any sword. His grip loosened as though the strength had been ripped from his body, and he stumbled back a step, staring at her as if she had become someone else entirely.

"Married…" His voice was barely audible, ragged with disbelief. "You—you gave yourself to another?"

Grace turned away, the tears she had fought finally slipping free. "Not just another. A Beloved. A man faithful and righteous."

The air between them thickened with more looming problems as Hunter's chest rose and fell with ragged breaths. His hand pressed against the railing as though he might crush it. His face twisted, torn between fury and despair.

"I wandered for centuries with your ghost haunting me," he choked out. "And now, when I find you...When I finally *find you.* You belong to another?"

Grace's voice broke. "Don't you think I wanted to forget you? Don't you think I prayed to be free from this ache. An ache for which I didn't understand, no memory? But I couldn't. Even when James held me, part of me was still reaching for you. Reaching for someone or something else. Yet I chose him, Hunter. Because he chose God first. Because he loved me the way you could not."

Hunter's eyes closed, pain carving across his face like a scar reopened. "Do you think I didn't love you? Even when that witch bound me, confused me, twisted my mind....I still loved you. I tried to finish building towers to reach the heavens just to drag you back. I warred against angels because I could not bear to lose you. Then God exiled me." The creek below gurgled on, indifferent to their torment. The silence stretched between them...

Hunter's eyes burned when they met hers again, softer now, wounded. "Then tell me, Aurariel. What do I do with this? With the centuries of longing, with the punishment that made no sense until this moment? I carried you in pieces all my life. And now that I see you whole, I am told to let you go again."

Grace's chest heaved, torn between past and present, desire and duty. She stepped closer, her hand hovering near his arm but not quite touching. "Then seek Him, Hunter. Don't seek me. It's the only way forward for either of us."

For a long moment, Hunter only stared at her, his jaw tight, his breath uneven. Then, with a sound like a wounded animal, he turned, bracing his hands hard on the railing. His shoulders shook….not from rage this time, but from something deeper. Grief.

And Grace knew, with a certainty, that the man before her was not just Hunter, nor Nimrod, nor king nor tyrant. He was a broken soul, still chained, still fighting ghosts he did not know how to bury.

Hunter's shoulders shook as he leaned hard into the railing, the wood groaning beneath his grip. For a moment, Grace thought he might snap it in two. But then the tension drained, and his hands slid down until his fingers curled uselessly over the weathered beam. His head bowed, auburn hair falling forward to shadow his face.

Grace stood still, her hands trembling at her sides, aching to reach for him and terrified of what would happen if she did. The time of centuries pressed between them…their forbidden love, her death, his punishment, her vow to another. None of it could be undone, and yet here he was, flesh and blood, broken before her.

The sound of water rushing beneath the bridge filled the silence, unrelenting and cruel in its indifference.

Hunter's voice broke through at last, hoarse and raw. "Do you know what it's like to wait lifetimes for someone, only to find them… untouchable?"

His throat worked as he swallowed hard. "Every step I've taken, every battle, every night I clawed myself out of despair…it was for the hope of you. To find out who you were to me. And now…"

He shook his head, laughing bitterly under his breath. "Now God is crueler than I ever imagined."

Grace's breath caught. "Don't say that."

"Why not?" He turned, and for the first time since she'd known him, his eyes, the fire that had once fueled an empire was dimmed, flickering with something far more human. "He took you from me once, and when He returned you, you belonged to another. Tell me, Grace, what mercy is there in that?" The use of her mortal name was not lost to her.

She wanted to reach for him, to hold him the way she once dreamed of, but James's name rang in her heart like a shield. She clasped her hands together tightly to keep them from betraying her.

"Mercy," she whispered, "is that He gave you back your memory. That He gave you a chance to repent before it is too late. That He has not abandoned you, even when you abandoned Him."

Hunter flinched at her words, as if her truth had struck him harder than any blade. For a long moment, neither spoke. The children's laughter drifted faintly from the park, distant and unreachable, a reminder that the world still turned no matter how shattered they felt.

Finally, Hunter straightened, dragging a hand across his face as if to wipe the desperation away. His jaw set, but his voice trembled as he forced the words out. "I don't know how to be anything other than what I am.

He paused for a moment. "And I don't know how to let go of you."

Grace's throat tightened, her vision blurring. She wanted to answer, but no words came. None that wouldn't undo her. Hunter looked at her one last time, his eyes a storm of longing and despair. Then, without another word, the giant of a man turned and walked away across the bridge.

Grace stood alone, the ache in her chest heavier than when she had first sat on the bench. She pressed a hand to her heart, whispering into the emptiness. The creek roared on below, carrying away his footsteps, her tears, and the fragile hope and the shadows of what might have been.

Chapter Fifteen

Eva

I watched Remiel as he carefully held our daughter, humming in that low, steady tone that seemed to calm even me. He paced slowly, his bare feet quiet against the floorboards, his shoulders curved protectively over her small frame. Fresh from the shower, I stood in the doorway longer than I should have, caught by the sight of him—this man who had once been untouchable, immortal, now mortal, undone by the simple weight of a crying child in his arms.

He must have felt my gaze, because he turned. Our eyes locked for an instant, and something electric passed between us. Too quickly, I tore mine away, busying myself with the towel at my hair.

He gave a small, apologetic smile. "I think she's hungry." I settled into the rocker, adjusting my robe before he stepped close. He lowered her into my arms with a tenderness that left my chest tight. His hand brushed against mine in the transfer, warm, lingering a second too long.

"I'll get your towel," he offered quietly, almost too quickly. "And some water?"

I raised my gaze. His eyes held mine, searching, almost pleading, though for what I couldn't say. My throat tightened. "Remiel... you don't have to. I can get it when I'm done."

The change in him was immediate, his jaw tightening, his shoulders straightening. A flicker of something raw crossed his face...hurt, anger, longing. All hidden again in a heartbeat.

"Remiel, I didn't mean...."

"It's fine, Eva." His reply was short, flat, but the sound of it cut deeper than I expected. Silence grew. I wanted to reach across it, to soften what I'd just broken, but I stayed still. I had been too cold, too careful, and yet every moment with him pulled me closer to a line I wasn't sure I should cross again.

He turned as if to step away, but paused, his hand brushing the doorframe. His back was to me, but I could feel everything unsaid hovering between us. His breath unsteady, his heartbeat loud enough that I imagined I could hear it in the quiet. And I could not decide if I wanted to hear it against my own chest.

When our daughter's hungry cries softened into soft breaths, I adjusted my robe and rose carefully from the rocker. Remiel lingered close, as if reluctant to step away, watching every movement with that quiet, protective intensity. I carried her into the nursery, laid her down in the crib, and smoothed her blanket. For a moment, I just stood there, gazing down at her….our fragile bridge between heaven and earth.

When I finally turned, Remiel was waiting in the hallway. I hadn't expected him so near, and we collided shoulder to chest, the narrow space drawing us flush together. His warmth radiated through me, igniting every restraint I'd tried to build between us.

"Eva," he said softly, my name breaking the silence. His eyes searched mine, full of shadows. "Do you want me to leave? Would that make you happy?"

The question that I was not prepared for. Guilt flared because yes, part of me thought I should want him gone, for his sake, for mine, for the forbidden bond we had no right to claim, but we did. But beneath it was the ache I couldn't bury, the ache that made my voice falter as I whispered, "If I say yes, will you?"

His jaw tightened, a muscle ticking as though the answer cut him. He leaned closer, not touching me, but the air between us throbbed with the pull of something neither of us dared name.

"I would," he murmured. "But it would be the end of me." His eyes were the same color as storm clouds. And they were threatening to let loose all the emotions that they held. The words unraveled me. Anger, betrayal, guilt, need…they collided all at once, leaving me raw and trembling.

I should have stepped back. Instead, I stood frozen in the hallway, caught between guilt and the unbearable truth that I did not want him to leave. The narrow hallway seemed to shrink around us. His nearness was intoxicating….his scent, his warmth, the way his breath brushed my cheek as though it belonged there.

"Remiel…" My voice broke, barely more than a whisper. I wanted to push him away, to build the walls back up. Instead, I found myself staring into the storm of his eyes, eyes that once had seen eternity and now carried the ache of mortality.

He leaned closer, his hand bracing against the wall beside my head. Not touching me, not yet, but close enough that every nerve in me trembled with the threat of it. "You haven't answered me," he murmured. "Do you want me to leave?"

I swallowed hard, my heart warring against my reason. The words that rose in me weren't the ones I should say. *Yes, leave. Undo what you've sacrificed.* But my lips betrayed me.

"No," I breathed. "I don't want you to go."

His chest shuddered with a ragged breath as he bowed his head. And for one unbearable heartbeat, I thought he might close the distance between us. His gaze moved to my mouth, and my pulse hammered so loud I was certain he could hear it.

"Eva…" My name was raw on his lips, both a plea and a warning. His hand hovered, inches from my face, trembling with the restraint it took not to touch me. The longing in his eyes was unbearable, a mirror of my own.

I swayed toward him before I realized it, but then the guilt crashed down… the cost of his fall, the betrayal of what he had chosen. I froze, my breath faltering and his hand dropped away, and the sudden distance felt like a wound.

He stepped back, jaw tight, forcing control back into the spaces we had almost broken. "Then I'll stay," he said, voice hoarse. "But don't ask me not to want what I can't have."

And with that, he stepped past me, leaving me trembling, knowing the only war being fought was my own heart tearing itself apart. I watched him disappear down the hallway, each step a silent cut across my chest. My hand rose unconsciously to my lips, as though trying to hold back the words I hadn't spoken.

Guilt hit me…..he had given up eternity, glory, *light itself* because of me. Every breath he drew in this earth was a reminder that his sacrifice was my doing. And yet, tangled with that guilt was something darker, something I couldn't name without flinching. Betrayal. He had chosen me, knowing it was forbidden, knowing it would brand us both. He hadn't asked if I wanted this burden…..he had simply bound himself to me, and now I was shackled to the weight of it.

But even in that raw betrayal, my heart whispered for him. Because the truth was unbearable. I pressed my palm flat against the wall, steadying myself against the silence he left behind. The space around me felt cold without him beside me, even for a moment. My heart ached for him and I couldn't bring myself to let go.

I had woken early, the house was quiet. Wanting a sense of normalcy, I busied myself in the kitchen, scrambling eggs, the scent of eggs and butter filling the air. I heard him before I saw him. I half-expected him to sit down and give me a half-smile like he had a habit of doing, when we didn't know what to talk about.

When he appeared in the doorway, he didn't look at me. "I'm heading to the stables," he said simply. No warmth, no softness.

I swallowed, setting the spoon down too quickly, the clang sharp in the silence. "Remiel—"

But he was already moving, the door closing behind him before I could gather the words. Through the window, I watched as he got in his truck to drive away.

It was midmorning before I gathered the courage to leave the house. I told myself it was nothing. He had gone to the stables simply to work. But the silence of the house gnawed at me until I found myself calling Mariana to watch the baby. I packed a small lunch for him and hoped that maybe I could fix some of the damage between us. If he wasn't going to leave and I wasn't going to ask him…then this needed to be fixed.

I had left the basket in the car, wanting to surprise him first. I wasn't sure if I would find him in the arena or the barn. So I started in the barn first. The sound of voices reached me first. Hers, flirting and sharp, seeping through the open barn doors. I stepped closer even though my mind was telling me to back away.

And then I saw it. Lisa stood far too near, her hand trailing up Remiel's arm as she leaned in. My chest seized as she tilted her face toward his. And she leaned in pressing her lips to his, her body to his. And for a breath, the world went still.

Then Remiel's hand shot up, firm against her shoulder, shoving her back with a flash of anger in his eyes. "No," he snapped, his voice low and cutting.

My feet froze, and my throat closed. The image of her leaning into him burned into me. He turned…too late. His eyes caught mine just as I backed away, every nerve screaming to flee. His lips parted, but I didn't wait to hear whatever words he might throw after me. I turned and walked away, my steps unsteady, my chest felt as if it might explode. I could hear him calling me but I continued to walk away.

He must have run to catch up to me because I felt him grab my elbow. "Hey, Eva, I am talking to you." His voice was harsh and angry.

Before I realized my hand struck out and I had slapped him. He was as stunned as I was. He dropped his hand and let me go. He didn't try to stop me as I got in my car and drove away.

The drive home was a blur. My hands clenched the wheel, but my mind was elsewhere, caught in that frozen image. I couldn't process it.

I let the Zaza stay at Mariana's a little bit longer. I was not sure what would be said or how I would react. I didn't want her to pick up on the tension. I wasn't home long before I heard his truck pulling into the yard. The air in the house was brittle, ready to shatter. I was in the living room when he came through the door fast, his boots loud against the floor, his eyes burning. I immediately started walking away.

"Eva," he said, raw and hoarse. "It's not what you think. She—"

"Don't," I snapped, whirling on him, the anger spilling over the fear and hurt clawing in my chest. "Don't stand there and make excuses. I *saw* her. I saw you!"

"And you saw me push her away!" he shot back, his voice rising. He had never yelled at me and it took me by surprise. Even before, when he first came home. He had raised his voice, but never actually yelled at me.

He closed the space between us in two strides, his hands clenched at his sides. "I don't want her, Eva. I've never wanted her."

My chest heaved, the tears I refused to shed burning in my throat. "Why—why does it feel like I can't trust any of this?"

"Because you won't let yourself," he answered, his voice breaking as he leaned closer, the fire in him colliding with the ache in me.

"Do you think I'd trade *you* for anything else when you and our daughter are the only reasons that I breathe in this mortal hell?" I stumbled back, but he followed, his words chasing me.

"I gave up heaven for you, Eva. Every chain I bear, every battle I fight—it's all because I *love* you. I've loved you when I shouldn't. I've loved you when it damned me. And I'd do it again."

The confession tore through me, breaking the emotional wall I'd tried to build. Anger and desire collided, too much to hold back. I shook my head, whispering, "We shouldn't have."

I tried to walk away, but his hands caught my arms, rough and desperate, pulling me closer until there was no space left between us. His face was a mere breath away from me. "I already have," he practically growled, and before I could argue again, his mouth was on mine. The kiss was raw, desperate, every ounce of fury and longing pouring into it.

I fought him at first, fists pushing against his chest, but my fight crumbled as the truth of him consumed me. My hands found his shirt, pulling him closer, answering with all I'd tried to bury. When we broke apart, breathless, his forehead pressed to mine, I realized that I could no longer deny… I didn't want him to leave. Not now. Not ever.

His arms circled me, pressing me to him. The world beyond the room disappeared…the baby, the house…..everything was gone, leaving only the two of us, bound to one another by a force neither of us could resist.

I pressed against him, letting go of every fear I had carried. I traced the line of his jaw, felt the tremble in his hands as he gripped me, as if he was afraid to let go even for a second. His lips trailed from mine to my cheek, to my neck, each touch scorching, claiming, leaving a trail of fire in its wake. My knees threatened to give way, but he held me steady, even as he burned every part of me.

Later as we lay tangled in the sheets, I rested my head against his chest, listening to the steady rhythm of his heart, each beat a reminder of the man who had returned to me, mortal and raw, but mine only. His hand traced slow, lazy circles along my shoulder, bringing me back to the present, soothing the lingering ache of longing and fear. There was a quiet around us, the room filled only with the soft whisper of our breaths and the warmth we shared.

I lifted my gaze to meet his, hesitating. "I…I'm sorry," I whispered, my voice barely audible. "For being so angry… with you. For telling you that I couldn't love you."

His thumb stroked the line of my arm, and I felt a small, almost wry tension in his chest under my ear. "You don't need to apologize," he murmured. "I was angry too. Jealous. Frustrated… and afraid. Afraid of losing you, afraid of what I couldn't control."

I pressed closer, letting his confession settle over me, mingling with my own guilt and relief. "I've been so scared too," I admitted. "Scared of losing you… of what we are… what we're not supposed to be. Even before Zariah was born."

His lips brushed the top of my head, soft and patient. "We're both human in this," he said, voice low, warm, and unwavering. "We're both vulnerable. But I promise you that I'm not going anywhere….not anymore."

I sighed against him, placing a gentle kiss on his chest before placing my cheek to his chest. Letting go of the uncertainty. I closed my eyes. For the first time in so long, I could breathe.

Chapter Sixteen

Psalm 32:3-5 (NIV):

"When I kept silent, my bones wasted away through my groaning all day long. For day and night your hand was heavy on me; my strength was sapped as in the heat of summer. Then I acknowledged my sin to you and did not cover up my iniquity. I said, 'I will confess my transgressions to the Lord.' And you forgave the guilt of my sin."

Remiel

Sunday afternoon

The church bells were still echoing in the air as the crowd spilled out into the parking lot. I lingered near the steps, watching Eva laugh gently at something Mariana had said, the baby cooing in her arms. For a moment, I let myself breathe, pretending there was not some darkness that loomed in the future.

Matthew appeared at my side, his expression tight, jaw clenched like he was bracing for a storm. He stepped closer, his voice low, urgent. "Remiel," he muttered, eyes never lifting from the pavement. "I need to tell you something before I lose my nerve."

Something in his tone chilled me. I turned slightly, keeping my face neutral though suspicion stirred in my gut. "What happened Matthew?" I said evenly, scanning the crowd.

He cut in, his voice cracking under the strain. "You deserve to know, and I can't keep hiding it."

My patience thinned. "Know what?" I wasn't sure why but I sensed that I really didn't want to know his confession. That this confession was something serious and could change lives.

He finally met my eyes, and what I saw there made my stomach knot. Shame. Fear. And something darker. Matthew swallowed, his throat dry. "Before… before you became mortal, I intercepted certain… situations. I made decisions that altered outcomes I wasn't supposed to touch. I tried to keep the balance, to prevent harm, but in doing so I interfered with lives. With Mariana's. I withheld information, manipulated circumstances. I thought I was helping but I was only… complicating everything."

I could feel my jaw clenched as I forced the words out. "You made choices about lives… without telling anyone? You are not God." My voice was low and restrained.

Matthew's gaze fell. "I thought I was doing the right thing. But I was wrong. I see that now. I see how my actions caused more harm than the dangers I thought I was preventing." There was a silence as he looked in Mariana's direction with all the sadness of a heartbroken man. Longing for something he could never have. I knew that longing and understood his pain.

"It was me," he whispered. "Carlos… he died because of me." The words felt like a hammer against stone, rattling everything inside me. I froze, blood roaring in my ears, even as people milled around us, smiling, shaking hands, oblivious to the blade he had just driven into me.

"You need to explain yourself but not here," I said, voice like iron. My hands clenched at my side, but I locked my jaw, forcing control. I was trying to hold back confusion, how I had not known about his part in Carlos's death. Why had that been hidden from me when I was still an angel.

Matthew's lips parted, but no sound came. He swallowed hard, his face pale, and finally managed, "Please…just believe me when I say I never meant for it to happen. I thought I was protecting him."

Disbelief crashed through me, but I glanced toward Eva….her gentle smile, the way Mariana leaned in close to whisper something…and forced myself still. The last thing I wanted was for her to see this, to feel the blow of it before I understood what Matthew was confessing.

I turned back to him, my voice low and sharp as a blade. "We will talk," I said. " You've carried this secret long enough. Tonight, you tell me everything."

His shoulders slumped with relief and dread all at once. "Tonight," he echoed, barely audible. I stepped back just as Eva turned, her eyes finding mine, warm and unsuspecting. The echo of Matthew's confession burned, but I forced myself to nod at her, to pretend nothing had changed. Yet everything had.

That night, I gave Eva an excuse that I had to run to town, but in reality it was to meet Matthew at his house. Sitting across from him, I could see his hands shaking as he found courage to speak.

Hunter sat down beside me, he had been staying with Matthew till his next mission. I could tell he was unsure whether he should be there or not, but he stayed. Finally, Matthew drew a shaky breath, his eyes locking on mine. "I have stood before the congregation," he said, voice low but urgent, "and I have preached of truth and lies… of sin and the fires of hell."

His voice wavered, almost cracking. "Every sermon, every warning I gave, I spoke with authority, while hiding a secret… a truth that could damn me for eternity."

I felt a chill run through me. Hunter shifted beside me, his brow furrowed, sensing the gravity of what Matthew was admitting.

"I've carried this for a year now," Matthew continued, gripping the edges of the table as if it were the only thing keeping him from collapsing. "I warned of lies, of deception, while concealing one of my own… one that could condemn my soul. I preached about hell while standing on the edge of my own."

Each word seemed to echo against the walls, echoing with the weight of his confession. "I cannot stand in front of others," he whispered, "when I have hidden this darkness inside myself. I… I am asking for your understanding, not absolution. Pray for me, for I fear the consequences of what I have kept buried."

I said nothing as I waited for him to continue. I knew— no I dreaded what was coming. But I had no choice but to sit still and listen.

"I saw it, Remiel. I saw Carlos dying….flashes, twisted metal, blood on the pavement. It came on me so suddenly I couldn't breathe. I thought it was a warning. I thought I was meant to save him."

His voice cracked, raw with guilt. "I had never seen visions like that. I had only felt when something might be off with someone. Then in time it started getting worse."

He looked at me as if I was judging him but I shook my head. "Explain, Matthew. What was getting worse."

"Everything," he whispered. "The death," His hands shook harder now. "I couldn't accept that being the only path."

Hunter frowned. "So you interfered?"

"Yes," Matthew admitted. "But this time… I wasn't alone."

"The Fallen noticed," he continued. "They always do when someone peers too long into what should remain unseen. They didn't block my sight— they *played with it.*"

His jaw clenched. "They showed me fragments. Overlapping outcomes. Roads splitting and rejoining. They made it impossible to tell which thread was true and which was bait."

My voice dropped. "And you believed them."

"I believed myself," he said bitterly. "That was the mistake."

He leaned forward, elbows braced on his knees. "The night of Carlos's accident, I saw a window—a moment where intervention could save him. A single decision. A single turn. I thought if I could guide him away from the impact point, everything else would realign."

"You nudged." I said simply.

"Yes," Matthew replied. "A suggestion. A whisper of instinct. I didn't force his hand—I redirected it."

My chest tightened with the unspoken understanding of what that meant.

"I thought I was sending him *away* from danger," he said, his voice breaking. "I thought the road I pushed him toward led to safety."

He covered his face briefly, fingers pressing into his eyes. "But the Fallen had altered what I was seeing. The safe road in the projection wasn't safe anymore. They shifted the variables just enough that I didn't notice."

Hunter muttered a curse under his breath.

Matthew looked up again, "I sent Carlos down the wrong road." The words fell into the room like a death sentence.

"I felt it the moment it happened," he went on. "The snap. The instant the future collapsed into something irreversible."

His voice dropped to a whisper. "That's when I knew I had been played."

My hands curled into fists. "And you said nothing."

"I couldn't," he said. "Because if I admitted it, I would have had to admit that I killed him—not with intent, but with arrogance."

My chest felt as if someone was continuously tightening a rope around it. As Matthew spoke, each word felt heavier than the last. I watched Hunter from the corner of my eye, searching his face for any sign that he already knew this truth—but his expression was carved from stone.

Matthew swallowed hard. "It didn't just start with Carlos." The words sounded as if they were scraped out of his very soul. "It started with *her*."

"What do you mean?" I asked. Unintentionally leaning forward.

"Eva," he said softly. "Every projection I saw— every true one —ended the same way. She dies."

None of us spoke for a second. My mind had immediately caught the words. *Dies, not died…*

"Sometimes it was fire. Sometimes falling. Sometimes her body simply… stopped. But no matter how I traced the threads of time and events, no matter how far back I pushed or how carefully I followed the paths —Eva never survived."

His hands trembled as he lifted them, palms open, as if the visions still burned there. "In one projection, all of them died. Then it changed."

I felt something cold move through my chest. "What did you do, Matthew?" I knew my words were hard.

"I couldn't accept it...by that time I was already close to Eva..." His words trailed off but I heard what he had not spoken. He loved Eva or had been in love with her at one point. Memories of my descent and the first night Eva came to me filled my head. I knew then that he loved her.

"You nudged fate for all of them?" I asked, my mind barely able to comprehend that he had been involved with Carlos's death.

Matthew took a deep breath before continuing. "No, I tried to *fix* it. I thought if I changed the variables, just small ones—I could break the outcome. I focused on Carlos because he was... close and the last one I saw die. I thought if I could save him, maybe the rest would shift. Maybe the timeline would bend."

My heart hurt for him, with him —with the pain he had hidden.

"Thanksgiving night—I saw it again. The wreck and death but it was just him that time. I didn't see Eva or Mariana. I went to him as he got into the car and begged him not to drive. I told him the road wasn't safe. He laughed. Said I worried too much."

Matthew shook his head. "So I interfered. I urged him to take the longer route. I thought I was pulling him *away* from the vision. Redirecting."

He looked up then, eyes glassy and hollow. "But the Fallen were watching."

The air felt heavier and I knew then exactly what had happened. They had used his gift and turned into a curse, into their weapon.

"The accident didn't happen where I first saw it—it happened on the road I made him take."

His shoulders collapsed inward as he leaned his elbows on the table and put his face in his hands. "I walked him straight into it. I felt it the moment it happened," he went on.

No one spoke. I couldn't speak. There were no words for the confession...

"Carlos died because I trusted what I was shown," Matthew whispered. "Because I believed I could outmaneuver fate. Because I tried to rewrite what Heaven had already sealed."

He covered his face with both hands. The room felt suffocating. "I didn't kill Carlos with my hands," he said, his voice barely sound. "I killed him with my curse. And I've been carrying his blood ever since."

He looked at me then— "How do I tell Mariana that I am responsible for killing Carlos, her husband, the father of her child?"

I sat frozen. Part of me wanted to strike him down, to make him feel the pain he had caused. Another part...the quieter part, understood too well how the Fallen worked, how they corrupted even the best intentions and turned them into ruin.

"I don't know how to live with it any longer but I don't know how to tell her." His confession tore at my soul.

Finally taking a deep breath, I gripped his shoulder, firm. "This is not your fault," I almost choked on the words but it was the truth. It wasn't. He had tried to save them, to save Carlos.

"Matthew. They used you as the weapon but you were not the mastermind. They used you, understand that. That means you're dangerous to them, or they wouldn't fear you enough to twist your sight. Do you understand?"

He shook his head, "What do I do now? Remiel, I love her and if she knows that I played the part of killing Carlos, she will never look at me the same again."

I understood his fear, all too well. "You stay close," I said. My voice was steady, though inside me something was storming. Confusion, anger, sadness…too many emotions, too much to understand.

"You protect Mariana and little Carlos. We will pray about the rest. God will reveal it to us." There was so much running through my mind, why had they wanted Carlos dead? Was it to destroy Matthew because he had chosen to be a messenger for God and not give into the evil side of the Nephilim? Did Mariana play a bigger part, a part that I had overlooked? Or was it the child? Or both? The more I sat there trying to piece it together, the messier it got.

I stood up, needing to leave. Needing to return to Eva. The fear that I tried to kill and bury was rising in me. I was halfway to the door when Matthew spoke again.

"Remiel," he said. Something in his voice stopped me cold—not panic this time, not guilt. Fear.

I turned back slowly. "If there's more," I warned, "you say it now."

He swallowed hard, his throat working like the words were lodged there, cutting him from the inside. His eyes flicked to Hunter, then back to me.

"There is still one projection…one vision," he said. "Only one that still appears."

The room seemed to narrow and the very air around us seemed to stop moving. He hesitated as if debating on whether he should say it.

"And?" I said.

"In it… Eva still dies." His words came crashing down on me. My chest felt as if someone had just stuck a hot brand to it, a sharp and all too familiar pain began flaring.

But then he shook his head, quick and desperate. "But you don't."

I froze. "What do you mean, I don't?"

Matthew's voice trembled now, stripped bare of restraint. "You live. You stay mortal. You endure the war of the realms." His hands clenched into fists. "She doesn't."

Chapter Seventeen

Eva

Grace hadn't called before coming. The knock on the door came just after sunrise, soft but steady. I opened it to find her standing there, a figure of quiet tension, her eyes heavy with things she wouldn't say. She smiled, but it didn't reach the shadows behind her gaze.

"Eva," she said, voice careful, as though each word had to be thought out. "I… I needed to see you. To get out for a moment."

I stepped aside. "Come in," I whispered, though I didn't know what I would say to her, or if anything I said could comfort her. She seemed really upset.

She paused in the doorway, before crossing the threshold. She set her purse down, folding her hands in front of her. After a long moment, she finally spoke. "I don't know who I am anymore," she admitted, voice low, almost broken.

"I don't know how to be… me, or how to… love James anymore. I am so torn. This shouldn't be real." Her eyes moved to mine, searching for understanding. "How can you love someone… who killed you?"

The words hung in the room. I felt them but I understood them, they were not just about Hunter, not just the past. But they reminded me of the love that persists through betrayal and brokenness, a love that sacrifices even when the cost is unbearable. A love that once died on the cross.

Her question carried a reflection of the love that had borne the weight of the world once, and still bore it silently, waiting for hearts to return. Grace's hands tightened around mine, and I felt the tremor in her fingers.

"I…I saw him again," she whispered, almost to herself. "Hunter. Just for a moment, but… it was like the past reached out and wouldn't let me go. And I… I don't know what to do with it."

Her voice was raw and hoarse from crying. "You don't have to have all the answers," I said gently. "You don't have to decide what to feel right now."

She shook her head, her gaze falling to the floor. "It's not just that. It's James. It's everything I thought I knew…I don't know anymore. How do I go back to what I was? How do I… how do I …without losing myself?"

I squeezed her hands. "You don't have to figure it all out at once. One step, one moment at a time." I felt the quiet ache of knowing the truth of the choices she made, the love she held. I held my silence, though.

"I thought distance might help," she continued, her voice barely above a whisper. "I thought if we stayed apart, if he stayed away…maybe I could forget. But the truth is… I can't. And I don't know if I *want* to forget…James knows something is wrong. He has asked me several times. We have had arguments. He left this morning to go purchase supplies. He said that we needed time apart, that it would do us good." The silence that followed her words…I understood what she meant. Her marriage was on the brink of failing.

Her hands fidgeted at her sides, twisting the edges of her sleeve. "I suppose that's why I came," she admitted, her eyes finally finding mine.

"I needed someone to hear it. Someone to understand that…" Her voice broke as she swallowed back the tears. She shook her head. "…that I don't know what to do with all of this."

I studied her as she sat there, hesitant and fragile, and yet… somehow still radiant. Grace was older now, the years lightly traced in her once brown hair, now peppered with strands of silver that caught the morning light. But her face remained youthful, untouched by the heaviness she carried in her heart. Her brown eyes shone with a sparkle that drew you in, a brightness that covered the grief lurking just beneath the surface.

She held the kind of beauty that wasn't just skin-deep but seemed to radiate from the way she moved, the way she held herself, the gentle warmth in her voice. How was I just now seeing this? Or maybe it was because before my spiritual eyes had not been opened? As Grace spoke, I found myself studying her again, not just her beauty. Because even in all that beauty, there was a sadness in her, that made her achingly human.

There had always been a distance between us, a quiet space that I had never understood. Not a lack of love… never that.. but something else. Something almost like a curtain but now I was beginning to understand. Grace sank further into the edge of the couch, her hands resting in her lap as if holding herself together. Her gaze stayed fixed on some point just beyond the room, lost in memory.

"I thought I understood love," she whispered, voice brittle. "I thought I knew what it meant to care for someone, to protect them…to forgive. But with Hunter… it's different. It's raw. It's dangerous. And it's still so alive inside me, no matter how much I try to bury it. Even then when he was king and I was a prophetess, I remember fighting my feelings for him."

She wasn't just struggling with memory or longing…she was wrestling everything she'd lived through, everything she had survived. I remembered the dream that I had of Grammy, the one where she told me Grace battled her own demons. Now I understood what her demons were.

"I tried with James," she continued, almost bitterly. "I thought that I could…fill the space, heal the cracks that I didn't understand why I had. But it didn't. It never could. My heart… my heart keeps pulling me back, no matter how far I try to push it away. Then when I saw Hunter again, I knew why."

She looked down at her hands, the faintest shimmer of tears in her eyes. "Because no matter what he became…no matter what I became …. something in me still remembers the man before the fall. The one who listened when God spoke." Her words hung in the air. And in that silence, I could see her truth clearly now.

Just then the back door opened and three sets of footsteps walked down the hallway to the living room. I knew who it was before I even saw them. I shot a quick glance at Grace, her body had frozen and a look of fear was on her face.

I stood up to meet them, to give her time to compose herself….but as I did, the air moved around me, almost like a strong wind. And something changed, not in the room—but in me. My pulse raced, heat rushing behind my eyes, my heartbeat drumming in my ears, suddenly the present slipped sideways.

I blinked—and I was no longer standing in my living room.

I was standing in a stone room with the sun shining through the window. Grace stood before me, but not as she was now. She was younger— radiant in a way that made my chest ache in sadness. Her hair fell loose down her back, dark and gleaming, her face unlined, her eyes alight with fire and faith. She wore simple white and blue robes, but there was no mistaking what she was.

The prophetess—Aurariel. The air around her felt *alive*, charged with purpose. Power hummed from her, restrained but immense. And across from her—Hunter. But not the man I knew. Not the fallen king, not the shadowed presence that haunted our lives. This Hunter was younger too and his eyes held only devotion and love. He was kneeling

"Aurariel." he said, voice steady but thick with emotion. "I was sent to guard the people and to guide them." His hands clenched at his sides. "But I have failed at one thing— to not love."

She stepped back, shaken. "Amraphel—"

"I love you," he said simply. "I am commanded not to. It is not permitted. But as I choose, my heart chooses to. I choose you."

The words echoed with terrible yet painful beauty. "I was not meant to love you," he said quietly.

Grace's breath caught. "Then don't," she whispered, though her voice betrayed her.

"Don't ask me to do that. For that is impossible," he said. "I have built cities. An empire."

His jaw tightened. "None of them have undone me the way you have."

He stepped closer, lowering his voice. "I will marry you."

Her eyes widened. "You already have a wife."

"A political bond," he snapped. "A crown bargain. Not a covenant of the soul."

She shook her head, fear and longing warring in her gaze. "You are king. I am consecrated. This will end in blood."

He reached for her hands, almost desperate. "Then let it be honest blood. Not cowardice."

"I will marry you," he continued, lifting his gaze to hers. "Not in secret. Not in defiance alone. I will ask God Himself if I must. But I will not deny what has been placed in me."

"You are a king, and I am a prophetess," she whispered.

He smiled—soft, fearless. "Then I would have a prophetess as my wife."

Her hands trembled as she reached for him—and then that world shattered. There was fire and smoke. The vision lurched forward violently, time and the sound was like the ripping of a cloth.

I gasped—and now Aurariel was older, bound in chains etched with witchcraft signs. Her robes were torn, stained with blood and ash. Her voice was muted, suffocated by spells woven by a dark breath but yet the divine power remained. She stood before a woman. Amraphel's wife. A witch. Her beauty was cold and deliberate—dark hair braided with charms, eyes sharp with victory. A dark power clung to her.

"You dared," the witch hissed. "You dared touch what was promised to me."

Aurariel lifted her chin, bruised but unbroken. Her voice barely audible, a quiet whisper. "He was never yours, he belongs to God almighty."

The witch laughed, a sound like breaking glass. "He chose me. He chose to rise to greatness. To be a god. And you?" Her smile sharpened. "You chose prophecy over obedience. Disobedience to your queen and goddess."

"You were never my queen and you will never be my goddess. You are a witch bound by the powers of Satan." Aurariel said with a certain defiance, her voice returning once more, then looking the woman directly in the eyes. "You are already destroyed."

The queen screeched an unholy sound as she raised her hand to strike her, but then she stopped and slowly she lowered her hand. "I condemn you," she said calmly.

"By blood and by binding. By silence and by time. You will be forgotten. Your voice will be buried. Your God will be unheard."

Grace cried out, not in fear, but in grief. She lifted her eyes toward the sky. Tears streamed down her face. "This shall be the curse for him and you shall be destroyed. God will always be heard. Everything you have wished and prayed for me, on my God, will return to you seventy times seven…"

"God will have no mercy on your soul," she whispered.

The witch's eyes flickered then—jealousy, rage. "That," she said softly, "is why you will suffer. Your disobedience and arrogance against your queen."

The vision flashed to Hunter, no… Amraphel. The blade moved before anyone could stop him. Steel flashed. Aurariel gasped—not in surprise, but in sorrow—as the blade drove through her. Hunter's eyes widened in horror at what his own anger and hand had done.

"Aurariel—!"

He caught her as she fell, dropping to his knees, pressing his hands against the wound as if he could force life back into her body as blood pooled around her.

"Please," he begged, voice cracking open. "Forgive me. I never stopped loving you. Never. I swear—"

Her hand lifted, trembling, brushing his cheek. "Turn to God while you still can. Before you lose everything," she whispered.

Then with her last breath, her strength was gone. Her hand slipped from his face. And she was still. That Hunter, that Amraphel— gathered her to his chest with a sound that was not quite human, rocking her, calling her name…as if she might answer, as if he could raise her from the dead.

Later—long after the screams had torn his throat raw—he laid her body upon the altar. For three days he knelt there, fasting, praying, bleeding, begging his god to give her back. He was answered but not with mercy. But with silence.

On the third day, God almighty finally spoke to him, God had named him Nimrod, for his rebellion against God. When he rose from where he knelt, he remembered nothing at all. He looked back at her body as he left the throne room, I understood then. That is why her face had haunted him all these years.

The vision collapsed—and I stumbled, gripping the doorframe, breath tearing from my lungs as the present slammed back into place. My heart beat violently. Behind me, Grace gasped. I turned slowly. She was staring at me, eyes wide, face drained of color. "You saw it, too." she whispered.

It wasn't a question.

The footsteps in the hall drew closer. And suddenly I understood the depth of what Grace carried—not just love, not just betrayal. But a promise made and a condemnation that had never truly ended.

Remiel

Matthew's voice was low, hesitant. Hunter followed a few steps behind, silent as his shadow. When they came around the cottage to where I was working, I knew something was wrong. Matthew had that look, shoulders drawn tight, eyes sunken like a man who'd rehearsed a goodbye he didn't want to give. Hunter's face was unreadable, but his hands were shoved deep into his jacket pockets, jaw set like stone. I straightened, brushing hay from my hands. "Morning," I said, though it came out flat.

Matthew didn't return the greeting. He stood there a moment, looking anywhere but at me, before clearing his throat. "I wanted to talk to Eva," he said finally. His voice cracked just enough to betray him.

"Explain… everything. I'm leaving and I don't want her to think I'm just walking out on Mariana without cause."

I frowned. "Leaving? Matthew, where are you going? I told you to stay for now. That we would figure this out. I know you aren't heading back west."

He shook his head. "No. I'm going to stay with my sister Sarah." He looked at the cottage, "The further I am from Mariana, the better. Once I tell her, she is going to hate me. I have already seen it. I can't stay here, knowing that."

Matthew exhaled slowly, as though bracing himself. "I can't stay here pretending everything's fine. I've kept too many secrets, Remiel. And the longer I do, the more it eats at me. Eva deserves the truth. Mariana too."

I studied him for a long moment. This man who had once stood so certain among the congregation, now stood falling apart under the weight of what he carried. "You think telling them everything will make it right?"

He met my gaze then, eyes haunted but resolute. "No. But at least it won't be a lie anymore."

Hunter made a sound … low, almost a growl. "Truth doesn't always fix things, Matthew. Sometimes it just burns down what little's left."

Matthew turned toward him, anger flashing for a heartbeat. "Maybe it needs to burn, Hunter. Maybe it's time."

The silence that followed was sharp as glass. The wind picked up, rustling the grass, and somewhere a crow called from the treeline. I turned back toward Nevada, stroking her neck absently to hide the tightening and worry that I felt in my chest. I looked back at him then — really looked — and saw the exhaustion in his eyes.

Hunter didn't respond. He just turned away, staring out toward the mist-covered hills. There were so many kinds of leaving, I thought. Some of them happened quietly, long before the person ever walked away. And sometimes, the hardest goodbyes weren't spoken, they were carried in the eyes of the ones who stayed.

Enough standing out here," I said finally, exhaling a breath I hadn't realized I was holding. "Let's at least have warmth from this wind, if we're going to wrestle with ghosts."

Hunter gave a low grunt that might've been an agreement. Matthew managed a faint smile, thin and uncertain. But the moment I stepped inside, everything in me went still. Someone was there and something was wrong.

As we entered the living room, Eva moved from where she had been standing but something was wrong. Her face was pale. "Give her a moment," Eva said quietly, her tone firm enough to halt even Hunter in his tracks. Every trace of his usual composure slipping. His jaw clenched, and I could almost hear the tremor in his breath.

"Grace…" he said, barely a whisper.

She didn't answer right away. The silence between them stretched. The years, the betrayals, the blood and mercy tangled together in ways no mortal could untangle.

Hunter took a step forward, his expression a mix of disbelief and anguish. "You shouldn't be here," he said… not in accusation, but in fear of what might be said or done.

"She's here because she needed to be," Eva said softly.

The air in the cottage felt full of ghosts and memories that it held. Hunter stood rooted to the spot, his eyes locked on Grace as though afraid she might vanish if he blinked. Eva's shoulders were squared, her hand still resting lightly on Grace's arm, the quiet protector between past and present.

I saw it before Grace did—before her breath caught, before her hand flew to her chest. Something inside her giving way beneath too much pressure. Her eyes lost focus, darting as if the walls had begun to close in.

"No," she whispered. "I can't—"

Eva had turned instantly. "Mom—"

But Hunter moved faster. He crossed the room in two long strides, hesitation stripped from him. One moment Grace was swaying, the next she was in his arms, pressed tight against his chest as if she belonged there. His hold was firm, protective—almost desperate.

"It's alright," he murmured, his voice low and urgent. One hand cradled the back of her head, the other her spine. "I've got you. You're safe. Breathe."

Grace gasped, fingers clutching at his shirt like he was the only solid thing left in the world. Her body trembled violently, the panic rippling through her in waves.

"I'm here," he said again, and this time his voice broke. "Nothing's going to hurt you. Not now." She clung to him. Not Grace the wife. Not Aurariel the prophetess. Just Grace—frightened, unraveling, human. Hunter tightened his hold instinctively, shielding her from everything. He lowered his head, his mouth brushing her hair.

"Look at me," he said softly.

When she couldn't—when her breath only shuttered harder—he gently took her hands, peeling her fingers from his shirt and threading them through his own. His hands were steady.

"You're safe," he said, slower now, deliberate. "Feel me. I'm right here. I'm not going anywhere."

Her eyes lifted to his, at last, glassy and terrified. "What are we doing here?" she whispered.

Something in his face shattered. "There is a reason, we are not through yet." he said fiercely.

Her shoulders sagged as the panic loosened its grip. Her breaths slowed, shaky but real. She leaned into him, resting her forehead against his chest. Hunter bowed his head, pressing his cheek to her hair, his eyes closing as though he knew their time together was short.

I cleared my throat, the sound abrupt in the stillness. I said softly but firmly. "Matthew came here to speak with Eva. Maybe Grace should—" I started to say leave but was cut off. .

"Should stay," Matthew interrupted before I could finish. "It's alright. She should stay."

All eyes turned to him. He hadn't moved from where he stood near the doorway, but something in his posture had changed, the indecision was gone. He looked at Grace. "She should stay," he repeated, quieter now. "What I have to say concerns her too."

Grace's brow furrowed. "Matthew?"

He shook his head. "No more hiding. No more walls between the living and the fallen."

I looked at him carefully. The man who'd come to me by the barn had been uncertain and confused. The one standing before me now had found something close to courage. Eva glanced back at Grace, her voice soft but cautious. "If it's about Mariana, Matthew, maybe this should wait—"

"It's not just about Mariana," Matthew said, and something in his voice finally gave way.

I felt it before he finished, the invasion of the confession. "It's about why I'm leaving."

Eva looked at him about to speak but I lifted a hand slightly, "Sit," I said quietly. "If we're going to tear this open, we do it properly."

I glanced at Eva. "Coffee?"

She nodded and moved away, though I could feel the tension radiating off her. Grace hesitated before taking the chair across from Hunter, her hands folding tightly in her lap. Hunter reached for her without looking, squeezing her fingers once. She didn't pull away.

Eva returned with the coffee pot and mug, after she had poured the coffee she quietly sat beside Grace. I took the end seat, placing myself directly across from Matthew. If he was going to confess, I would bear it. Matthew's eyes flicked between us, then settled on Grace. His expression softened, heavy with regret.

"It starts with James," he said. "He's… not what we believed." There were exchanged glances around the table before Matthew continued. "He's Nephilim."

Grace inhaled sharply but stayed still. Eva stiffened beside her, and I felt the moment land like an ax blade on the chopping block.

Eva turned to me slowly. The accusation burned in her eyes before she spoke it aloud. "You knew," she said. "And you let him near me? Near Mariana?"

I rubbed my face, already knowing no answer would be enough. "I knew what he might be," I admitted. "Not what he would become in all this. I thought shielding you was the lesser danger—until I could control the fallout." The word barely left my mouth before Hunter slammed his fist into the table.

"Control?" he snapped. "You speak of control?" His gaze cut to Grace, sharp and filled with jealousy. "You married a Nephilim not a Beloved? You pledged yourself to the Light—how does that vow survive when you share your bed with—"

"Enough," Grace said. Her voice trembled but it was firm. "I loved him," she continued softly. "Before I understood what he was. And after I married him, I knew something was different. But I didn't yet understand how."

She lifted her eyes to Hunter, holding his gaze without flinching. "But James is not the enemy," she said. "He is not *your* enemy."

Something dark flickered across Hunter's face. "Not my enemy?" he echoed, a humorless edge slipping into his voice. "You speak his name like..."

"Like what, Hunter? Like he is my husband because by law and under God he is. Despite everything else between us."

His jaw tightened. "He shared your life. Your bed. While I—" He stopped himself, inhaling sharply, eyes burning with something dangerously close to grief. "While I was buried under years I couldn't remember. While your face haunted me."

Grace didn't retreat. "I will not apologize for loving a man who stood beside me." she said quietly. "And I won't let you turn that love into a weapon either."

Hunter's gaze dropped to her hands, then lifted again, raw and unguarded. "You defend him," he said. "After everything. After knowing what he is."

"I defend the truth," she replied. "Not what you fear it means." The silence between them pulsed. Jealousy tangled with longing, possession with regret. "James has never harmed me nor Eva." She finished the sentence by looking at Eva.

Matthew leaned forward, voice tight with urgency. "There's more," he said. "And this is where I failed."

The room stilled. As all eyes landed on him. "James was part of why my visions were warped the night Carlos died," Matthew said. "I didn't understand it then. I thought the distortion was emotion—fear. But I see it now." His jaw tightened. "Dagon was using him."

Grace's breath caught. "Using him how? What do you mean visions?"

Matthew said quickly. "I am Nephilim as well, only I chose to follow the light and not the dark. With that there is a connection that allows us to feel or sense the Fallen or other Nephilim." He allowed his words to sink in before continuing. "James knew of the Fallen's plans. He didn't act on them— but that knowledge clung to him. It echoed. And that echo bled into my seeing. The Fallen manipulated that even though James had no part in it."

I felt the pieces lock together with sickening clarity.

"In the projections, my visions…" Matthew continued, voice shaking now, "Carlos, he —" He let his words trail off. Rethinking how much of the vision, he needed to describe. "Over and over. No matter what I shifted, he died. Till my last one, I thought I could send him down the other direction. That is why I left here shortly after he did. I found him and tried to redirect him back or have him ride with me."

His eyes flicked to me. "I panicked," Matthew whispered. "I tried to fix what was inevitable. I went to help Carlos—but the Fallen twisted my sight. I sent him down the wrong road."

Grace covered her mouth, a quiet sound breaking from her. Eva grasped her mother's hand.

"He wasn't meant to die," Matthew said. "I never intended that."

I nodded slowly. "James confessed to me later. He told me he saw Dagon at the cottage that night when you went to stay with Grace—but he said that he didn't see him till after they had returned."

I closed my eyes briefly. "He didn't want any part in it. But the presence still resonated off of him. I should have told you, Eva."

Eva's shoulders trembled once. Then she drew in a breath that sounded like it hurt. "And I never said anything to you," she whispered.

The admission didn't come with defensiveness—only exhaustion from holding the truth hidden. "I didn't know how," she continued, lifting her eyes to mine at last. "We weren't… we weren't right then, Remiel."

Her voice didn't break. "You were distant. Cold. Every time I asked about the missions, you shut down. You wouldn't let me in."

The words struck deeper than accusation ever could. "You were already gone half the time," she said softly. "And when you were here, you felt unreachable. I didn't want to add one more thing—one more demon, to the darkness we were fighting."

She looked down at her coffee mug before meeting my eyes."I thought if I told you about Dagon," she went on, "it would push you further away." The room faded around us. All I could hear was the quiet truth in her voice. Knowing that my distance, my refusal to let her see the cost of what I carried—had taught her to carry her fear alone.

"I should have come to you," she said.

"No, Eva. I knew and I should have asked you." We had both been trying to protect each other. And in doing so, we had left the door open for something else to walk in.

Hunter laughed bitterly, cutting through the silence. "You let a dark Nephilim sit at your table?"

Grace turned on him then, fire in her eyes. "He did not choose his blood any more than you chose your crown." The words struck deep. Hunter didn't speak anymore but hesitantly and gently he took Grace's hand, apologetically. And I understood then…fully, painfully, that this was not one failure. There were many. Matthew's seeing. James's silence. My protection that had become concealment.

Matthew spoke again, interrupting Eva, but softer this time, but every word precise. "James' original plan…before he ever loved Grace, was to get close to Eva. Dagon wanted him to manipulate her, and he followed the orders at first. But then… he fell in love with Grace. And being with her changed him. It didn't erase the past, but it shifted his path."

Grace's lips pressed into a thin line. "He did change…I didn't know from what but I sensed it."

Hunter's hands clenched into fists. "And what about the vows? Your promise to the Light? The guardians? How can that survive?"

Grace looked down, a quiet sorrow in her eyes. "Love doesn't cancel loyalty, Hunter. It gave him a chance to fight what he was born with rather than succumb to it. I do not know about the rest. And perhaps it is best that I do not know."

Hunter's voice was harsher this time just as his truth was. "What if his Nephilim nature wins?" Grace looked at Hunter, she didn't have to answer him. Her silence did.

We all sat there, waiting for someone to speak either in anger or forgiveness. Eva finally stood up and walked to Matthew, she bent over and hugged him. "I am so sorry that you carried all of that by yourself for so long."

Matthew clung to her as she was his saving grace. You could see his entire body breathe with relief. When Eva straightened, she placed her hand on his shoulder. "Matthew, I understand how hard this is for you and why you wish to leave, but you need to tell Mariana. She loves you and deserves to know the truth."

Matthew shook his head, looking up at her. "How can I tell her? How can I tell her that I am the reason her husband was killed?"

Her hand tightened briefly on his shoulder. "If you leave without telling her, you leave her alone with ghosts and the uncertainties that she will never understand. If you stay, if you explain—then at least she can choose how to carry her grief."

Matthew finally nodded in agreement. "You are right, Eva. I have to tell her."

Part of me was relieved that Eva knew, but I also noticed that Matthew had not mentioned that Mariana and Eva had been in the visions. Would this be another thing that I would have to confess later to her that I knew, but had kept from her as well?

Chapter Eighteen

Eva

I watched as Grace walked toward the door and I knew immediately Hunter was going to follow her. I stood up to follow them but Remiel softly grabbed my wrist. "Eva, let them go. They need to sort things out without interference."

I watched as they walked out, Hunter holding the door open as Grace walked underneath his arm. It wasn't hard to see the love in Hunter's eyes, what he carried for Grace. My heart ached for her, for them as I watched as they got in Grace's car and drove off.

Matthew had left already and it was just Remiel and I. I watched as he sat there, so calmly, holding our beautiful baby girl. He motioned for me to sit down beside him on the sofa. I slowly sank into the couch, grabbing one of the cushions and putting my face into it. Slowly releasing a muffled scream.

I heard Remiel chuckling beside me and I looked up at him. "Why is this so funny to you?" I asked sarcastically. "You do realize we are living in a very tangled mess of realms and supernatural beings. Nobody on this Earth would believe this."

Remiel reached out with his free hand and brushed the curls out my face. "It is not for everyone to understand."

His quietness soothed my anxiety for one second. I leaned into his arm as he pulled me close. He gently kissed the top of my head before resting his cheek there. "Eva, we know what we fight against."

"Do we, though?" I asked softly, letting my head rest against his shoulder. "Because it feels like everything is moving faster than I can keep up with. I feel like I'm being swept along by a current I didn't choose," I continued, voice barely above a whisper. "Like every time I try to plant my feet in something solid… it changes beneath me."

I folded my arms across my stomach as if to hold something in place…gravity, peace, or maybe simply *myself.* "It wasn't supposed to be like this. I don't even know what it is anymore. One moment, I'm a normal child and the next I'm remembering battles I've never fought. I hear voices in my dreams…memories that aren't mine."

The words tumbled out now, faster than I could catch them. His arm tightened slightly around me, but he still didn't speak. Maybe he was giving me space to unravel or maybe he didn't have the words either. I ran my hand over our baby's tiny back, amazed at how wonderful she was made..

"And everything just keeps changing. Grace, she's carrying all this weight. Hunter remembers things that broke him. Matthew's out there ready to run. And you…." I lifted my head then, just enough to meet his eyes, "you look at me like that…but I still feel so unworthy of your love and your sacrifices." Tears blurred my vision, but I forced a smile.

"You keep saying you don't know what to do," he murmured, brushing his thumb across my face, wiping the tears away.. "But you love. Even when it hurts you and you don't know what else to do….. That's more than most would ever dare."

He placed his finger under my chin, lifting my face to meet his. "You are more than worthy of my love. Do not forget that. We have crossed realms to find each other. Maybe it is I, who is unworthy of you."

I shook my head as I laid it on his shoulder and sighed, exhaustion settling into my body. The kind that sleep could never fix. I thought about our battles—how strangely similar they were, even if they looked nothing alike from the outside.

While he had been away fighting demons that threatened our earthly realm, I had been here… fighting the ones that lived inside of me.

He battled things with claws and teeth, ancient things that knew how to tear flesh from bone. And monsters that haunted you in nightmares.
I battled grief that hollowed out my chest from the inside. Memories

that whispered– I was not enough. A voice that sounded like my own, but spoke only condemnation.

Loss had not come to me all at once—it came slowly, mercilessly, taking pieces of me until I didn't recognize what remained. First hope. Then joy. Then the quiet confidence that God had made me with purpose. Depression had wrapped itself around my spirit like chains, convincing me that even breathing was a burden I placed on the world.

And still… I was meant to guide others to Him.

I swallowed hard, thinking of every person, every young woman who had ever sat across from me, their eyes swollen from tears, their voices shaking as they confessed they felt forgotten by God. They came to me looking for answers, for reassurance, for proof that the darkness they were drowning in would not last forever.

And I gave it to them.

I spoke of redemption. Of grace. Of a love that did not falter when we did. All that while wondering if that same love could ever truly reach me.

Because what testimony did I have to offer, when I had spent so many nights begging God to take the pain away and hearing nothing but silence in return? What right did I have when I had struggled daily to believe I had one of my own? My voice had also trembled in the dark, asking if my existence was a mistake. I closed my eyes as the ache pressed deeper into my chest. But Jesus had shown me that I was worth his life and so much more. Looking up at Remiel, I knew we had been blessed, even if our blessing looked like a curse on the outside.
He fought demons to save the world and I fought the lies that the lost believed– that the enemy tells them that they are not worth saving.

I felt Remiel shift his weight slightly, the gentle sway of his arm coaxing her back to calm. "She's so peaceful," I whispered. "How is that even possible? With everything in motion, how does she rest?"

"Because she trusts," Remiel said. His tone was thoughtful,"She doesn't know what she's waking into. She just knows she's held."

I let out a long sigh. "I want to be like that," I said quietly. "Just for one night. To breathe without being afraid."

He looked at me then. And I realized…he did understand. He wasn't free from fear. But he chose steadiness anyway. Not because he wasn't afraid….but because he loved something more than his fear.

"You will be," he said softly. "But you have to stop trying to carry yourself alone."

"I'm not the only one," I replied gently. "You keep a lot to yourself too."

He blinked and for a moment, surprised. "I'm just trying to—"

"I know," I interrupted softly. "Protect me. But I'm not made of glass, Remiel." He didn't protest.

"I forget sometimes," he said, voice quiet but firm. "You're not just someone to protect."

"I'm someone to *fight alongside you*," I finished for him. A small smile curved his lips. He leaned in, forehead resting against mine. "We don't have to be unbreakable," he whispered. "Just unyielding."

Mariana called me two days later, asking me to watch Carlos. She and Matthew were going out for dinner. She sounded so excited but my heart sank, not because I didn't want to help….but because I knew exactly what this dinner really was. His confession. "Yes mam, I can take him, bring that sweet baby." I told her, even though my voice came out softer than I meant. "Bring him by whenever you're ready."

"Thank you," she breathed, and before I could say another word, she hung up. I stared at my phone for a long second before sitting it down. Zariah gurgled in her bassinet nearby, kicking her legs, trying to free herself of the blanket. I prayed quietly that Mariana would have the courage to forgive Matthew. And that Matthew would have the courage to tell her the truth but his truth wasn't normal. It wasn't clean or easy or something you could fold up neatly and store in a drawer.

How does a man explain to the woman he loves that he can see beyond the earthly realm? That he can sense the fallen or nephilim? That he was used as a weapon by the fallen? I didn't know how he'd do it. But I hoped, desperately, that he would try.

Remiel stepped into the room then. He glanced at me, reading everything on my face without me needing to say a word. "What happened?" he asked gently.

"Mariana and Matthew are going out tonight," I said. "She asked me to watch Carlos." Understanding flickered in his eyes. Then a hint of concern. Not for them but for me.

"You're afraid for her," he said.

"I'm afraid for both of them," I admitted. "If she can't accept who he is now… if he can't explain without scaring her…" I exhaled slowly. "They could lose each other."

Remiel sat beside me, "Love does not disappear because of fear," he said quietly. "But fear can keep people from walking toward what's meant for them."

I leaned into him, closing my eyes. "They deserve peace."

"They do, and they deserve love," he agreed. "But peace usually comes after truth. And truth is rarely gentle. And love can be dangerous."

We sat that way for a while, his arms wrapped around me, and me needing him more and more. I had dozed off when I heard a soft knock come from the front door. Mariana, she was little early but then she was probably nervous.

"Ready?" Remiel asked softly. No, I wanted to say. Not at all.

But I nodded anyway. "Yeah. Let's do this."

He smiled a little. "One step at a time, Eva." I stood and walked toward the door, praying tonight would be the night everything changed for them and not in the way that breaks people forever. I prayed my friend would have the courage to forgive Matthew. I wasn't sure how he was going to explain his ability to sense or see.

Mariana came back just after nine, keys jingling in her hand, her expression already tight. I felt the tension before she even stepped through the doorway. She had come in and tried to make small talk while gathering the diaper bag and Carlos. When I tried to ask how the night went, she completely changed the subject.

Then Matthew's truck was pulling into the drive and he was walking up the porch. Just as she was trying to walk out. She was doing everything in such a hurry, I had a hard time trying to keep up with what was going on. She brushed past Matthew heading to the steps, but Matthew was right behind her on the porch. "Mariana…please. Just listen to me."

She didn't turn. "I listened, Matthew. I listened for two hours while you talked in circles.

"It's not circles," he said, running a hand through his hair. He looked exhausted—frustrated. He looked at me for help before turning back to her. "I'm trying to tell you the truth."

"The truth?" She spun on him so fast he flinched. "You can *see things*, Matthew? You can *sense danger*? You can *feel demons*? Do you hear yourself?"

Matthew's jaw tightened, but he didn't back down. "I'm not crazy. Ask Eva. Ask her what she's seen."

Mariana scoffed. "Oh, I'm sorry—are we all supernatural now? Is that what this is?"

"Mariana," I stepped forward gently, "he isn't lying. I wish he were, but—"

She held up a hand. "Don't, Eva. Please. I love you, but don't."

Matthew reached for her arm. "Wait…just wait. Let me *show* you. I can't lose you over this."

She jerked away as if his touch burned. "You already did." Matthew's face crumpled.

Remiel stepped forward then, his voice calm so calm, that it seemed to still the air. "Mariana. Fear clouds discernment. You are hurt, yes…but not because he deceived you. You are hurt because what he said demands you reshape what you believe about the world."

She stared at him, startled by the clarity of his words—but only for a moment. "Who even *are* you?" she whispered, suddenly afraid.

Remiel fell silent and looked at me for help. How could we reason with someone who was determined not to believe. I loved Mariana but I also knew how stubborn she could be.

Mariana shook her head, blinking fast as if the whole night was blurring. "I can't do this. Not tonight."

"Mariana—" Matthew tried again, voice breaking.

But she was already walking down the steps with Carlos on her hip and the diaper bag slung on her shoulder.

"Mariana, please," Matthew called, stepping after her. "Don't walk away like this. Just talk to me. I'm not asking you to understand everything…just don't shut me out."

She opened her car door without a word, and put Her eyes were glossy, but her face told it all. Matthew reached the edge of the driveway as she started the engine.

"I love you," he said desperately. "You can be mad…just don't give up on us." For half a heartbeat, it looked like she might pause. Then she pulled away, tires rolling over gravel, tail lights bleeding into the night.

Matthew stood there, breathing hard, staring after her as if the road might give her back. "I shouldn't have told her," he choked. Matthew dragged a hand over his face. "I just wanted her to believe me."

"She will," Remiel said. "But only when she is ready. And you know yourself that readiness rarely comes wrapped in comfort."

Matthew didn't speak. He just watched the empty road, chest rising and falling with the ache of someone losing the person they love. The truth was nothing but fair when it came to love…

Then something happened, a shadow crossed through the night air. Remiel stepped forward, placing a hand on Matthew's shoulder. "Prepare yourself. Something is coming."

He lifted his head to the sky, eyes blazing. I felt it too, something was coming. I walked down the porch to be close to Remiel but even that couldn't take away the feeling that something was wrong….very wrong. I watched as Remiel turned and I gasped at the shadows I had never seen before. For the first time since he became mortal, the shadow of wings flickered across the ground behind him..like a memory trying to return. And I knew something was wrong, something was very wrong.

Matthew's face went pale. "Remiel…?"

But before he could finish, a loud horrific animal sound was let out, one sharp enough to rattle the air. I felt it deep in my bones, like the world exhaling something foul. *Something terrible had just crossed into our earthly realm.* The wind slowed. The insects stopped. The sky darkened even though sunset was long gone.

Remiel stiffened first. He lifted his head like he heard something beneath the earth. His eyes narrowed, scanning the treeline. "Eva," he murmured, "get inside."

"What? Why? What's—"

The treeline split open. A jagged seam tore down the air like lightning but stayed, suspended, edges burning with black flame. Shadows spilled through it in thick tendrils, pooling, gathering, forming. At first the shape that stepped through, looked like a huge gigantic black wolf but then the shadows twisted upward, shaping into a colossal beast…huge. Misshapen. Shadow-bound. Its limbs unfurled unnaturally, black smoke dripping off its form like liquid venom, just as I'd seen in Dagon's vision, wings dripping darkness that sizzled against the ground.

Matthew took a step toward Remiel's side to face the beast with him, but he suddenly froze. "She is in danger." Matthew's voice was low now. Terrified. "I—I can feel her. Mariana. She's not just upset. Something's wrong."

Remiel didn't question it. "Go for her, it's the Fallen." he commanded. "NOW!" He bellowed before stepping back and shoving me behind him.

Matthew didn't wait. He bolted for his truck, looking one more time at Remiel before cranking the truck, gravel spitting beneath the tires as he tore down the road into the dark. I knew he was praying he could get to Mariana.

The beast turned its hollow gaze toward the direction Matthew had gone… then toward me. My stomach dropped and my blood froze. "It's… it's the same one," I whispered, barely able to speak. "Remiel…. the …the vision."

The beast lifted its head, nostrils flaring as if scenting him. Remiel moved instinctively, stepping in front of me. The beast's hollow gaze fixed on him and *only him.* Because this had been sent. An executioner wearing a shadow, this was a signature of Dagon's wrath and promise.

"Remiel," I breathed, "Dagon sent it." A low, rumbling snarl vibrated across the ground, rattling the porch beneath my boots. The tear behind the beast pulsed like a heartbeat…steady, intentional, waiting.

"Eva," Remiel said without looking back. Then the beast lunged. Remiel shoved me away just before it struck. The creature's claws scraped across his ribs, flinging him several feet. He rolled, gasping, stunned.

"REMIEL!" I screamed before I realized it. The beast roared and advanced once more. And then everything exploded. Light exploded from Remiel with a violent, blinding crack. His body arched as if something inside him tore free. His breath came out —half pain, half release. Power rolled off him in waves so strong the ground trembled.

The beast staggered back as if he recognized this form, the mortal who stood in front of him.. Remiel stared at the beast. Suddenly the beast lunged, and Remiel threw himself forward with a burst of light, tackling it, the two of them slamming into the yard with impossible force. Their battle ignited the night. But as I watched them collide…I felt it. A stabbing, sudden jolt through my chest. Zariah. Her cry. Her fear. Something touching her. "No!" I gasped, turning. "Zariah!"

I ran back into the house, heart thundering so hard it blurred my vision. Down the hall. Into the nursery. And froze. Someone stood over the bassinet. Someone who shouldn't be here.

"A… Alysson?" My voice was barely a whisper. She turned slowly, smiling softly. But her eyes were no longer green but black. This wasn't right. This wasn't reality. And Alysson and that beast outside, shouldn't be here. They should be in the realms….not here.

"You left her alone," she whispered gently, like a scolding mother. "You left your daughter unguarded."

Cold horror ripped down my spine. "Alysson," I said, shaking, "step away from my baby."

Her smile widened, slow and knowing. "Eva," she cooed softly, "she shouldn't belong to you."

Pain struck my chest like a physical blow as Zariah whimpered, her tiny cry slicing straight through me. "Alysson, don't touch her!"

But Alysson didn't look at me. Instead she leaned closer to the bassinet, her voice dropping to a whisper, as if she were standing at an altar instead of over my child. I tried to move toward her—but an invisible weight slammed into my chest, crushing the air from my lungs and driving me to my knees.

Outside, the beast roared. Remiel shouted something, my name, maybe—but it all blurred into nothing. All I could see was Alysson, her shadow spilling over the bassinet, her fingers hovering just above Zariah's face.

"She should have been mine," Alysson murmured.

I started praying—out loud, broken, desperate—begging God for strength, for mercy, for anything at all. Alysson finally looked up at me, her eyes gleaming with something terrible.

"Eva," she said gently. "Sweet Eva. Do you know how you got your name?" She traced the side of Zariah's face.

My heart pounded so hard I thought it might tear itself free. "Don't," I whispered. "Don't you dare."

But she smiled wider. "I gave it to you."

The room tilted and I felt sick, physically sick.

"You were supposed to be the first," Alysson continued calmly, as if she were recounting a forgotten bedtime story. "The first sacrifice."

I shook my head violently. "You're lying."

"No," she said softly. "I named you *Eva* because you were meant to begin it all. The start of my power. Only you delayed it." Her face turned into one of disgust as she looked at me.

My stomach turned as bile burned my throat. Alysson straightened slowly, her gaze drifting somewhere far beyond the room, beyond time.

"Your mother—Faith—she didn't understand at first. None of them ever do. She thought she was following God. She thought obedience meant silence. I tried to show her another way…" Alysson's voice faltered for the first time, something sharp and bitter cutting through it. "But when she realized what she was about to give me… when she understood what *you* were meant for…"

Her fingers curled into her palms. "She ran."

I sucked in a broken breath but continued to pray. I could feel the pressure beginning to leave me.

"She took you and fled," Alysson went on. "She brought you to Grace. To hide you. To *protect* you." A humorless laugh slipped from her lips. "Grace still carried the power of a guardian then—though she didn't know it. Not consciously. But power recognizes power."

Alysson's eyes snapped back to me. "I couldn't touch you."

My chest heaved as the truth crashed over me in waves. "So she left," I whispered, the words tasting like ash. "Faith left because—"

"Because she was ashamed," Alysson finished. "Ashamed of what she had almost done. Ashamed that it had nearly cost her child's life. She ran and went back to serving your God. She threw it all away with all the power she could have had."

I shook my head, "No my mother left to save me—from you."

Zariah whimpered again, and Alysson's gaze flicked down to her, hunger flashing across her face before she masked it. Then I realized what my dreams had been trying to tell me. "You wanted what my mother had. What Faith had, you didn't just want me. You wanted her life. You betrayed her friendship just as you betrayed mine. You lied to everyone these years, letting them believe you were young and that your mother had run off and abandoned you. The entire time it was you."

She hesitated for just a second, "When I pledged myself to the darkness, I didn't know," she said fiercely. "They never tell you what they'll take. They only tell you what you'll gain—power, protection, answers. I thought I was offering my loyalty. My voice. My skill." A broken laugh slipped from her throat. "I didn't know I was offering my womb. My ability to have children."

"It was written into me," she went on, her voice cracking now. "A clause I didn't read because it wasn't spoken aloud. I was never meant to bring life into the world. Only to take it." Tears welled in her eyes, spilling over despite her attempt to blink them back.

"Do you know what it's like," she asked hoarsely, "to feel your body betray you over and over again? To realize too late that the thing you wanted most was the very thing you had signed away?"

Zariah let out a soft, hiccupping cry. My heart was racing. I had to reach her.

Alysson had also flinched. "Why do you think your father drank himself to death? Because he couldn't deal with the reality of what he had done. He wasn't strong enough so he caved to the weakness."

I bowed my head once, just once, and whispered a prayer—not for escape, not for rescue, but for strength. When I lifted my head again, something inside snapped. I stood. Each step toward the bassinet felt like walking through water, the pressure still heavy but no longer crushing. I kept my voice steady as I moved closer, careful, deliberate, hoping my words would reach her before my body ever could.

"It took years of sacrificing," I said quietly, "years of bleeding yourself dry to become as strong as you are now."

Alysson's shoulders stiffened.

"And for what?" I pressed on.

Her smile faltered. Slowly, she looked down at Zariah. Not with hunger this time—but with a longing so naked it startled me. Alysson's hand moved on instinct, pressing against her stomach as if her body remembered something her mind and heart had tried desperately to forget.

"For power," she said automatically.

I shook my head. "No," I whispered. "For emptiness." Her jaw clenched. The air around us shuddered with the truth.

"You gave everything," I went on, taking another step closer, "your future, your body, your children—things you didn't even know were being taken from you. And all they left you with was this moment."

Alysson inhaled sharply. "That's not true."

"It is true. Look at you. You were promised greatness," I said softly. "But all you were ever given was loss."

She turned her face away, but I saw it—the way her eyes shone with unshed tears, the way her mouth trembled before she forced it still.

"They lied to you," I said, my voice barely more than a breath now. "And you paid the price with every child you never got to hold."

Her hand pressed against her chest, knuckles whitening. "Stop," she hissed, but there was no strength behind it. Only pain.

"You didn't choose to be barren," I continued. "They took it without your consent so they could force you into doing their dirty work. Allowing you to believe that in the end you would get what you always desired. And now they're asking you to do it again…the only thing you were ever allowed to do, take instead of love."

Silence fell heavy between us. Alysson looked at Zariah again, her expression breaking completely. "I just wanted one," she whispered. "Just one to stay."

I stepped closer—close enough now that I could feel the cold radiating off her skin.

"And what happens after?" I asked gently. "After you take her? Are you to sacrifice her so they will give you back what they stole from you?"

Alysson's breath came sharp and uneven, because she knew the truth without speaking it. So I spoke it out loud for her. "They won't," I said. "Because they never intended to. Your beauty and youth was just a cover up for what they needed you to do."

Her hand slid from her stomach and hovered over the bassinet again—but this time, it shook. For the first time, Alysson didn't look like a vessel of darkness. She looked like a mother who had never been allowed to hold her one of her own.

"Dagon did not love you, he used you." I continued.

Alysson nodded slowly in agreement. "He could never love me, because all he wanted was you. You held that one little peace of light that he wanted so badly but could never have. And me, all I ever held was darkness. Something he already had."

I took a tentative step forward, my hands trembling but open. "Alysson," I said softly, "it doesn't have to be like this. You don't have to give in to them. You don't have to be this person." I swallowed hard. "There is another way."

I prayed in my mind—silently but fiercely—that my words would find whatever place was still alive inside her that might hold some sort of light.

Alysson lifted a shaking hand and wiped at her cheek, surprised by the tear there as she stared at it. When she spoke, her voice was different, quieter, stripped bare. It sounded like the Alysson I had once known.

"I wish that were true," she whispered. "But God would never forgive me."

"That's not true," I said quickly, panic threading my voice. Outside, the sounds of fighting had stopped. No roaring. No shouting. The silence pressed in, heavy and wrong. And still—I was no closer to my daughter.

Alysson swallowed, her throat working. "If there were a way back," she said, voice breaking, "I would take it. I would." Her eyes lifted to mine, filled with fear, not fury. "But the moment I turn away from him… they will come for me."

"Let them," I said without hesitation. "You don't have to belong to him anymore. Alysson, you can be free. Free from this darkness. Free from what they made you."

She closed her eyes—just for a heartbeat. But it was enough.

The shadows around her loosened, recoiling as if burned by the thought alone. I didn't hesitate. I lunged forward, throwing my weight into her. We crashed to the floor in a tangle of limbs, her body hitting hard with a hollow, final thud.

I expected her to fight. She didn't. She just stayed there. Still. Silent. Like something inside her had finally broken beyond repair—or release. Like she was too tired to hold herself together anymore.

I scrambled to the bassinet, my hands shaking as I scooped Zariah into my arms. She whimpered once, then settled against my chest. I bolted toward the front door, my pulse roaring in my ears. The air behind me felt thick, coiling, angry—as if the darkness itself were reaching for what it had lost.

I waited for Alysson to rise and come after me. For her to scream. To strike me from behind. She didn't.

"Go," she whispered hoarsely from the floor. The word stopped me cold. It wasn't a command. It wasn't a threat. I turned slowly. She hadn't lifted her head. Her face was pressed to the floor, her shoulders shaking like someone finally laying down a weapon they'd carried too long.

"I won't take her," she said, her voice breaking completely now. "I won't take anyone's child ever again."

The shadows writhed around her, angry, tightening—but she didn't look at them. "I am so tired," she whispered.

The air seemed to shake from the sound of her words. Alysson stayed on the floor as I backed away, cradling my daughter. When I crossed the threshold, I felt it…something dark tearing free from her, screaming soundlessly as it lost its hold.

Outside, something crashed….a reminder that Remiel was still out there, and God only knew what was happening to him. I tightened my hold on Zariah. I glanced one last time at Alysson, but she continued to stay on the floor, staring at nothing. Broken, emptied, undone.

"I'm sorry," she breathed, so soft I almost wasn't sure I'd heard it. I didn't wait to hear more. I pushed through the front door, into the cold air, with my daughter clutched against me… praying that I wasn't already too late. A cry–Remiel's cry.
 Not of victory. But of pain.

He was on one knee near the side fence, his sword, the one that he always tried to keep hidden from me, lay several feet away, broken and half-buried in the dirt. "Remiel—" I started forward. He lifted his hand in warning without   even   looking   at   me.
 "Stay back," he rasped. Something moved in the darkness behind him. Not footsteps. Not breathing. The creature slammed into him with a force that cracked the fence behind him. Remiel gasped, knees buckling, but he pushed off the ground and drove his fist into the creature's jaw — once, twice — each strike deeper, heavier, fueled by something more than strength.

The beast reeled, snarling. Remiel didn't let up. He grabbed the thing by its throat or where a throat should've been, and hurled it across the yard, both of them crashing through the wooden fence. The explosion of splintered wood made Zariah scream in my arms.

"Remiel!" I sobbed.

He staggered out of the wreckage, breath ragged, shoulders heaving. His shirt was torn open, skin slashed and bruised, bleeding, but his eyes–his eyes burned. Not with angelic glory.
But with sheer, human refusal to let us die.

The monster rose again, hissing, body reforming like smoke and bone. Remiel didn't wait. He charged full speed, like a man who knew he wouldn't survive the next blow but intended to land his own anyway. They collided. The creature's claws tore across Remiel's ribs. Remiel drove his knee into its gut. The thing shrieked. He grabbed its head and slammed it down on the gravel.

For a moment…just a moment…he was winning. I started praying and asking for a miracle. I prayed, trying to understand what was going on but trying to figure out how to save my husband and keep my daughter safe. I finally cried out. "Lord, what…why?! Do you not see us suffering, please God, I am begging you in Jesus name. Help us!"

The sound of my prayer sent the beast shrieking and the shadows around the creature surged upward like a wave, swallowing his legs, dragging Remiel off balance.

"NO!" I tried to run toward him, but the darkness lunged for me too. Remiel saw it. He threw himself between us.

The creature's claws raked across his chest—deep. But even then, he stayed in front of me, shielding us with everything he had left. "Eva… run," he gasped.

The thing struck again. This time Remiel didn't block it. He couldn't. He collapsed to the ground, the impact echoing. The creature, that hideous beast loomed over him and then it backed up, its surrounding shadows twisting, preparing the final blow.

"REMIEL!" I screamed, voice breaking. I knelt down beside him. He lifted his head once—just enough to look at me. He gathered his strength to stand up, in doing so he shoved us away from him.

"Eva, run," Remiel forced out. His voice was strained, fading. "Take her and run."

"I'm not leaving you!" I whispered fiercely.

"You have to." The shadows behind him twisted upward, forming something tall and thin… then collapsing again. Hunting. Searching.

My stomach dropped."Remiel?" He didn't answer. He couldn't. Because the beast surged suddenly toward him, slamming him once more into the ground. Zariah whimpered in my arms. Remiel groaned, choking on a breath that didn't fully come. "Go!"

Suddenly a sound rang out making my ears hurt. The sound was sharp. Almost unhuman. But it was real. The darkness recoiled. A familiar voice rang out, rough and furious. "HEY." Hunter stepped in front of me, eyes locked on the beast as if it were nothing more than another enemy to be put down. He didn't hesitate. He didn't flinch.

He *charged*. And suddenly Grace was beside me, trying to help me stand but I couldn't stand. My knees wouldn't move.

"Get away from them!" he shouted. The beast turned, enraged.

But before it could strike—Grace dropped to her knees beside me. Her hands were shaking but her voice was not.

She pressed one palm to the ground, the other to her chest, and began to pray. Not softly. Not timidly. "In the name of Jesus Christ," she said, her voice ringing with sudden authority, "I rebuke you. You unholy entity of darkness."

The air stopped moving and the shadows stilled. The cottage groaned as if waking from a long sleep. Light began to bleed from the walls, seeping through wood and stone, threading through the cracks like veins of gold. Grace lifted her head. And I gasped.

She was no longer only Grace. Light unfurled behind her, spilling upward in shimmering waves, greens and violets, blues and golds—like the living fire of the Aurora Borealis dancing across the sky. Power wrapped around her form, ancient and holy, settling onto her as she reclaimed it.

A guardian. Whole. Awakened. She rose to her feet, radiant, terrible, beautiful."This ground," Grace declared, her voice layered now—hers and something older, "is *holy*."

The beast shrieked as the shadows around it recoiled, tearing at itself. Grace lifted her hands, eyes blazing. "You have no claim here. No authority. No dominion."

And then—other beings of light came. Light burst through as the figures emerged, one by one— I *recognized* them. The forgotten guardians. The cast down. The once silenced. They had returned.

They formed a living wall of radiance behind Grace, their combined power surging forward like a tide. The air filled with sound—not screams, not roars—but the deep, resonant hum of creation itself pushing back against the dark void.

Hunter slammed into the beast again, driving it backward as Grace raised her voice one final time.

"In the name of Jesus," she cried, " You must GO! You are forbidden from crossing into this realm anymore."

And then I saw them. We were not alone…We never had been. They stood encamped around us in a vast, unbroken circle—row upon row of angels, their forms towering and radiant, their presence humming with restrained power. Their wings arched high, overlapping like living ramparts, feathers catching the light and scattering it into gold and fire. Each held a sword. The blades burned—not with flame that consumed, but with holy fire that purified, blazing white at the core and edged in molten gold. The air vibrated with their readiness, not frantic, not furious…but steady.

Protective. Unyielding. Waiting for the call to war.

Some knelt, their swords planted into the earth as if sealing it. Others stood with weapons raised, eyes fixed beyond us, guarding every angle, every shadow, every possible breach. Darkness recoiled at their perimeter, unable to cross the boundary of light. Where it pressed forward, it burned away, unraveling into nothing.

One of the angels turned his gaze toward me. *You are covered, Beloved.* The words weren't spoken aloud, yet they settled my heart. Zariah stirred against my chest, and as she did, the circle tightened, blades flaring brighter in response to her movement—as if the entire host leaned inward to shield her.

A sob broke free from me, not of terror this time, but of relief. We were not abandoned and we were not forgotten. The light did not disappear all at once. It settled.

The roar of battle ebbed into a sacred hush as the angels lowered their swords, their blazing blades dimming to embers of gold. One by one, they stepped back, fading into the unseen, leaving the night quiet and whole again. I stood frozen, Zariah pressed to my chest, my legs trembling now that fear no longer held me upright.

Grace remained. She no longer blazed like the aurora, yet the light still lived in her—soft, steady, unmistakable. She turned to me and smiled. A mother's smile.

"Eva," she said gently.

I swallowed hard. "You're going back."

She nodded. "To my seat." There was no sorrow in her voice…only a longing to be where she belonged. Completion.

She stepped closer and touched my cheek, her hand warm, grounding. "You are stronger than you know," she said. "And you have never walked without covering." Her gaze dropped to Zariah, and something tender passed through her eyes.

"She is a Beloved," Grace whispered. "Nothing that comes for her will come unseen nor shall it prosper."

Behind her, Hunter stood motionless, watching—no longer tense, no longer guarded. Just…waiting. Grace turned toward him. "This is where I leave you," she said softly.

Hunter's breath caught. "Grace—my Aurariel."

She lifted a hand, stopping him as he moved toward her. "I love you and I forgive you," she said, kind but firm. "But that is not the forgiveness you need."

The truth of it landed like a bell tolling. Hunter bowed his head, shoulders shaking. For a long moment, he said nothing. Then his voice broke.

"My God…in your son's holy name. The name of Jesus," he whispered. The name sounded unfamiliar on his tongue—unused, unguarded.

"I never asked you," he said hoarsely. "I blamed you. I ran from you." His hands opened at his sides, as if trying to release the pain. "I did terrible things. I became someone I hated." He paused, as if unsure if he should continue. "I'm sorry," Hunter said, tears spilling freely now. "Forgive me, Lord."

Nothing thundered. Nothing blazed. But something *happened, something lifted off of him.* Hunter gasped as if a weight he'd carried for lifetimes suddenly loosened, his breath rushing out in a sob that shook his entire body. He dropped to his knees, pressing his forehead to the earth.

Grace watched, tears shining in her eyes. When he finally looked up, she smiled. "He has forgiven you." she said. Then she stepped back.

The light gathered around her once more, gentle but insistent, drawing her upward. As she rose, the colors of the aurora flared again— greens and violets folding into gold.

Grace met my eyes one last time. "Goodbye, my daughter," she said.

And then she was gone—ascending into the realms, returning to the seat that had waited for her. The night closed softly in her absence.

Hunter stood and came to my side without a word. Together, we turned. There in front of us, Remiel lay motionless on the ground, his body unnaturally still. Hunter put his hand on my shoulder to steady me. My heart began to race. Hunter walked beside me, steady, silent. We didn't speak the words that we both feared were true.

Echoes of Redemption
Book Three
Chapter One
The Lord is close to the broken hearted.

Eva

The sky was gray and drizzling rain as I drove to the cemetery, windshield wipers tapping a slow, mournful rhythm. Zariah slept in her car seat behind me, her tiny breaths steady, unaware of the sadness of the world around us. I pulled into the long gravel drive, tires crunching over stone. The old iron gates already stood open, waiting.

I parked beneath the old oak tree. For a long moment, I couldn't move. I let the song on Klove play out before I looked at the flowers. My hands slowly closed around the bouquet of Christmas poinsettias, resting in the passenger seat. I forced myself to take the flowers, open the door, and step into the cold wet morning air.

The path to the grave was short, close enough that I could make it there and back before Zariah ever stirred. I could see the car the whole time. I didn't want her out in this weather. Not around this place. Not for this. The wind swept past me as I moved between the headstones, carrying the scent of wet earth and wilted grass, like the whole cemetery was breathing in slowly, and letting out tired exhales.

My vision blurred with tears, but I blinked hard, trying to stay steady. I stopped in front of the grave. Kneeling slowly, I placed the flowers down, brushing my fingers over the cold stone. My voice trembled but I forced the words out. "I miss you," I whispered. The wind whispered back, soft but empty. I closed my eyes, letting the ache rise. I placed my hand on my chest as the wind blew once more, reminding me of how cruel and cold life could really be.

"I wish you could see her," I whispered. My eyes drifted toward the car where Zariah slept.

"You always said everything happens for a reason." I laughed quietly under my breath. "I'm still trying to believe that." The rain tapped softly against the stone in front of me.

"I keep thinking about the things you told me." I traced the edge of the headstone slowly with my fingers. My voice softened.

"You always looked at me like you were protecting me from something." The wind moved through the cemetery again, brushing damp hair across my cheek.

"Maybe you were." My throat tightened. I blinked away fresh tears. The silence stretched.

"I don't know what I'm supposed to do now," I admitted. "I feel like I lost my way somewhere." My hand rested against the cold stone. "But you always believed I'd find it again." My voice trembled. "So I guess I'm trying to believe that too."

I glanced back toward the car again. Zariah stirred slightly in her seat but didn't wake. For a long moment, I simply stood there, listening to the quiet rain and the distant hum of traffic beyond the cemetery gates. Then I sighed and brushed moisture from my face. "I should go." My fingers lingered on the stone. "I just wanted to visit you today." I stepped back slowly. The flowers looked bright against the gray morning.

The drive home felt longer than usual. The rain slowed to a thin mist that clung to the windshield as the tires hummed steadily along the road. Zariah slept the entire way, her tiny chest rising and falling softly in the rearview mirror. I was grateful for the quiet. Grateful for the space to breathe again. The cemetery always left something heavy in my chest, like part of me had been buried there too.

By the time I turned onto the narrow road leading toward the house, the clouds had begun to thin slightly. Pale gray light filtered through the trees lining the drive.

For a moment, everything looked almost peaceful. Until I saw the truck. It was parked beside the fence line near the pasture. My foot eased off the gas. Hunter stood a few yards away, hammer in one hand, a bundle of fresh wooden boards stacked nearby. The section of fencing that had been torn apart weeks earlier was half rebuilt now.

I hadn't realized how much damage had actually been done until seeing it like this. The broken posts. The splintered wood. The deep gouges in the earth where something massive had crashed through the pasture.

The memory sent a chill through me. That night still felt unreal.Like a nightmare I couldn't fully remember. I parked beside the house and stepped out quietly, careful not to wake Zariah.

Hunter noticed me immediately. He set the hammer down and wiped his hands on his jeans before walking over.

"Good morning," he said. His voice carried the same calm steadiness it always had since that night. It reminded me so much of Remiel's.

"Morning." For a moment neither of us spoke. The silence between us felt strange. Not hostile. Just… complicated.

Hunter glanced toward the car. "She is asleep?"

I nodded. "Finally. The car ride helped."

He smiled faintly. "Babies do tend to like that."

My eyes drifted back toward the fence. "You didn't have to do this."

Hunter followed my gaze. "Yes, I do." The answer came without hesitation. "That mess out there… part of it's on me."

I crossed my arms against the chill. "None of that was your fault."

Hunter didn't respond right away. Instead he studied the half-finished fence line for a long moment. "You'd be surprised how often trouble follows me around," he said quietly.

Something about the way he said it made my stomach tighten. I looked at him more carefully. Hunter had always carried a certain pain in his eyes. A heaviness that didn't belong to an ordinary man. But today it seemed deeper somehow. Like he was remembering things he couldn't say out loud. My gaze drifted back to the pasture again. The rye grass had grown over most of the damage now, but I could still see where the ground had been torn apart. Where that creature had stood. Where the fight had happened. Where everything had changed.

"You remember more about that night than I do," I said quietly.

Hunter looked back at me. "Maybe."

"What was that thing?" I asked. The question slipped out before I could stop it.

Hunter's expression tightened slightly. For a moment I thought he might avoid the question. Instead he leaned against the car, folding his arms. "Something that shouldn't exist in this world," he said.

"That's not exactly comforting." I said, because I knew of several things that shouldn't exist in this world but they did.

"No," he admitted. "It isn't."

The wind moved gently through the trees around the property, rustling the branches. For a moment the only sound was the quiet creaking of the unfinished fence posts. "Where did it go?" I asked.

Hunter's gaze lifted toward the tree line. "Gone."

"That's it?" I asked.

"That's it." He answered. "Aurariel and your prayers caused it to go back where it came from."

Something about the certainty in his voice made me uneasy. I studied his face again. "You're not telling me everything."

A faint smile touched the corner of his mouth. "Probably not."

"That doesn't bother you?" I asked, wondering how he could just stand there and lie with such ease.

"Sometimes," he said. "But sometimes the truth causes more problems than it solves."

I shook my head slightly. "That sounds like something someone says when they're hiding something."

Hunter chuckled softly. "Maybe." He pushed away from the truck and picked up the hammer again. "I'll have the rest of this finished by the afternoon."

"You don't have to stay that long." I said, trying to protest against it.

He simply shrugged, "I know." He positioned one of the boards against the post and began hammering it into place. The steady rhythm echoed across the quiet pasture. For a moment I just watched him work. Strong. Focused. Sometimes I wondered if that was how he dealt with the past. Repairing whatever he could in the present.

"You know," he said without looking up, "most people would have moved away after something like that happened."

I frowned slightly. "After what happened?"

Hunter gestured vaguely toward the field. "That."

I glanced out across the pasture again. The place still felt like home. Even after everything.

"I'm not most people," I said quietly.

Hunter drove another nail into the wood before answering. "No," he said. "You're not."

There was something thoughtful in his tone. Almost like he understood something about me that I didn't fully understand myself. I turned toward the house. "I'm going to bring Zariah inside before she wakes up."

Hunter nodded. "I'll be here."

I opened the car door carefully and lifted Zariah from her seat. She stirred slightly but didn't wake. Her small hand curled gently against my shoulder as I carried her toward the front door. Behind me, the steady sound of the hammer continued. Wood against metal. Rhythmic. Patient. Fixing what had been broken. But as I reached the porch steps, a strange feeling settled over me again.

The same feeling I'd had at the cemetery. Like someone was watching. I glanced back toward the pasture. Hunter was still working on the fence. Nothing unusual. Nothing threatening. Just a quiet morning at home. Still…

Zariah stirred slightly as I stepped inside the house, but she didn't wake. The warmth of the house wrapped around us the moment I closed the door behind me, shutting out the cold damp air. For a second I simply stood there in the quiet entryway, listening.

The house had always had its own kind of silence. Not empty. Just peaceful. Today it felt heavier somehow. I adjusted Zariah against my shoulder and walked slowly down the hallway toward the nursery. The pale morning light filtered through the small window above the crib, casting a soft glow across the room.

I laid her gently into the crib, careful not to wake her. Her tiny hand curled instinctively around the edge of the blanket as she settled deeper into sleep.

I smiled faintly. "You really do sleep through everything," I whispered. For a moment I just stood there watching her. Her breathing was slow and steady, the soft rhythm of it calming something inside me that had been restless all morning.

Outside, faint through the walls, I could still hear the steady tapping of Hunter's hammer as he worked on the fence. Fixing what had been broken. I pulled the nursery door mostly closed and made my way down the hallway toward the kitchen. The house felt strangely quiet now. Not unsettling exactly. Just… still. I pushed the thought away and opened the refrigerator, studying what was inside.

Hunter had been working outside in the cold all morning. The least I could do was make him something warm to eat. I gathered a few things from the shelves—bread, cheese, a couple of tomatoes—and set them on the counter. A simple lunch would do.

The familiar routine helped settle my thoughts. I sliced the bread carefully and placed it into the pan, adding a bit of butter and the cheese before setting it on the stove. The faint sizzle filled the quiet kitchen as the sandwich began to toast. For a moment the normalcy of it all felt comforting.

Just a house. Just lunch. Just an ordinary day. But the memory of the broken fence and the gouged earth in the pasture lingered in the back of my mind. Nothing about the past few weeks had been ordinary. I flipped the sandwich carefully and added a small pot of soup to warm beside it.

Outside the hammering stopped. The sudden silence made me glance toward the kitchen window. Hunter stood near the fence line, examining the work he'd done so far. After a moment he bent down to pick up another board. The hammering started again. I exhaled quietly and turned back to the stove. A few minutes later I set the sandwich and bowl of soup on a plate and placed it on the kitchen table. The smell of toasted bread and warm broth filled the room.

"Not bad," I murmured to myself. Just as I reached for another plate—I heard something.

A faint sound. I froze. The sound had come from down the hallway. At first I thought it might have been the house settling. Old houses made noises sometimes. But then it came again. A quiet movement. From the direction of the bedroom. My stomach tightened slightly.

Hunter was outside. Zariah was asleep in the nursery. Which meant... I stood there for a moment, listening carefully. Nothing.

The silence stretched long enough that I almost convinced myself I had imagined it. Maybe grief and exhaustion were finally catching up with me. I wiped my hands slowly on the kitchen towel and stepped out of the room. I took a few slow steps down the hallway. Another faint sound came from the bedroom. My breath caught in my throat as slowly...I stepped forward to see what was there.